Praise for Leigh Greenwood

"Leigh Greenwood continues to be a shining star of the genre!"

—Literary Times

"Leigh Greenwood remains one of the forces to be reckoned with in Americana romance."

—Affaire de Coeur

"Greenwood's books are bound to become classics."

—Rendezvous

"Leigh Greenwood is one of the best."

—RT Book Reviews

"What more could we want? More cowboys!"

—*RT Book Reviews*

"Greenwood's plot flows like paint across the canvas of a master. He reveals his characters with the skill of a diamond cutter, one facet at a time."

—*Rendezvous*

When Love Comes

"Leigh Greenwood NEVER disappoints. The characters are finely drawn, the plots always created with just the right amount of spice to pathos and always, always, a guaranteed good read!"

—*Heartland Critiques*

Someone Like You

"Greenwood never disappoints. His latest Night Riders romance is a tangle of lust, greed, and betrayal. Continuous action, sharp intrigue, and well-rounded characters captivate."

—*RT Book Reviews*

"This is a love story that will keep your interest from the first sentence until the last page. Enjoy!"

—*A Romance Review*

Born to Love

"The characters are complex and add a rich element to this Western romance."

—*RT Book Reviews*

"[Greenwood] has a nice sense of place, and his ability to write interesting, flawed characters dealing with real issues is admirable."

—*Rendezvous*

Heart of a Texan

A Night Riders Romance

LEIGH GREENWOOD

Published by Sourcebooks Casablanca, an imprint of Sourcebooks, Inc.
P.O. Box 4410, Naperville, Illinois 60567-4410
(630) 961-3900
Fax: (630) 961-2168
www.sourcebooks.com

Printed and bound in Canada.
WC 10 9 8 7 6 5 4 3 2 1

To Brandon Moretz Lowry, my first grandchild.
March 3, 2012

Prologue

South Texas, 1873

"You want me to hit the Tryon place?" He didn't like doing business with a man he couldn't see, but the offer was too good to pass up.

"Yes." The man who called himself Gilbert Travis remained deep in the shadows. Not even his eyes were visible.

"What do you want me to do?"

"Blow a hole in the dam, trample the crops, and burn the barn. I want nothing left standing but the house."

"I won't touch the woman." Hurt an innocent woman, and you might as well put a noose around your neck. He wasn't ready to die.

"I don't want her hurt. Just shoot the old man."

"I don't kill nobody."

"Then I guess I'll have to do it for you." Travis's voice was laced with such scorn he flinched. A hat landed at his feet. "Make sure you leave this where she can find it."

It was Nate Dolan's hat.

Chapter One

ROBERTA TRYON WASN'T SURE WHAT WOKE HER. IT wasn't a sound so much as a feeling there was a sound she ought to have heard. Yet the night was still, soundless—so quiet she could hear her father's snoring at the other end of the house. She attempted to go back to sleep. She turned on her left side, but it wasn't long before she shifted to her right. Instead of feeling sleepy, it made her more awake. She couldn't shake the nagging feeling something was wrong.

In frustration, she got out of bed and looked out the window. The night was overcast with clouds hiding the crescent moon. She could barely make out the silhouette of the trees that grew alongside the creek that flowed through their farm, the creek that carried water the ranchers depended on. Some distance away—too far for the sound to carry—water tumbled over the dam her father had built. After the ranchers blew up the first one, her father retaliated by building an even bigger one.

She hated the strain between ranchers and anyone who attempted to farm more than an acre of ground. The ranchers admired someone like Nate Dolan, a handsome young man rich enough to buy the largest ranch in the county, yet filled with such hatred he spent most of his time searching for the man he said was responsible for his brother's death. It was no secret that Nate intended to kill Laveau diViere if he could. Apparently he didn't care that meant he'd hang. Stupid. Idiotic. Typically Texan.

But she didn't want to think about Nate Dolan, the dam, the farm, or the ranchers. She was tired and needed to sleep. She turned back and crawled into bed. She'd hardly adjusted the blankets when her father stuck his head through the doorway.

"There's somebody outside," he whispered.

She threw back the covers and slid her feet into her slippers. "What are they doing?"

"I don't know, but I expect it's one of those fool ranchers nosing around to see what damage he can do. I'm going to put a stop to it. Stay here."

She wanted to go with him, but she'd never used a rifle, shotgun, or pistol. And no Texan who called himself a man paid any attention to a woman.

"Don't light the lamp," her father warned when she followed him to the kitchen. "I don't want them to know I'm on to 'em."

A premonition of danger gripped Roberta. "Don't go." A light flickering through the window warned of something else. "I think they've set fire to the barn."

Muttering a string of curses, her father strapped on a holster carrying a single pistol. Then he grabbed his shotgun from the shelf and stuffed the pockets of his robe with shells. "I'll teach the sons of bitches to try to burn my barn," he swore.

Deaf to all her pleas that he stay in the house, he disappeared through the doorway.

She had never felt so helpless in her life. She had spent her first fourteen years in Virginia, where people didn't blow up dams or consider slinging on a gun an essential part of getting dressed. Shotguns in Virginia were used for birds and squirrels, rifles for deer and wild hogs. Horses pulled wagons. Cows were docile and milked twice a day. Men came home for supper rather than spend their evenings drinking and gambling. Women cooked and cared for their families. They didn't ride horses or use firearms. Even after five years in her new home, Texas was an alien universe.

Two shots in quick succession changed the direction of her thoughts. She rushed to the window, but the cloud cover was so heavy she couldn't see her father or anyone else. After trying a second window without success, she ran to the door and wrenched it open.

The blackness of night closed around her like a blanket thrown over her head. Shouts, occasional gunfire, and the grunts of horses came at her out of the murky shadows. Fear followed quickly on their heels. She heard her father calling the invaders cowards, bastards, scum of the earth. Blasts from his shotgun accompanied his insults. The bark of answering rifles was accompanied by curses that amazed Roberta by their variety and inventiveness.

The fire blazed higher. She could see silhouettes of several hooded figures stoking the flames until they engulfed the whole side of the barn. Others rode their horses through her father's fields, destroying the crops. Her father barreled forward into this melee, a feeble force against so many. She called him to come back but had no expectation he could hear her, or that he would heed her if he did. He thrived on opposition. It didn't matter that he was badly outnumbered. That only made him more determined.

Unable to stand around doing nothing, Roberta went inside and straight for the rifle her father had hung on pegs in the wall. She'd never handled a rifle before, but all she had to do was pull the trigger. Even a useless female could manage that.

Yet after she'd returned to the doorway, she couldn't decide what to do. Even if she could overcome her natural repugnance at the thought of killing anyone, the men at the barn and in the fields were too far away. Shooting at them would mostly likely draw fire in her direction. Still, she couldn't go back in the house. She couldn't just watch, while everything her father had built during the last five years was destroyed.

Deciding to stand alongside him, she headed toward the spot where he'd plunged into a potato field. She was only halfway there when she heard a howl of pain.

"You damned son of a bitch!" someone shouted. "You shot me."

He sounded surprised. Surely he couldn't have thought her father would fire into the air in a futile attempt to scare him off. Not even a Texas cowboy could be that dumb!

There was just enough light for her to see the man

take a shot at her father. It missed. The rider cursed and fired another shot that missed.

"Get back doing what you're supposed to do."

The raspy voice—clearly in the habit of giving commands—sounded vaguely familiar. Roberta looked around to see where it had come from, but it was too dark, there were too many people, and everyone was in constant motion. She turned back to find her father running toward the barn. A break in clouds allowed enough light for her to see that several hooded riders had trampled much of the field. She was tempted to shoot the first person she got close to.

A lasso spun out of the darkness and settled over her father. A second lasso pinned his arms to his sides. Keeping her father immobile between them, the riders forced him to watch as they drove his livestock from the barn. Driven by their inherent fear of fire, the mules quickly disappeared into the night, but the pigs milled around senselessly, allowing the hooded figures to make a game of shooting at them. Fortunately, someone opened the gate to their pen, and the survivors of the massacre fled into the night. The squeals of the wounded animals formed a piteous backdrop to the attack. Despite her rage at the brutal shooting of helpless animals, Roberta was relieved when the last wounded pig was put out of its misery. Intent on further destruction, a rider pulled down the chicken coop, sending the squawking hens flapping into the darkness. Her father could do nothing but watch helplessly as five years of work was systematically devastated.

A hooded rider who had watched until now rode

up to one of the men holding a lasso. At a signal, both riders let their ropes go slack. At that moment, the late arrival drew his gun and shot her father in the chest. Then he calmly turned and rode away as her father staggered a few steps before slumping to the ground.

For a moment, Roberta's mind went blank. When she next became aware of her surroundings, she was bending over her father, calling his name, begging someone to help get him to a doctor. But there was no one left to hear her.

Ripping a strip from her nightgown, Roberta struggled to stanch the flow of blood, but the bullet had pierced her father's lung. When he tried to speak, he choked on his own blood. She could do nothing but cradle him while, bathed by her tears, he died in her arms.

Driven beyond reason by the horrific events, she reached for the gun in her father's holster. Whirling around at the sound of an approaching horse, she didn't care that the man wasn't wearing a mask, or that he was coming from the direction of town. Blinded by tears and in the grip of helpless rage, she fired in his direction. Certain she had missed, and beyond caring if she had, she flung the gun aside, and covered her father's body with her own.

Roberta didn't know how long she lay there before the shock began to wear off. At first she was aware only of the silence. After the horror of the last minutes, it seemed enormous, unending, as though she was the only person left on earth. Gradually a mixture of sounds penetrated her consciousness.

Voices. Hooves. Wagons. Running footsteps. They must have seen the fire from town.

"Grab a bucket," someone shouted. "There's a water tank behind the barn."

Roberta knew there weren't enough buckets and not enough water to put out the fire.

More and more people arrived, all moving around her, shouting instructions, asking questions, wondering who had led the attack and why. The thunder of an explosion in the distance brought the activity to a halt.

"Clear out!" a man shouted. "They just blew up the dam."

Someone took hold of Roberta's shoulder and tried to lift her to her feet, but she clung to her father's body.

"You've got to move," a gentle female voice urged. "People say there's a lot of water behind that dam."

Roberta knew there was no need to panic. A relatively small hole in the middle would achieve the same effect as blowing up the whole dam, and it wouldn't endanger anyone. Still, she allowed herself to be brought to her feet. She was too grief-stricken to pay attention to the arms that enveloped her or to attempt to identify the men who carried her father's body toward the house.

"Lay him in his bed."

Roberta recognized the voice of Boone Riggins, a man who asked her to marry him at least once a month. She had refused his offers, but now his was a friendly face in this night of unbelievable horror. With an anguished cry, she flung herself at him and burst into tears. Even though she couldn't stop crying long enough to put together a coherent sentence, she poured out everything that had happened. When she finally stopped, her body was racked by painful hiccups.

"Here, drink this." The gentle female voice.

Roberta grasped a dipper in two hands, brought it to her mouth, and drank. After she'd drained the dipper, she took a deep, steadying breath. Then, for the first time since she had seen her father fall, she was able to take note of her surroundings. The room was full of people, half of whom she didn't recognize, all facing her, waiting for her response.

"Thank you for taking care of my father. I would never have been able to move him by myself."

"What happened?"

"Who did this?"

"Did you recognize anybody?"

Questions were thrown at her from every corner of the room until they sank of their own weight.

"I don't know who did this," she managed to say. "They all wore hoods, but the killing of my father was deliberate. They held him between two ropes and forced him to watch while they tried to destroy everything he'd built. Then a man who seemed to be the leader shot him."

"Who blew a hole in the dam?"

She whipped around to face a middle-aged man standing in the doorway. "Where have you been the last four years?" Roberta cried. "The ranchers have done everything they could to run us out ever since my father built that second dam."

"Threats are one thing, but killing a man…" Sheriff Bryce Kelly entered the house. "I don't know a single rancher in the county who'd do such a thing."

"Well, somebody did it," Roberta said. "Who else would have a reason?"

"It could have been strangers," someone suggested.

"Strangers would have looted the place. Those men didn't take anything."

"What are you going to do now?" the sheriff asked.

Roberta hadn't had time to think about that, but once the question had been asked, she knew the answer. "I'm going to put this farm back together. I'm going to see that the man who killed my father hangs. *Then* I'm moving back to Virginia."

"You can't run this farm by yourself," the sheriff said.

"Why not?"

"You're a woman."

Roberta didn't have the energy to say half the things that sprang to mind. "I'll worry about that after I bury my father."

An awkward silence followed. Roberta was thankful for the concern of the people gathered in the room, but she needed to be alone.

A soot-streaked man came to the door. "The fire's out, but there's not much of the barn left. When we ran out of water, we just threw dirt on it. Worked better than we expected." He moved aside to let the town doctor come in.

"I need a bed," the doctor said to Roberta. "I've got a man out here who's badly wounded."

"Who?" Bryce asked.

"Nate Dolan."

Chapter Two

THE LYING, BACKSTABBING, BARN-BURNING, LIVESTOCK-killing traitor. Nate Dolan had been the only rancher Roberta thought had some sympathy for her father. He'd advised him against building the dam, against trying to farm in such dry country, and against making enemies of some of the most powerful men in the county, but he'd defended her father's right to do what he wanted with his land, no matter how stupid he thought it. She might have been able to admire Nate if he hadn't been so eaten up with hatred.

"No!" It came out as a cry of anguish. How could the doctor even think of bringing one of the attackers into her house? It was too much to ask of even the most forgiving woman. "I won't have him in my home."

"Can't you take him to town?" the sheriff asked.

"He's hurt too badly to make the trip. It's more than a mile to town, and the ruts are deep enough to break an axle."

"I don't care if he dies." That wasn't really how she felt, but she couldn't face the idea of offering shelter to one of the men who helped kill her father. How could anyone expect it of her?

"Well I care, young woman," the doctor stated. "I've seen too many men die, and I don't intend to see this one follow the rest if I can help it. I'll put him in a bed if you have one. I'll put him on the floor if you don't, but he's going to stay in this house until he's well enough to be moved. Then, if you can prove he's one of the men who killed your father, the sheriff can put him in jail."

"There are only two beds in the house, and my father is lying in one of them."

"We can take your father's body into town," the sheriff offered.

For a moment she was speechless with shock and rage. How could anyone think she would allow her father's body to be taken away so this man could have his bed? It was a travesty, a sacrilege, an unimaginable affront. "Don't you touch my father's body."

"He must be prepared for burial. Wouldn't it be better to do it now?"

Roberta recognized the voice of Mrs. Pender, the woman who'd spoken to her earlier. "How can you ask me to put *that man* in my father's bed?"

"I'm not. I'm just thinking of your father."

"It's the only practical solution," the sheriff said.

"I don't care if it's the *only* solution. I won't have that man in my house." She had barely launched into a list of reasons why it was inhuman to ask this of her when four men carrying Nate Dolan walked through the doorway. "Where do we put him?"

"Through there," the sheriff directed.

Roberta moved to position herself in front of her father's door and dare anyone to enter, but she could tell from the sheriff's attitude that he wouldn't hesitate to remove her forcibly. There didn't seem to be anyone to whom she could appeal for support. This was cow country, and people had little sympathy for her father's stand.

"Can't you take him somewhere else?" Boone Riggins asked the doctor.

"No." His answer was flat and unequivocal.

It looked like she didn't have much choice, but she didn't intend to have anything to do with Nate Dolan. Let the doctor see to him. "Who's going to feed him and look after him?"

"You are. Did you expect anyone else?"

Roberta couldn't believe what she was hearing. "I'm not touching him. In fact, I wish he were dead."

The sheriff ignored her. "We've got to move her father's body first," he said to the men carrying Nate.

Roberta wanted to scream, shout, threaten violence, but no one showed any likelihood of listening. Moments later, several men emerged from her father's bedroom with his body.

"We'll take him to the doctor's office," the sheriff told her. "He can stay there until you've made the funeral arrangements."

Seeing her father carried out almost caused her to break down again. She wanted to wipe the blood from his lips, straighten his clothes, put slippers on his bare feet. Allowing him to be carried into town in such a state felt like the worst kind of disrespect. She ran to his bedroom and returned with his pillow and the spread from his bed. "Cover him. I don't want people to see him like that."

"Take my buckboard," Boone Riggins offered.

Roberta followed as they carried her father outside and laid him in Boone's buckboard. She put the pillow under his head. Not until his body was positioned properly did she allow them to cover him with the spread.

"Don't drive too fast," she directed the driver. "I don't want him bounced all the way." She turned to Sheriff Kelly. "I'll go into town later today. I want the funeral to be tomorrow."

"I'll make the arrangements."

There didn't seem to be anything more to say. As she watched the buckboard leave, she experienced a slight thread of resentment that her father was leaving the farm while she was condemned to stay. She told herself that was a horrible way to feel. She'd have been happy to stay in Texas for the rest of her life if it meant her father could still be alive.

"You've got to move into town. I'll hire someone to look after Dolan."

She had forgotten Boone had followed her outside. She forced herself to think. "I've got to stay here."

"Why? The place has been destroyed."

"Not the house."

"You can't fix the damage to your fields, and there's not enough left of the barn to keep. Half your pigs have been shot, the cows and mules have escaped, and there isn't a chicken in sight."

"Will you ask if someone in town would take the pigs that were killed? It seems a shame to let that meat go to waste."

"Roberta, stop thinking about the pigs and think of yourself. You can't stay here."

"If you think I'm letting Nate Dolan stay in my house without me, you're out of your mind. The ranchers keep trying to run us out, and I won't let them win."

"You can't make me believe you want to take care of Dolan. If he dies, people will wonder if you killed him."

Nate Dolan's presence wasn't the only reason Roberta wouldn't leave. She couldn't allow Boone to hire someone to take care of Nate any more than she could allow him to pay for her to stay in town. Doing so would encourage him to think her feelings for him were stronger than they were. She had her father's aversion to incurring a debt she couldn't pay and her own aversion to raising hopes she couldn't fulfill.

"They'd be right. I think I'm the one who shot him."

Boone looked startled. "You didn't say anything about shooting someone."

"I forgot. It was just after my father had been shot. I heard someone ride up. I didn't know who it was. I was crying so hard I could hardly see, but I do remember a blue shirt."

"Don't say anything," Boone advised. "Since he was one of the attackers, no one will care who shot him."

But Roberta did. As much as she hated what the ranchers had done, she couldn't accept that she might have killed a man. She wasn't a murderer. She didn't believe in violence. "I need to talk to the doctor. I have to know what to do."

"Let me stay here with you."

"You know that's impossible. Think of the gossip."

"You're already staying alone with a man."

"One who's unconscious. I don't think people will start any rumors over that." She noticed the sky was getting lighter. "It'll soon be time to open your restaurant. People must have their breakfast." Boone was a nice man who owned the most successful restaurant and most popular saloon in town. No woman in her right mind would have turned him down, yet Roberta had. She couldn't marry a Texan when she intended to return to Virginia as soon as possible.

"I'll check on you tonight."

"That's not necessary." She turned away before he could attempt to convince her she was necessary to his happiness. Unfortunately, he wasn't necessary for hers.

She was reluctant to enter the house, but she had never been one to avoid bad news or difficult decisions. She was stuck with Nate Dolan, so she wanted to know how to make him well as quickly as she could. No one Boone could hire would look after him as conscientiously as she because she wanted him out of her house as soon as possible.

She thought everyone had gone until she heard the doctor talking to someone. When she reached the bedroom, the doctor was bending over Nate's body. He looked up when she stepped into the room.

"Glad you're back. Mrs. Pender gets queasy at the sight of blood. I need you to help me extract the bullet."

"What do you want me to do?" She hadn't thought the sight of blood bothered her, but seeing it smeared over Nate's chest made her stomach queasy. She resolutely fought the feeling. She expected she'd see more blood before she saw the last of Nate Dolan.

She took the pan of water Mrs. Pender had been holding, dipped a cloth in it, and started to clean the blood from Nate's chest. A little oozed out of the wound, but it didn't take long before he was clean.

Much against her will, she became aware of him in a way that was unsettling. Nate's chest was completely smooth except for a little hair around his nipples, and a trail that disappeared at his waist. His broad shoulders tapered down to slim hips. Even in repose, it was easy to see the muscles that enabled him to wrestle full-grown steers to the ground. Like every Texas cowman, his face and neck were deeply tanned, but his chest was practically white. Nate wasn't wearing any long underwear. In fact, he wasn't wearing anything. The doctor had undressed him while she was gone.

Knowing she was in the room with a naked man was something of a shock. It didn't matter that he was unconscious. He was naked, he was a man, and he was in her house. He wasn't her father, her husband, her brother, or a relative. He was a stranger, a man she knew mostly by reputation. She doubted the doctor would dress him before he left.

"Pay attention."

The doctor's probing had caused Nate's wound to start bleeding again.

"That's better," the doctor said when she'd wiped away the blood. "You're not going to faint on me, are you?"

"No."

"Then why are you looking so strange?"

"She's been through a terrible experience."

Roberta had forgotten Mrs. Pender was still in the room. "I'm surprised she's still on her feet."

"I'm not. She's stronger than she looks. Ah! I think I found it." Seconds later the doctor extracted a bullet that he held up. He squinted at the blood-covered bit of gray metal. "That didn't come from a rifle. He was shot with a pistol."

Roberta's stomach clinched. She *had* shot Nate.

"He ought to be okay now," the doctor said, "but you'll have to watch him. I wouldn't be surprised if he develops a fever. He could have gotten a concussion when he fell out of the saddle."

"What do you do for a concussion?" Roberta asked.

"You keep him on his feet and awake until you're sure he's okay."

"He's unconscious and unable to move."

"Then you'd better hope he doesn't have a concussion. We don't need the biggest rancher in the area suffering from brain damage."

Roberta felt faint. "What can I do?"

"Watch him. If he wakes up, send someone to let me know."

"I'm the only one here."

The doctor looked thoughtful. "I guess you are. Well, take your father's shotgun and fire away. After today's ruckus, that ought to bring someone from town, and they can fetch me."

She was so infuriated that he would refer to the murderous attack as *today's ruckus* she nearly said something rude. Remembering her father was dead was almost like hearing it for the first time. It was still hard to believe only a few hours ago her father had kissed her good night and gone off to bed with plans to pick beans and tomatoes early the next morning. Boone had promised to buy all the vegetables her father produced. Roberta didn't know if he needed that much produce, or whether he was trying to buy her affection.

"What do I feed him? When do I feed him?"

"Don't feed him anything until he wakes up, or you'll probably drown him. After that, a clear broth for a day or two. Vegetable broth will do, but beef or chicken would be better."

"I don't have any beef, and the chickens were scattered."

"I'll make some broth," Mrs. Pender offered.

"Once everybody hears he's here, you'll probably have every unmarried woman in town offering food," the doctor said. "He's got to be one of the most eligible bachelors in Texas."

"I would expect her to receive offers of food from *every* woman, unmarried or not." Mrs. Pender's tone was less than respectful. "The citizens of Slender Creek are always quick to help anyone in need or distress."

"So they are." The doctor wasn't quailed by Mrs. Pender's reprimand. "Roberta will need it since some of Slender Creek's citizens are responsible for her present situation."

"It couldn't have been anyone in town, I'm sure," Mrs. Pender stated with certitude. "Now unless you need me," she said to Roberta, "I'll be going. My men would starve if I weren't there to feed them."

"Remarkable woman," the doctor said after Mrs. Pender had left. "Very remarkable. I'm just glad she's not my wife."

Dr. Danforth was a widower. Much to the distress of several hopeful women, he had shown no interest in changing his marital state. He said his patients were as much of a family as he wanted.

"How long do you think he'll be here?" Roberta asked as the doctor was putting the last touches on the bandage.

"A week if things go well. Maybe two if they don't."

"What do you mean—*if things don't go well?*"

"Fever or infection, but he looks like the kind of healthy young man who will bounce back quickly if you take good care of him. If he comes through the next day okay, you ought to be able to relax."

"How can I relax with a sick man in my house for at least a week?"

The doctor looked at Nate's unmoving body. "I don't think he'll be getting in your way."

"He's in my way just by being here."

"Well, he can't be moved just yet, so you'll have to get used to it. Now I have to go. Mrs. Millican's baby has jaundice, and Mrs. Grady's third boy broke his arm... *again*. Good thing I never had a hankering to be a rich man. This town would be in a mess of trouble if I left." The doctor gathered his equipment, stuffed everything into one oversized bag, and walked out the door. "At least your patient is young and handsome," he called over his shoulder. "Be glad it's not old Mr. Grunwald. I can't find a nurse who can last half a day without wanting to suffocate him."

How did he know she didn't want to suffocate Nate Dolan? Just because he hadn't shot her father didn't mean he wasn't as responsible as every one of those masked cowards for her father's death. And where were all those citizens of Slender Creek who were so anxious to help people in trouble? They should have been standing in line to bring food, help clear away the wreckage, to help feed and care for Nate Dolan.

She turned back into the house and closed the door. They were probably afraid to help. This part of Texas was dominated by ranchers. No one wanted to offend them because the town depended on them. Her father's insistence in farming despite the ranchers' objections had caused many people to avoid them. Considering the murderous nature of the attack, she wouldn't be surprised if she was now completely isolated.

That didn't bother her. What to do about the farm did. She didn't know if the crops could be saved, but she was determined to put the farm back on its feet. She would not let the ranchers win. The farm would thrive once again. *Then* she would go back to Virginia.

Roberta had never been a slacker, but trying to save her crops had forced her to work harder than she had in her whole life. Yet she was grateful—it was the only way she could keep the grief and shock of her father's death at bay. She could push it aside for a short while, but then it would hit her again with the force of a physical blow. She would never be able to forget the sight of her father sinking to the ground, blood running from between his lips as he died in her arms. What made it even more horrible was the way he'd been shot. It was like an execution, cold and deliberate. Who could have hated her father enough to do something like that?

On the verge of breaking down, she forced her mind back to her work. Another bout of tears would needlessly increase her physical exhaustion. She'd reached emotional exhaustion long ago.

The damage to the crops wasn't as bad as it first appeared. She was hopeful of being able to save enough to survive. The biggest hurdle was that she had to deal with the problem one plant at a time. Her father had planted more than five acres in corn alone. That didn't count the beans, tomatoes, squash… the list went on. She was only one person. It was impossible to do all this work alone, but she couldn't afford to pay anyone to help her. So she reached for the next corn stalk that hadn't been knocked over, stood it up, and packed dirt around the roots to hold it in place. She tossed the ruined corn aside. She would use it to feed the pigs when they came back… *if* they came back. The two mules had been returned, one by a tongue-tied cowhand, and another by a little boy who said his mama had told him to run it out of her garden.

Roberta felt uncomfortable leaving Nate alone. As much as she resented having to take care of him, she couldn't square it with her conscience to ignore him. She'd gone to the house every hour to check on him. She didn't know whether he was still unconscious or just sleeping, but he hadn't moved all day. If it hadn't been for the bandage, she would have thought he hadn't been hurt. It was hard to believe a man who had been shot could look that handsome.

It bothered her that she liked looking at him. She should hate him. But if evil was as handsome as Nate Dolan, no wonder so many people got into trouble.

She reached the end of the row. Standing and stretching her back muscles, she was pleased to see how much corn she'd been able to save. The hooded cowards hadn't been as successful as she'd thought. She was contemplating how much work she could do before her body gave out when she heard an approaching vehicle. She was dismayed to see Prudence Goodfellow driving the small trap she used when she went anywhere. It was pulled by a shaggy-haired pony that remained a curiosity in the eyes of the children in Slender Creek.

"I would have come sooner, but I've been over Sligo way taking care of Mrs. Wingate. She's down with a fever and no one to look after her brood." Prudence eyed the damage to the cornfield. "Wicked." She shook her head. "Just plain wicked, but your pa knew what would happen if he rebuilt that dam."

"That doesn't make it right." Prudence was the soul of kindness, but her opinions—delivered in her forthright manner—often made that hard to remember.

"No, it doesn't," Prudence agreed as she climbed out of the trap. "You look exhausted. You have no business doing all this work yourself. There ought to be dozens of people from town helping you."

"Mrs. Pender brought some soup, but no one else has come by."

"I'll take care of that as soon as I get back to town," Prudence declared. "Now it's time for you to rest. Let me walk you up to the house."

Roberta would have liked nothing better than to go back to the house, collapse in a chair, and not move for hours, but she didn't dare as long as Prudence was here. If that straitlaced woman found out there was a man in her house, she was likely to move in to protect Roberta's honor. It didn't matter that Nate was unable to sit up in bed. He was a man, and his mere presence was a danger that must be guarded against.

"I can't stop," Roberta told Prudence. "Everything I have is in these fields. If I don't save every plant I can, I'll be broke."

"Why should that matter? You've always said you intended to go back to Virginia. There's nothing to keep you here now." Prudence didn't approve of Virginia. It was too far north and too proud of its past.

Roberta massaged a muscle that had been throbbing for the last hour. "I've got two things to keep me here. First, I intend to find out who killed my father."

"It had to be the work of vagrants," Prudence said. "No one from Slender Creek would do anything like this."

"It was the ranchers. I just don't know which one pulled the trigger."

Prudence didn't look happy. "What's your other reason for staying?"

"To get this farm working again. I'm determined to show them they can't drive me out. What kind of coward would I be if I ran away?"

"A sensible one."

Roberta didn't know why that struck her as funny, but she laughed. "I know it sounds crazy, but I feel like it would dishonor my father if I left."

Prudence looked at the charred remains of the barn, glanced over the devastated fields, then back at Roberta. "You can't do all of this yourself."

"I can't pay anyone to help me."

"There's lots of kids in town with nothing to do."

"You know people are afraid of helping me for fear of what the ranchers might do. If lightning had struck the barn, they'd have a new one up by tomorrow. As it is, they won't touch it."

Patience surveyed the damage. "It's just wicked."

Roberta thought having someone agree with her would help. Instead, it just made her feel tired. "I don't mean to run you off, but I've got a lot of work to do while it's still daylight."

"I'll help you. There's not a man in this county who would dare lay a hand on me."

She was probably right. Except for Joe, every man Roberta knew was scared to death of Prudence.

"If you want to do something for me, you can make the arrangements for my father's funeral tomorrow."

"I'll be happy to. What time do you want it?"

"In the morning. I don't know that anybody will come, but it should be before it gets too hot."

"I'll see to it. I'll also see that everybody in town is present."

"I don't want people there saying things they don't mean."

"They'll be there, and they'll mean it. Now I have

to go if I'm going to make sure all the arrangements are done properly."

Roberta didn't say any more. It was nearly impossible to dissuade Prudence once she made up her mind. Besides, Roberta had more than enough to worry about. She turned to start on the next row of corn. She hoped to get the field done before it was time to fix supper.

Nate wasn't sure whether he'd woken up or regained consciousness. It probably didn't matter. His mind was fuzzy, his vision was blurred, his body hurt, and he had no idea where he was. The last thing he remembered was seeing what he thought was a fire. He must have gone to help. But try as he might, he couldn't remember whether he'd found the fire, or what he'd done after he got there.

Exhaustion gripped his body. He felt incapable of lifting his arm, even turning his head, but he was thirty-one years old and supposed to be in his prime. He'd just spent two weeks in the saddle trying to cross the trail of Laveau diViere. He couldn't be incapable of sitting up.

But he was. What had happened, and why did his chest feel like it was in a vise?

He turned his head to the left and then the right. He was in a small but well-furnished bedroom. It appeared to be a man's bedroom, but it wasn't his bedroom or one he recognized. The walls were without pictures or decoration, their monotony broken up by two doors and a window. The blank spaces in-between were taken up by pieces of furniture and hooks on which hung coats, hats, shirts, even a pair of saddlebags.

He listened intently, but he couldn't hear any sound. As much as the mystery of where he was and why he was there unsettled him, he felt safe. Whatever had happened, someone was taking care of him. He would stop looking for answers just now. He needed to rest more. Maybe then he could sit up.

Her father had always said that after a productive day, he felt great even if he was so tired he could hardly stand up. Roberta was so exhausted after a productive day, she felt like she was going to die. She was too tired to think. She was even too tired to be hungry. After she'd checked on Nate, it had taken what remained of her flagging energy to clean up and drag herself to a rocking chair on the front porch. Now all she wanted to do was soak up the cool of the evening, until she could summon the energy to drag her tired body to bed.

A light breeze provided a refreshing contrast to the heat of the day. The sun had set, but it would be light for about another hour. Swallows darted through the air in their erratic flight to catch insects. She suspected some of the airborne predators were bats. She didn't like bats, but they were certainly more welcome than the man driving an approaching buckboard. She recognized Nate's foreman long before he reached the house. If Nate was said to be built along the lines of a greyhound, then Russ McCoy was modeled after a bulldog. There wasn't a man in three counties with shoulders that wide or a neck so thick.

"What do you want?" she asked when Russ brought the buckboard to a stop.

"I've come to take Nate home."

"What took you so long?"

"I didn't know he was here. Hell, I didn't even know he had come back until Gill Pender told me his wife had taken some beef broth to you for him."

"If you know that much, you know the doctor said he can't be moved. I'm not going to have people saying I was so anxious to get rid of him I killed him."

Russ had gotten down from the buckboard and come up to the porch. He was probably an inch or two shorter that Nate, but his bulk made him look bigger. It was said half the men in Slender Creek stayed out of his way, but Roberta wasn't intimidated. She was too tired.

"Taking him home can't be half as dangerous as leaving him here with no one but you to look after him. Hell, I wouldn't put it past you to poison him. If I thought you could hit the broad side of a barn, I'd swear you were the one who shot him."

"If I had, it would have been no more than he deserved for being one of the cowards who murdered my father."

"Nate thought your father was a fool for rebuilding that dam—I heard him say that to your father's face—but he would never be part of what happened last night. I don't know how he came to be here. He's been off hunting Laveau diViere."

"If your boss is so anxious to kill diViere that he goes looking for him, why should he hesitate to shoot a farmer using water he thinks of as his own?"

"DiViere is a traitor who killed Nate's brother. Your father was just a fool." Russ didn't appear to care that it was considered uncivil to criticize a dead man, especially to his daughter.

"The doctor will tell you when you can take your boss home. I'll do everything I can to make sure he survives his stay here. After that, I intend to see that every man involved in the attack hangs."

"They were masked. How can you know who they were?"

"I'll find out." She didn't know how, but she didn't intend to give up until she did.

"I'm not leaving until I see the boss."

"He's sleeping."

"How can I know that without seeing for myself?"

Roberta wasn't sure she could summon the energy to get to her feet, but somehow she managed. "Okay, one look. Then I want you out of my house and off my land."

An agitated voice was heard from inside the house. "Russ, get your butt in here before that woman kills me."

Chapter Three

EVERY VESTIGE OF CIVILITY LEFT RUSS'S FACE. "WHAT have you done to him?"

"Nothing." Roberta couldn't understand why Nate would make such an accusation. "Every time I've looked in on him, he's been sleeping."

Russ pushed by Roberta to go inside. "Where is he?"

"In my father's bedroom."

The house was built in an "L" pattern with a bedroom, parlor, and bedroom across the front. Behind the bedroom on the left were the dining room and kitchen, both of which opened onto a porch that could also be reached from the parlor. Russ covered the distance to her father's bedroom in half the steps it took Roberta. When she reached the bedroom, Nate lifted his arm and pointed at her.

"Why did you shoot me?"

Roberta wasn't ready to admit she'd shot Nate, but his blunt accusation threw her off stride. "I... you... who says I shot you?"

"I do." Nate was emphatic. "I saw you pick up a gun and aim it at me."

"If you know that, then you know why I shot you."

"I can't remember everything that happened, but I remember seeing what I thought was a fire. When I got here, it looked like there were men all over the place trying to put it out. It was so dark I couldn't see their faces, but the clouds parted just enough for me to see you bending over somebody. That's when you picked up the gun and shot me."

"You got some of it right, but you missed the important parts. You did see a fire, but they were building it up, not trying to put it out. Men were all over the place because they were riding through my father's fields. You saw me bending over my father. He'd just been killed by one of the men whose faces you didn't recognize because they were wearing hoods. I shot at the first man I saw because I was hysterical with grief and shaking with rage. I wanted to kill every man who rode here that night. Oh, I almost forgot. They blew a hole in the dam."

"I didn't come here to blow up the dam, destroy crops, burn the barn, or kill your father," Nate insisted. "I don't know anything about what happened. I've been gone."

"I know. You've been looking for a man you intend to kill on sight. So of course you wouldn't do anything to hurt a man who was stealing *your* water."

Nate struggled to sit up but failed. "I thought your father was making a mistake, and I told him so, but I wouldn't shoot him or blow up his dam."

"Then why were you with those men?"

"I wasn't. Didn't you say they were wearing masks? Well, I wasn't."

That had been bothering Roberta all day, but she

wasn't ready to back down yet. "Maybe you took it off so you could see better. Maybe you didn't think I would recognize you. Maybe you think you're so rich and powerful it wouldn't matter if I did. Who'd take the word of a mere woman against that of the most important rancher in the county?"

"I'm taking you home," Russ said to Nate.

"I'm not the most important rancher," Nate objected.

"You're the richest with the largest ranch. Who else would you recommend?"

"Can you sit up?" Russ asked Nate.

"Do you think I'd be flat on my back if I could?"

"I can carry you to the buckboard."

"You can't move him," Roberta insisted. "He'd never survive the trip back to his ranch."

"He has a better chance than surviving your care."

"I'm not a murderer."

"You shot him. It's a miracle he didn't die."

"I wasn't trying to shoot *him*," Roberta clarified. "I just shot *at* somebody."

"A distinction I find hard to appreciate," Nate muttered.

"Well, it's a distinction nonetheless. If I'd known it was you trying to kill my father, I'd have shot you because I wanted to shoot *you*. Not that I would have hit you," she added. "I've never touched a gun in my life. I didn't think I'd actually hit anybody."

"I wasn't trying to kill your father," Nate insisted. "I didn't even know where he was."

"I don't believe you."

"We don't believe *you*," Russ said. "Now move so I can get the boss out of your house."

"No one is moving my patient anywhere until I say so."

Roberta hadn't heard the doctor enter the house. He elbowed Russ aside.

"Why are you arguing like children when the man ought to be sleeping? You want to set his recovery back a week?"

"Not by so much as a minute," Roberta declared. "I can't wait to get him out of my house."

"I'm in total agreement," Russ growled.

"Then you'll go home and take care of his ranch," the doctor said to Russ. "And you," he said, turning to Roberta, "will fetch the broth Mrs. Pender sent. This man must be starving by now."

Roberta fled the room, embarrassed at having been caught in a pointless argument. She knew it was fueled by guilt. She hadn't really wanted anyone dead. Her guilt was made worse by the suspicion that Nate might be telling the truth. There was one other thing she couldn't understand. One of the men cleaning up after the attack had found two hats for Nate. Whoever heard of a man wearing two hats? She was too emotionally exhausted to sort through everything. Just thinking of her father's brutal murder made her want to punish every man within ten miles of Slender Creek. In one way or another, they'd all contributed to his death.

Realizing she was about to be overcome with grief, she pushed those thoughts aside and reached for the broth she'd kept warm on the stove. She ladled some into a bowl and hurried back to the bedroom.

Nate was sitting up when she returned. The doctor

had removed the bandages and was inspecting the wound. "Feed him," he ordered without looking up.

Russ reached for the bowl. "I'll do it."

"Let Roberta do it," the doctor said. "Men like you are good in the saddle, but you can't feed yourselves without making a mess."

Roberta grinned at Russ's startled protests. Even Nate managed a faint smile.

"Open your mouth," Roberta told Nate. "I don't want to be accused of being as messy as a man."

"What is that?" Nate demanded as soon as he'd managed to swallow. "It tastes like water."

"It's a nourishing beef broth," the doctor said.

"I'm wounded, not dying," Nate protested. "Put some actual beef in it."

"You'll eat nothing solid until tomorrow," the doctor said.

"I'm fine."

"No, you're not. You have a low-grade fever, your wound is still draining, and you can't sit up without help. Swallow all that broth then see if you can sleep through the night. Feed him more in the morning," the doctor said to Roberta. "Feed him the same at midday. I'll come back as soon as I can. Depending on how he's doing, maybe he can have some solid food."

"When can I take him home?" Russ wanted to know.

"I can't say," the doctor replied. "But if you want to make it longer, keep arguing over him."

Russ seemed angry at the doctor's strictures on their behavior, but Roberta was chagrined. She didn't have to like Nate Dolan, she didn't even have to believe him, but she did have to behave in a manner she could respect.

"Let me know when he can eat real food," Russ said. "I'll see he has three hot meals a day as long as he's stuck here."

"I can feed him," Roberta said.

"I wouldn't want to keep you from your work," Russ sneered.

Nate opened his mouth to say something, and Roberta filled it with broth.

"Smart girl," the doctor said with a grin. "You," he said to Russ, "out of here now. I know you're trying to take care of your boss—from what I hear he's too good for that rascally bunch you call cowhands—but you're just causing needless anxiety. Send someone else with those meals. I expect you've got plenty of work to keep you busy. You," he said to Roberta, "make sure he eats a full bowl of broth at each meal. You can check on him occasionally, but leave him alone to get as much rest as possible. You," he said turning to Nate, "are to ignore both of them and concentrate on getting well. Now I have to go. I have other patients who actually deserve my attention."

The doctor left quickly, taking Russ with him, which left Roberta facing Nate with what was left of the bowl of broth.

"You're going to make me eat the rest of it, aren't you?" he asked.

"You heard the doctor."

"He's gone."

"But I'm here, and I intend to make sure no one

can say I didn't do everything I could to make you well. Now eat."

"No wonder you're not married. Any husband of yours would be so henpecked he wouldn't have a thought to call his own."

"The man I marry will love me so much he'll be eager to do anything he can to make me happy."

"You're not looking for a man. You're looking for a slave."

"I'll post a notice in town tomorrow." She shoved a spoonful of broth into Nate's mouth before he could reply.

&

Gilbert Travis cursed in three languages. "Why couldn't the damned woman shoot straight?" he demanded. "That would have been a perfect solution."

"Did you know Dolan was going to be there?"

"Would I have had you drop his hat if I did? Would I have wasted time shooting that foolish farmer?"

He thought it was wiser not to answer. He wished he'd never gotten involved with Travis. It was becoming clear he would stop at nothing to get what he wanted. He was uneasy about his own safety once he was no longer useful. He suspected Travis had no use for those who worked for him once their usefulness was over.

"Are you sure he's in her house?"

"Yes."

"He won't have the good sense to die from his injury, so I'll have to think of something else…"

Despite being so tired she could hardly move, Roberta couldn't sleep. She'd checked on Nate twice that evening, and his temperature still hadn't gone down. Now he was talking in his sleep, which meant he was having a bad dream or was delirious.

Groaning from the effort, she got out of bed. Modesty caused her to put on a robe, though she couldn't say why she was worried about a man who wouldn't know she was there. He probably wouldn't care. A man as handsome and rich as Nate Dolan had probably been with enough women to populate a small town. He certainly had shown no signs of being impressed by her. Not that she wanted to impress him. She wouldn't have been interested if she'd been positive he had nothing to do with her father's death.

Locating the matches she kept near her bedside, she lit her lamp. She settled the globe over the lamp and left her room. Her bare feet made soft plopping sounds on the wood floor of the parlor. Turning the flame down as low as possible, she entered her father's bedroom.

She could tell right away Nate's temperature hadn't gone down. He was restless. His lips looked chapped, his skin unnaturally dry. Despite the restrictive bandage, he'd managed to throw off the sheet. Only his legs below his knees were covered. Roberta didn't need to turn up the flame in her lamp to know she was looking at a nearly perfect male body.

For a moment, shock held her motionless. She was familiar with the basics of male anatomy, but she'd never been exposed to one so openly. There was nothing to keep her from staring as long as she wanted. No one to tell her that a *nice* woman would avert her gaze until she had replaced the sheet. No one to tell her that a *nice* woman wouldn't want to look at a man's body, not even if that man were her husband.

Despite her desire to prolong the pleasure of looking at Nate, Roberta reached for the sheet. As she did so, her hand brushed against Nate's knee. She had never given any thought to the aesthetics of a man's knee—she couldn't remember that she'd ever seen one—but Nate's knee held a fascination all out of proportion to its humble position on the body. Maybe because it connected a well-rounded calf to a powerful thigh. Most likely it was the scar that ran from above his knee halfway down his calf. At one time, Nate had been seriously injured.

Even though she was quick to pull the sheet up to his shoulders, it was impossible not to take note of what rested between his legs. It was almost as frightening as it was impressive. It was safer to concentrate on his broad chest and muscled shoulders. Safer, but not nearly as titillating.

She chastised herself for taking such unfair advantage of Nate, but she knew she would do it again. What unsettled her even more was how much she *wanted* to do it again. She forced her fingers to release the sheet before sheer impulse made her lower it again.

Only hours before she'd said she wouldn't have cared if he had died. Now she was struggling to prevent unwelcome images from springing to vivid life in her mind. Taking a deep breath to slow her heart rate and decrease the tension in her shoulders, she leaned against the wall for support. She was here because Nate was feverish. Nothing else was important. She'd never been interested in Nate despite his looks, his money, and his popularity. She wasn't about to change now.

Feeling more in control, she pushed off from the wall and moved to the side of the bed. She placed her hand on Nate's forehead. He was hot. Too hot. She needed to bring his temperature down. She left the bedroom and returned shortly with a basin of water she'd drawn from the well. Setting the basin on a table next to the bed, she drew up a chair. She soaked a cloth in water, wrung most of it out, folded the cloth, and placed it on Nate's forehead.

Nate moaned and threw his head to one side. Roberta dipped the cloth in water and applied it to his forehead again. Over the next several minutes she repeated the motion until the water in the basin had become lukewarm. When she returned from the second trip to get water, Nate had pushed the sheet down to his waist. Having gotten herself under control, she decided to leave it there.

When she put the compress on his forehead, he pushed it away. She put it back and held it in place when he pushed at it again.

"Caleb."

Roberta didn't know who Nate was talking about. She didn't know anyone named Caleb.

"No! No!"

Nate became more and more agitated. When she tried to hold the cloth in place, he pushed her so hard she nearly fell out of her chair. He stopped fighting as abruptly as he started. Moments later, tears rolled down his cheeks. His lips formed words she couldn't decipher. He seemed to withdraw into himself, sink deeper into the bed.

During the next two hours Nate talked in spurts, sometimes in short angry bursts and other times with a sense of helpless doom. She learned that Caleb was his brother and that he was dead. She couldn't decide whether Laveau diViere had killed Caleb or had just been responsible for his death. She did know Nate hated diViere with a vehemence that caused his temperature to spike.

Three hours later, Roberta was so tired she could barely stay awake. She was afraid the doctor would arrive in the morning to find Nate suffering from a raging fever while she was asleep in the chair. Her back ached. Her shoulders were in knots. Her hands were shriveled from so much time in water. She barely stifled one yawn before another took hold. She found herself dozing off, the damp cloth slipping from her grasp. Once she nearly let the pan slip off her lap. Despite going through a half dozen pans of water, Nate's fever didn't break. If nothing else worked, she'd start pouring basins of water over his whole body.

At first, Nate's ramblings had helped to keep her awake, but he said the same things so many times she stopped listening. So it was a jolt when she heard him say *fire*. He repeated the word several times without saying anything else. What did he mean? Had he seen a fire? Had he set a fire? Had he been in a fire?

"Got to help Robert."

Roberta sat bolt upright, all thought of sleep forgotten.

"Got to help Robert."

There was no mistaking what his words meant. He'd seen the fire and had come to help her father. She had shot an innocent man.

If Roberta hadn't been on the verge of passing out from exhaustion, she might have been horrified by what she'd done. As it was, she felt little more than the deadening weight of guilt. All she could do now was sit up with Nate until his fever broke. After that, she'd see what she could do about learning to live with herself.

৵

"Wake up. What kind of nurse are you?"

Someone was shaking Roberta. She mumbled in protest, hoping they would go away and let her sleep.

"Young woman, I order you to wake up this instant. You've got Crazy Joe pulling apart what's left of your barn, and a sick man in need of his breakfast. There's no time to sleep in a chair that will probably ruin your back."

Roberta fought off the deadening weight of sleep that threatened to pull her into unconsciousness once more. She recognized the doctor's voice. She just couldn't open her eyes to see him.

"He had a fever," she managed to say. "I meant to change the sheets, but…" She opened her eyes, and blinked at the doctor. "I must have fallen asleep after his fever broke."

"How long were you up?"

"I remember it was getting light."

"Then you can't have had more than two hours of sleep. Take yourself off to bed. Crazy Joe is working for you."

"I've got to help him."

"You'll do nothing of the sort. Your father's being buried this morning. Give Crazy Joe whatever instructions he needs, then get back in here and eat breakfast before you dress for the funeral. I'll drive you into town."

"Why is Joe here? Who told him to come?"

"You'll have to ask him. I can never get more than two words out of him. Sometimes not that many."

Roberta struggled to her feet. Most people didn't understand Joe. He wasn't crazy. He was just slow. He was also big, powerful, and able to understand when people made fun of him. People had learned to leave him alone.

Roberta dragged herself past the rows of ruined crops until she reached the barn. The men from town had managed to save the roof and two sides. The third side was badly damaged, but the fourth was gone. Joe was pulling down the charred timbers.

"What are you doing?" Roberta asked.

"Miss Prudence told Joe to fix your barn," Joe replied. "She said everybody else is afraid. Joe is not afraid."

"I know you're not, but I want you to do something else."

"Did Joe do something wrong?"

"Of course not. I just want you to go through the fields and set up the plants that are still alive."

"Joe is good with plants."

Joe tended Prudence's garden. It made other gardens in Slender Creek look like wasteland.

"I have to go to town for my father's funeral, but I'll help you when I get back."

"Joe doesn't like funerals."

Joe had been forced to watch both parents and his sister be buried. Whenever there was a funeral in town, Joe would hide. "You don't have to go. I'll fix us something to eat when I get back."

"Miss Annie feeds Joe. He's not hungry."

Roberta had never understood why Joe spoke of himself in the third person. Maybe if he could talk about Joe like he was another person, he didn't have to feel the pain of *being* Joe.

"I really appreciate your help," Roberta told Joe, "but you have to work at the saloon."

"Miss Prudence said Joe was to stay here. She said she didn't care if the saloon dried up and blew away. Joe doesn't want the saloon to blow away. Joe likes the saloon."

"I'll talk to Prudence when I'm in town."

"Joe does what Miss Prudence tells Joe to do."

"I'm sure you do. I'll see you when I get back."

"Joe is good with plants."

Maybe Joe should have been the farmer.

❧

Roberta was surprised that nearly everyone in town turned out for her father's funeral. She was not surprised most of them left without speaking to her.

"Prudence went door to door," Mrs. Pender

explained with one of her rare smiles. "People are more afraid of her than the ranchers."

Yet it was the ranchers who offered their condolences. Some volunteered to help clear away the remains of the barn. It was hard to accept their false sympathy without saying any of the things that burned on the end of her tongue, but she was determined her revenge would be in deeds rather than words.

"Thanks for your offer, but I'll worry about the barn later," she told Frank Porter, a self-important little man who bullied his wife and three daughters. "Joe and I are busy trying to save my crops."

"I was told everything had been destroyed," his wife said.

"Not everything. I'm hoping I'll have enough to feed myself until I can replant."

"You're keeping the farm?" Frank Porter asked.

"Of course. It was my father's dream, and I intend to see it fulfilled."

"You can't do that without water."

"There's plenty of water in the creek."

Frank Porter turned red in the face. "Are you saying you plan to rebuild the dam?"

"I'm not saying I *won't* rebuild it," she replied.

"Are you crazy?" Frank exclaimed. "You know somebody will just blow it up again."

That was too much. The tight rein she'd kept on her temper snapped. "My father's dead. Will you have your men kill me this time?"

Frank's wife gasped in shock. He turned still redder. "I had nothing to do with your father's death."

"My father's *murder*. Let's make sure we use the right words."

"Regardless of how he died, I had nothing to do with it."

She spun around to face some of the others waiting to speak to her. "How about you, Ches Hale? Was it your men in those masks?" She didn't wait for an answer before turning to Ezra Kemp. "Are your men good at setting fires, or are they better at trampling crops?" Ezra sputtered with rage, but she turned to Jess Reilly, the man who'd been most outspoken in his objection to her father's dam. "Are you the one who shot my father?"

Each man furiously denied having any part in the attack.

"So who did kill my father and blow up his dam? I suppose you want me to believe some strangers happened to be wandering by and thought it would be fun to shoot up a farm." She pointed a finger at Frank Porter then turned in a circle until she'd indicated every rancher present. "You're the ones who blew up the first dam. You're the ones who threatened my father when he decided to rebuild it. You're the ones who tried to drive him out." She turned on Mead Ryan. "You even tried to get the bank to foreclose on his property. When you found out my father owned his farm outright, you put pressure on Boone Riggins and everyone else in town to stop buying from him."

"I'm not ashamed to admit it," Mead blustered. "All of us depend on the water in that creek. Your father had no right to dam it, but I had nothing to do with what happened. I thought your father was a hard-headed fool who would fail if given enough time."

"So when he didn't fail soon enough, you decided to do something about it."

"I didn't kill your father."

"I'm going to find out who's responsible," Roberta stated. "I don't care if it's one or all of you. When I do, I'm going to make sure you hang."

"You'd better be careful what charges you throw at people," Mead Ryan said.

Roberta walked up to him, looked him in the eye. "Are you threatening me? Is my house going to mysteriously catch fire one night, or are some more strangers going to wander by looking for someone to shoot?"

Mead backed away a step. "No decent man would lay a hand on a woman, but that don't mean you can go around saying anything you want."

"I'm saying someone killed my father. It wasn't an accident. I saw it. I'm saying the ranchers are the only ones I know who had a reason to want the farm and the dam destroyed. I'm saying I intend to find out who's responsible. If you know of any reason why I shouldn't say those things, now would be a good time to tell me."

"My husband couldn't have had anything to do with it," Mrs. Kemp said. "Our hands were at the ranch that night."

"So were mine," Ches Hale insisted. "I didn't let them go into town because I wanted them up early the next morning."

Alibis came at her from every direction, but

Roberta didn't back down. "The fact remains that someone *didn't* stay home that night. Someone *did* attack our farm."

"You don't believe me?" Mrs. Kemp asked.

"Would you believe me if you were in my position?"

Mrs. Kemp paused. "No, I guess I wouldn't, but our men were at the ranch that evening. We had a party for my son's birthday."

"Did you check to see that they were still at the ranch three hours after midnight?" Roberta asked.

"Of course not."

"Then you don't know they weren't involved."

≈

Roberta had gotten through the funeral service without breaking down. Prudence had arranged everything beautifully, even telling the preacher what to say. Listening to the litany of praise from the pulpit made her quite proud to be his daughter. But her emotions took a sharp turn when she watched them lower her father's casket into the ground. The finality of death was indisputable. He had ceased to exist in the only form in which she could know him.

With tears running down her cheeks, she endured the final words spoken at the graveside. She was shaken but stalwart when the first shovel of dirt hit her father's coffin, but when a little girl dropped a single daisy into the open grave, she couldn't hold back any longer. All the grief and loneliness came pouring out. She didn't know when Prudence took her by the shoulders and led her to a chair. She didn't know when the men finished filling in the grave. She was relieved when, after refusing several offers to rest in a home or accept a ride back to the farm, everyone except Prudence had left. It wasn't easy to convince Prudence she wanted to walk the half mile to the farm by herself, but she was so insistent Prudence finally give in.

It had been one of those rare springs in south Texas when the rains had come in sufficient quantities and at regular intervals. With the scorching heat of summer held at bay, the earth was green, the skies clear, and the breeze soft and gentle. On such a day, in such a season, how was such tragedy possible?

She wouldn't forget her father any more than she had forgotten her mother, but she couldn't let his death weigh her down until she became mired in self-pity or in useless railing against his murderers. She had to rebuild the farm, and she had to find out who killed him. Only then could she decide what to do with the rest of her life.

The walk had been a good idea. The clear skies and warm sun helped to lighten the load of sadness that threatened to engulf her. The green of the prairie stretching around her on all sides held out the promise of new life. She had to begin again, acquire new skills, learn new lessons, but she wouldn't stop. She couldn't give up. If she did, they would win. By the time she reached the turn in the lane that brought her house into view, she was ready and eager to tackle the work ahead.

She was startled to see a man on horseback dismounting in front of her house. She was too far away to recognize, but he didn't look like anyone she knew. Rather than climb the steps and knock on the door, he disappeared around the far side of the house. His movements gave the impression of stealth. That was odd. What was he looking for? Why did he feel he couldn't approach the front door?

She didn't like the feeling that was creeping along her spine. Nate was in the house alone and asleep. She couldn't imagine why anyone would be looking for him, or why a man would be sneaking behind the house. Now she wished she'd accepted the sheriff's offer to see her home, but it was too late for regrets.

She increased her pace. The longer the man remained out of sight, the more apprehensive she became. When he did reappear—looking through the window of the bedroom where Nate slept—she wasn't reassured. He looked too long, his interest too riveted.

Now she was walking so fast she was almost running. The man was so focused on what he was doing, he didn't appear to be aware that she was approaching. He left the window and walked around to the front of the house. As he ascended the steps, she saw him push back his coat to reveal a holstered pistol.

He was going into the house to kill Nate!

Chapter Four

She wasn't close enough to stop him, so she called out, "Can I help you?"

The man froze. His hand dropped to his side. When he turned to face Roberta, he was like a different person. He came down the steps with the easy stride of a man confident of his welcome.

"This is my house." Roberta wheezed, while trying to catch her breath. "What do you want?"

The man came toward her, flashing a genial smile, and with outstretched hand. "You must be Miss Roberta Tryon," he said. "I'm so sorry to hear about your father."

Roberta ignored the outstretched hand. "Then why weren't you at his funeral?" She thought she saw a flash of something deep in his black eyes, but it was gone too quickly for her to be sure.

"I didn't know your father personally. I didn't feel it was appropriate for me to attend the funeral."

"That doesn't matter in Texas. Everybody goes to funerals."

"I was not brought up to do that."

There was something about him that was foreign.

It wasn't his English, which was perfect. It wasn't his clothes, though they were too dandified for anybody outside of San Antonio. It wasn't even his features. There were too many different nationalities represented in Texas for there to be a typical look. Yet there was something about him that set him apart.

"Why were you sneaking into my house?"

"I heard about the attack and your father's death. Being an unmarried woman with no family close by, I thought you might be interested in selling your farm. I'm interested in buying it."

"I'm not interested in selling, and I still want to know why you were trying to sneak into my house."

"I heard a noise inside the house. Or I thought I did. I circled around hoping to locate and identify the sound, but failed to do so. Unable to tolerate the thought that someone might be robbing you while you were seeing your father into the next world, I was preparing to enter the house to make certain there was no thief inside."

It was a perfectly acceptable explanation, but Roberta couldn't forget the change that had come over him when she called out. His posture was too practiced, his bearing too formal, his explanation too high-handed. He watched her with eyes that seemed never to blink. It was as though he was trying to overwhelm her with the force of his personality. But Roberta couldn't be unsettled by a penetrating gaze or an aloof, aristocratic attitude.

"Thank you for your concern, but I'm certain there's no thief in the house. Since I have no intention of selling my farm, we have nothing to talk about."

"You haven't heard my offer. Maybe we could go inside, have a cup of coffee, and talk it over."

"Mister... I don't even know your name."

"Gilbert Travis at your service." He made a bow, which seemed ridiculously out of place in the middle of a Texas farm.

"Mr. Travis, I've just come from my father's funeral. I've had to be polite and control my emotions in front of a lot of people. Right now I'm perilously close to being rude. I need to go inside, close the door, and spend the next several hours trying to decide what I'm going to do with the rest of my life."

"If you will accept my offer, you will have a lot more choices."

"I'm sure I would, but I'm not going to. Now please leave."

She didn't give him time to object. She walked up the steps, through the door, and closed it. Only then did the tension in her shoulders ease. Who was that man and what did he really want? She had no reason to doubt anything he said, but she couldn't rid herself of the feeling that something was amiss. She looked through the window and was relieved to see him mount his horse and ride away. She tensed when he stopped at the head of the lane. She locked the door when it looked like he might turn back, but after a moment, he rode away.

She had a sudden need to assure herself that Nate was all right. She didn't stop to take her hat off, but went straight to the bedroom. He awoke when he heard her enter.

"You're back."

She was relieved to see him just as she had left him. Nate must have had a dream that caused him to make the sound Mr. Travis heard. If they were as terrible as the dreams that haunted her, she wasn't surprised he had cried out. "How are you feeling?"

"Much better until I had a dream that woke me up."

She removed her hat and set it on the dresser. "Was it about the attack?"

"No. I dreamed I saw Laveau diViere looking in the window."

She had several things to tell him—that she'd fix him some broth as soon as she could heat it, that she had decided he hadn't been one of the men who'd attacked the farm—but she couldn't get the unusual behavior of Mr. Travis out of her mind. "What does Laveau diViere look like?"

Nate's mouth clamped down until his lips almost disappeared. His brows bunched over eyes that narrowed and turned as hard as blue ice. His hands clawed the sheets like a hawk impaling its prey. Even his lank, brown hair seemed to recoil at the mention of the hated name. "He looks like the Devil himself."

His reaction was so intense, she was sorry she'd asked. "Don't try to sit up. You're not strong enough yet."

Ignoring her, Nate struggled until he'd raised his body from the bed.

Roberta pushed two pillows behind him. "If the doctor were to come in now, he'd have a fit."

Nate collapsed against the pillows. "Thinking about diViere would raise me from my death bed. What made you ask what he looks like?"

"When I got back, there was a man here who said he was Gilbert Travis."

"I don't know anybody by that name."

"I don't either, but he was looking in your window. It was probably him you saw."

Nate tensed. "What did he look like?"

"I'm not very good at describing people."

"Try."

"He had black hair parted in the middle and was clean-shaven except for a small mustache. His skin was almost white, his face kind of pinched, like someone had put their hands on either side of his head and squeezed. Still, I imagine he is quite handsome when he smiles."

"What color were his eyes?"

"Black."

"Did they blink?"

"They must have, but I felt like they never did—just stared at me like he was trying to see inside my head."

"How was he dressed? Was he short or tall?"

Nate was becoming so agitated Roberta was uneasy. "I'm sorry I said anything. I'm sure he was—" She was about to turn away when Nate grabbed her wrist.

"How was he dressed?" It wasn't a request. It was a demand.

"He was about as tall as you, about your build, and dressed like he had just stepped out of a hotel in San Antonio." She pried his fingers loose from her wrist. "Why are you so upset?"

"I wasn't dreaming. You've just described Laveau diViere."

"But he said he was Gilbert Travis."

"That's probably one of the names he uses when he's putting together one of his schemes to cheat people. What was he doing?"

"He said he wanted to buy my farm."

"I don't care what he *said*. What was he *doing*?"

Roberta wished she didn't have to tell Nate what she'd seen. It would only upset him more.

"Are you sure he was reaching for a gun?" Nate asked after she'd described diViere's movements.

"That's what it looked like."

"He was here to kill me. I'm surprised he didn't shoot me through the window."

"Why would he do something like that?"

"I've been following him for two years. I've busted up some of his schemes. I tell every law officer I meet that he's wanted for murder in Overlin. The Reconstruction government is about to go. Once we elect men of honor, Laveau will lose his protection. He knows an honest Texas jury would hang him."

Roberta wasn't thinking about a jury. She was thinking about Nate being alone in the house while she worked in the fields, of both of them being vulnerable while they slept.

"I need a gun," Nate said.

"You need to rest. You're far from well."

"I'll be even further from well if Laveau shoots me. I want a gun, and I want something over that window. Can you lock your door?"

"Yes."

"Make sure you lock it every time you leave, even if it's only to feed the chickens or pick up the eggs."

A few chickens had returned to roost in a peach tree her father had planted, but she had no idea where they might be laying their eggs. "I can't leave you."

"If you do what I ask, you can go anywhere you want. I've got enough cowhands to watch the place around the clock, but you've got to be careful. Laveau won't hesitate to kill you if that's what he has to do to get to me."

"Does he hate you that much?"

"Yes."

Roberta found it hard to believe anyone could be that evil, but she couldn't forget the feeling she got before she called out to diViere.

"You look surprised," Nate said.

"Wouldn't you be if someone had just told you that you could be shot in your own home?"

"I've always known Laveau would kill me if he got the chance."

"Then why did you keep following him?"

"I lost my brother and twenty-three friends because Laveau was determined to be on the winning side. One man who survived got half his face shot off. I'll never stop until one of us is dead. Could you?"

Roberta opened her mouth to deny that she could ever pursue such a goal. She closed it when she realized she couldn't say that about the man who'd killed her father. "I don't know. I shot you because, at the time, I felt as you do."

"Have you changed your mind?"

She wanted to look away, but she didn't. "I changed it about you."

Nate's expression showed surprise. "Why?"

"You talked in your sleep when you were feverish."

"What did I say?"

"That you saw a fire. That you had to help Robert."

"Was that all you needed to convince you I wasn't one of the attackers?"

"You weren't wearing a mask like the others." She glanced away. "I always thought you were dumb for spending all your time following that man, but you never threatened Papa."

"Did I say anything else?"

"You talked about someone named Caleb. Was that your brother?"

Nate's look softened, turned sad. "He was a year younger, twice as good-looking, and full of fun. Everybody loved him. My mother worshipped him. I used to get jealous, but Caleb would put his arm around my shoulder and tell me he loved me enough to make up for two mothers. Maybe he did because he wouldn't let me go off to war without him. We joined the Night Riders together. Our captain was so successful at keeping everybody safe I couldn't make Caleb understand we weren't playing a game. He didn't want to kill anybody or steal anything. He would get so excited after a successful raid that it was all I could do to keep him from giving away our position. He would *sing*. Can you believe that? Always some stupid song Ma had taught him when he was a kid. I swear half the troop thought he was nuts, but whenever there was any fun to be had, Caleb was part of it."

"He sounds like a good brother."

"He was spoiled and often careless, but I loved him more than myself. Hearing of his death killed Ma. Pa followed not long after."

"Do you have other family?"

"Nobody close enough to make me go back to Arkansas."

Roberta would have wanted to go back to Virginia even if her closest relative had been a second cousin. She gave herself a mental shake. "I almost forgot. You need to eat."

"Give me something besides that flavored water."

"Not until the doctor says I can."

"Can I bribe you?"

There was something about the way he looked at her that gave Roberta's spirits a lift. "What have you got to offer?"

"What will get me soup with beef and vegetables? I'll settle for stewed chicken. How about eggs and sausage? Milk?"

"Both milk cows are gone, the chickens are running loose, and I don't have any sausage. If I give you beef and your fever comes back, your foreman will swear I'm trying to kill you."

"I'll talk to Russ. I'm his boss so he'll do anything I say."

"Sorry. I'm more afraid of the doctor than of you. I'll be back as soon as I change my clothes and heat the broth."

"I'll agree to swallow the broth if you'll bring me my gun."

Roberta walked over to the bureau, opened the top drawer, took out a holster and gun, and handed them to Nate. "Russ took your rifle and saddlebags when he took your horse."

"Put it next to me so I can reach it."

Roberta reached across Nate to slide the gun under the sheet. "I figure it needs to be where no one can see it."

"You're a smart woman. Now I'd appreciate it if you would bring me that broth. I am kinda hungry."

"I was hoping you'd have a change of heart," Nate said when she returned and placed the bowl before him.

"Your bribe wasn't good enough."

Nate eyed the broth with disfavor. "I'll have to work on that." He grimaced. "Do you have any idea how embarrassing it is to have to be fed by a woman?"

"Would you rather Russ do it?"

Nate looked aghast. "I'd never be able to face my men."

"Then stop complaining and eat."

"I'm only doing this for fear that if I don't you'll shoot me again."

"Don't tempt me."

Much to her surprise, they both laughed. "That's really not funny."

"I know. I'm the one being fed broth."

"I mean about me shooting you again. I'd never have shot you if I hadn't been in shock."

"If I could have found Laveau after Caleb died, I'd have stabbed him, strangled him, and mutilated his body."

"That would have stained your soul, and it wouldn't have brought your brother back."

The look Nate directed toward her was so full of bottled fury she nearly moved back.

"I wouldn't have cared."

Roberta hoped Nate didn't mean what he said, but she had no reason to believe he wasn't serious. "You'd better eat. I have to help Joe. If I don't save some of my crops, I'll have to accept Boone Riggins's offer to work in his saloon."

Nate nearly choked in his rush to say, "Don't."

She fed him another spoonful of broth. "It's not something I'm looking forward to, but neither is starvation."

"The people of Slender Creek won't let you starve."

"They're too afraid to help me. One way or another, most of them depend on the ranchers for their living."

"Fine, then *I* won't let you starve." He looked at her with such intensity a shiver went up her spine.

"I'd rather save my crops."

He pushed away the spoon she held to his mouth. "Do you hate me that much?"

"No," she said after a moment's thought. "I don't think I hate anyone but the man who shot my father."

"The sheriff will find out who did it."

"I expect the sheriff is just as beholden to the ranchers as anyone else." She put a spoonful of broth into his mouth. "I'll do it myself."

"How?"

"I don't know, but working in the fields will give me plenty of time to come up with a plan. Farming doesn't take a lot of thinking."

"Neither does ranching. My parents managed two stores, a livery stable, and owned part of a bank. That took a lot of thinking and a lot of work. I used the money they left to buy a ranch because it would give me time to follow Laveau."

"You don't care about ranching?"

He swallowed a mouthful of broth. "I didn't in the beginning, but I'm starting to."

"But you're still going to spend most of your time looking for diViere."

"I won't have much choice if he's decided to come after me." He pushed away the next spoonful of broth. "That's enough unless you want to help me to the chamber pot."

Roberta felt herself blush. "I'll leave that for Russ. Now I need to help Joe. Are you sure you'll be okay?"

"I've got my gun, and I'm not going to lie down until you put something over that window."

"I'll have Joe do it right away."

"Are you sure you can trust that man? Most people say he's crazy. Some even think he's dangerous."

"Joe doesn't trust people because they've been cruel to him, but he wouldn't hurt me or Prudence."

"I wouldn't hurt Prudence. That woman scares me."

Roberta grinned. "She is rather severe, but she's got a good heart."

"I'll take your word for it. Just don't let her in here."

Roberta lost all desire to laugh. "If she ever finds I'm alone with a man, even one who's unable to sit up without help, she won't leave. I expect the doctor will be by before supper. Maybe you can convince him to let you have something other than broth."

"Don't forget to lock the door and get Crazy Joe to cover this window."

She started to object to the way he referred to Joe but decided to do that later. Right now she had to take care of the window. Thinking of what diViere would have done if she'd been five minutes later made her shudder.

&

"If you insist on working until you're ready to drop, you might as well work in my saloon," Boone said to Roberta. "At least you won't have to dig in the dirt."

Roberta had toiled in the hot sun the whole afternoon. Joe had set the chicken coop to rights and nailed boards over Nate's window. One of the cows had returned, so he put together a rough corral for her and the two mules. Joe would catch the hens when they went to roost. That would mean stock to be fed, a cow to be milked, and eggs to be gathered as well as fixing supper for her and Nate. Thinking about all she had left to do put her in no mood to deal with Boone.

"If I hadn't sworn to make a success of this farm, I'd be tempted to consider your offer," she told him, "but right now I'm too tired to think about anything."

"If you'd marry me, you wouldn't have to think."

Roberta didn't look up from the tomato plant she was staking. "Marriage is the most important decision any woman can make. That requires more thinking than all the rest."

"Otis Parker told me he turned down your request for a loan. How are you going to survive without money?"

Roberta stood up to face Boone. "He had no business talking to you about my private affairs."

"I needed to know if he'd given you a loan because I was going to offer."

Roberta placed her hand on her hips. "Otis is positive the ranchers will blow up the dam if I rebuild it. You'd lose your money just like he would."

"I don't care about the money. I'd give it to you. It's not right for you to work in this field like a hired hand."

"I appreciate your offer, but I can't accept it."

"What if I make it a loan with interest?"

"I'd be obligated to you, and I won't be obligated to anyone."

"You were willing to be obligated to Otis."

"I would have been obligated to the bank. That's different."

"I don't see how."

Roberta turned to Joe, who'd been working quietly alongside her. "We've done about all we can today, so I'm going to the house to clean up. By the time you've milked the cow and done the feeding, I'll have supper ready."

"Joe eats supper at the restaurant," Joe said.

"I know, but you've spent the day working for me. I owe you supper."

"Annie cooks his favorites all the time," Boone told her. "If he's not there, she's liable to throw a fit and not cook for anybody. Half of Slender Creek would go hungry."

"I feel like I ought to pay him something."

"He wouldn't know what to do with it. Prudence collects his salary. Suppose I set you up in a dress shop?"

Roberta left the field and started toward the house. "Someone would still need to work the farm."

"Then give it up."

"I can't let the attackers think they succeeded. This is Texas. A person is supposed to be able to do what he wants."

"Look at you. Your dress covered with dirt, your hair escaping your bonnet and plastered to your forehead, and your hands covered with whatever it is that rubbed off those plants. Are you really doing what you want?"

Roberta didn't shorten her stride. The thought of getting to the house and cleaning up gave her extra energy. "If you dislike the way I look, why do you want to marry me?"

"I don't dislike it. I just hate that you have to work so hard."

"I don't mind. I won't have to do it forever."

"You mean you won't have to do it when you go back to Virginia, but I don't want you to go back. You don't belong there anymore. You're a Texan. What other woman would be stubborn enough to try to handle this farm by herself?"

Roberta had already been prey to doubts on that very score, but she wasn't going to let Boone know. Before she could decide how to respond, she rounded the corner of the charred remains of the barn to see Russ McCoy attacking the door of her house with his booted foot. "Stop!" she yelled.

"It's stuck," Russ yelled back.

"It's not stuck. I locked it."

"Why the hell for?"

She didn't answer until she'd reached the house. "Because your boss asked me to."

"Why would he do that?"

"Laveau diViere was here this morning."

"What makes you think it was diViere?"

"When I described him, Nate said it had to be diViere. He'd seen him at the window but thought it was a dream."

"His window is boarded up."

"He wanted it that way. Both of you stay here. As soon as I change my dress and fix my hair, I'll let you in."

Roberta trudged around to the back of the house. She left her dirt-encrusted shoes on the porch, hung her sweat-soaked bonnet on a peg, unlocked the kitchen door, and went inside. She would have liked nothing better than to cool her head under the pump, but she would have to do with the relief of being out of the sun. She quickly washed up, changed her dress, and ran a comb through her hair. Tugging on a pair of slippers, she went through the house to the parlor.

"Is that you?" Nate called before she reached the door.

Changing her path, she walked to the bedroom. Nate was propped up, his gun in his hand. He relaxed when he saw her. "I guess I don't need this." He indicated the gun that he slipped back under the sheet covering him.

"I was hoping you'd be asleep."

"I was until I heard someone trying to break down the door."

"That was Russ. I had to tell him about diViere to keep him from kicking it in."

"What took you so long?" Russ asked when she unlocked the door.

Boone responded angrily. "Roberta doesn't have to answer to you in her own home."

"She does as long as my boss is here. The doctor just drove up," Russ said over his shoulder as he headed toward Nate's bedroom.

"You don't have to put up with that man's rudeness," Boone said.

"He's just concerned about his boss."

"You mean he's concerned about his job. Nobody else would pay him so much for doing so little."

"You having a party here?" Dr. Danforth asked when he entered the house. "I hope I'm welcome."

"You're more than welcome if you've come to get that man out of Roberta's house," Boone said. "If you can get him out tonight, you can eat free at the restaurant for a week."

"That's a tempting offer, but it depends on my patient."

"He's probably pretending to be worse than he is."

The doctor eyed Boone with a cocked eyebrow. "Why would you say that?"

"Who would you rather have looking after you, Russ or Roberta?"

The doctor winked at Roberta. "I see what you mean, but I suspect Nate would rather not have been shot."

Roberta's father often said his bedroom was too big for one man, but it was crowded by the time four people had gathered around Nate's bed.

"I hope you're not planning to turn this into a

wake," Nate joked. "I'm not ready to cash in my chips yet."

Dr. Danforth pushed Russ aside. "It seems I'm the only one not trying to get you out of this house."

Nate cast an injured look at Roberta. "I'll see that you get a new window."

"I'm not trying to get rid of you," she protested.

"You ought to be," Boone said. "You shouldn't have to be responsible for him."

"She won't be as soon as I can get him back to the ranch," Russ said.

"Both of you wait outside," the doctor said. "He'll get well a lot faster without you fighting over him. You stay," he said, when Roberta started to follow the two men. "He's not going anywhere for the next day or two. I'm not happy with how he's looking. What's he doing sitting up?"

The doctor wasn't any happier when Roberta explained about diViere. "Nate is going to have Russ set up a guard on the house."

"Don't let them stand watch in this room. You have to keep Nate as quiet as possible if you want him to go home soon."

"He can stay as long as he needs to." Both men stared at her in a way that made her fidgety. "I don't believe he was one of the attackers. I think he was coming to help." They didn't stop staring. "I'm sorry I shot him." It was a lame ending, but she had nothing else to say.

The doctor recovered his businesslike attitude. "I'm glad you got that cleared up. Now, here's what I want you to do for the next two days."

"Unless you want me to die of hunger, let her feed me something besides broth," Nate begged.

"I guess if he's strong enough to sit up all afternoon, he's ready for some solid food," Dr. Danforth told Roberta. "Just don't start him on a diet of steak and beans. Some baked chicken ought to perk up your appetite."

The physician had just finished going over what he wanted Roberta to do for the next couple of days when the bedroom door was flung open, and Prudence Goodfellow appeared like a bad fairy.

"What is that man doing here?" She sounded like a demigod passing judgment on fallible mankind. "He must leave at once."

Chapter Five

"HE CAN'T LEAVE UNTIL I SAY SO," THE DOCTOR SAID. "Now go bother someone else."

"He was shot during the attack," Roberta said, trying to reassure Prudence. "He has to stay here until he's well enough to go back to his ranch."

"If he's one of the attackers, he belongs in jail," Prudence declared. "I'll have the sheriff remove him."

"He was coming to help," Roberta admitted. "I shot him by mistake."

That revelation gave Prudence pause. "I don't believe you. You're not a violent woman."

"I'd just seen my father shot. I didn't know what I was doing." Roberta followed Prudence's gaze, which was fastened on Nate's bare chest.

"It's not proper for a respectable woman to be in a house alone with an undressed man unless it's her husband."

"I'm changing his bandage," the doctor said. "If you don't like what you see, don't look."

"I don't care about myself, but Roberta, who shouldn't be exposed to…" Prudence seemed at a loss for words.

"Am I so ugly I offend her?" Nate asked.

"It's not a question of attractiveness," Prudence asserted. "No young woman can be alone with a man without endangering her reputation."

"I can barely sit up without help," Nate pointed out. "How can I possibly endanger her reputation?"

"You're a man," Prudence declared.

"Blame that on my parents," Nate said. "I had nothing to do with it."

"You're a good woman," the doctor told Prudence, "but right now you sound like you have less sense than Crazy Joe. Do something about her, Roberta, before I give her an injection."

"Come on," Roberta said to Prudence.

"I'm not leaving this house while he's here," Prudence stated as Roberta pushed her out of the room. "You never know what a man is capable of, even one who's been shot."

Russ, who had been waiting impatiently in the parlor, took exception to Prudence's aspersion on his boss. "I'll warrant he won't be a danger to you."

"I'm here to see he's not a danger to Roberta," Boone added.

"Russ is going to send someone to watch Nate at night," Roberta told Prudence. "I promise to keep my door fastened. Joe arrives early every morning so I'll be safe."

"I mean to take Nate back to the ranch as soon as the doctor says he can be moved," Russ said to Prudence. "I don't want him here any more than you do."

"Do you think Roberta's incapable of taking care of him?" Boone demanded.

When the two men started to argue, Roberta couldn't stand it any longer. "Stop, all of you. Nate is going to remain here until the doctor says he can go home, and all your fussing isn't going to change that. One of his men will be here from now on, so it's unlikely that I'll poison him or that he'll attack me. The doctor will make sure I give Nate the care he needs, and Joe will protect my virtue. I think that covers everything, so you can go home. Boone has his saloon to run, Russ has to organize the watch, and Prudence has to get home before dark. I'm depending on the two of you to see that she gets there safely."

It would have been hard to say who was more dismayed, Russ or Boone.

"Come on," Russ said to Prudence in a very ungallant manner. "I've got to get somebody over here quick."

"She can go with me," Boone offered. "I'd hate for you to have to go out of your way."

"Fine." Russ turned to Roberta. "If anything happens to the boss, I'm holding you responsible."

"Since I'm the one prescribing for him, you might as well hold me responsible, too." The doctor regarded Russ like he was a small, misbehaving boy. Since Russ was six inches taller and about twice his size, Roberta found it amusing.

Russ muttered a curse and stalked from the house, slamming the door behind him.

"Ignore him," the doctor said to Roberta. "He's just worried about his boss."

"About his job you mean," Boone said.

"That too. Now both of you get out of here so Nate can get some rest," Dr. Danforth ordered.

"I will be back in the morning," Prudence assured Roberta.

Boone said he intended to check on Roberta just as often.

"Don't let whatever cowhand Russ sends spend the night in Nate's room," the doctor reminded Roberta after Boone and Prudence had left. "He needs his rest. Now that the window has been boarded up, there's nothing the fella can't do from out here."

"Is it really okay for me to give him some chicken?" Roberta asked.

The doctor heaved a sigh. "He should probably stick to broth one more day, but I dare say his stomach can handle chicken. Young men these days don't care what they eat. He could probably digest leather. Just don't let him eat too much, and don't let him have anything sweet. He can have plenty of that once he's strong enough to go home."

"How long will that be?"

"Are you still wanting him out as soon as possible?"

"Yes and no."

The doctor grinned. "Are you going to explain?"

"I want him out because I don't have time to take care of him, and I'm tired of Russ McCoy pushing his way in here twice a day accusing me of wanting to poison him. Still, I'm the one who shot him, so I should be the one to make sure he gets well."

"What made you change your mind about him being one of the attackers?"

"He talked in his sleep about seeing the fire and coming to help my father. Besides, he wasn't wearing a mask like the others."

"Glad to hear it. I don't know him well, but I always liked him." The doctor cocked his head. "Maybe you ought to get to know him. You might like him, too."

"Don't try putting any romantic notions in my head. I'm not interested in a man who spends half his time playing cat-and-mouse with a murderer."

"I heard you told the ranchers you intend to keep farming."

"I also intend to find out who murdered my father."

"Shouldn't you leave that to the sheriff?"

"As long as the ranchers stick together, the sheriff can't do anything."

"Talk to Nate about this. I think he's as interested as you in finding out who's behind it."

"He's a rancher."

"The attack caused him to get shot. I doubt he's too happy about that. Think about it," he said when Roberta was slow to answer. "There's a lot more to that young man than you think."

❧

"This is good," Nate said. "If you ever need a job, you can cook for me."

Roberta had boiled a chicken, made a sauce from the stock, and served it over rice. The way Nate was wolfing it down, you'd think he'd never had a decent meal. "If you had made biscuits and gravy, the meal would be perfect."

"I'm not your private cook."

"You could be."

"Can you see me surrounded by all those men? Prudence would have a heart attack."

"How is that different from working in Boone's saloon?"

"One is public, and one isn't."

"I could invite Prudence to chaperon."

"Now you're being ridiculous. Apparently you're recovering faster than the doctor expected. Maybe you can go home tomorrow."

"Why are you so anxious to get rid of me?"

Roberta took her time preparing the next mouthful of chicken. "It's not *you* I want to leave. It would be anybody. I've got a lot to do."

"Have you ever thought of asking for help?"

"I asked Otis Parker for a loan, but he turned me down. I thought the sheriff would have some information about who murdered my father by now, but I haven't seen him since the funeral."

"I expect it's too soon to know anything."

"It has to be the ranchers. All he needs to do is find one person who will tell the truth."

"If everybody is as afraid of them as you believe, that won't be easy."

"That's why I've decided to do it myself."

Nate pushed away the food she offered him. "You don't know anything about chasing murderers. It's extremely dangerous. Anyone willing to kill your father the way he did wouldn't hesitate to shoot you."

Roberta put the spoon back in the bowl and set it on the table. "Then what do you suggest I do?"

"Let the sheriff handle it."

"And if he can't?"

"We'll think of something."

"*We?*"

"Don't you think I'm as anxious as you to know who's behind this?"

"Why should you be? Your father didn't get killed."

"No, but I got shot because of it. Besides, I don't like knowing there's a cold-blooded murderer in my community."

"It's hardly *your* community when you're gone most of the year."

"I'm not going anywhere with Laveau in the area now."

"Why should he want to kill you?"

"Because I want to see him hang."

"You said something about him when you were delirious, but I didn't understand it."

"Laveau and I served in the same troop during the war. When it became clear the South wasn't going to win, Laveau betrayed us to the Union Army."

"What happened?"

"The Union troops ambushed us in our sleep. If our captain hadn't sensed something wrong, none of us would have survived. Twenty-four men died that day. One was my brother. Laveau might as well have been the one to put that bullet in his head. I'll never be able to rest until he's dead. Don't you feel the same way about the man who shot your father?"

Roberta didn't know what to say. She wanted justice for her father, but she didn't know that she could shoot someone to kill. Did that make her a spineless female who talked big but would back down when push came to shove? "I don't know what I would do. I guess I was out of my mind when I snatched up Papa's gun and shot you. I don't believe I even thought about killing you."

"In other words, if you'd had time to think, you wouldn't have shot me."

"No."

"Would you have shot the man who killed your father? Would you have wanted to kill him?"

"Yes." She didn't know whether she was ashamed or relieved to make that admission, but it was the truth.

"Good. I was beginning to think you didn't have any spunk at all, that this insistence on keeping your father's farm going was just a lot of talk."

Roberta had been feeling less annoyed by Nate's presence, but that changed in a flash. "I may not be as ready to use a gun as a man, but that doesn't mean I can't stand my ground."

"Good. You're much too beautiful to be spineless."

A flush of pleasure ran through her at the compliment. Not even Boone had ever called her beautiful.

"That's just the fever talking now," she murmured. Roberta rose from where she'd been sitting next to Nate's bed.

He held her gaze for a moment. "Don't forget to leave the door unlocked, so my night guard can get in."

"I'll wait up for him. And I'll leave the chicken on the stove. He can bring you more food if you're hungry later."

Nate's grin was slightly crooked. "A good cowhand can stay in the saddle for a day and a half, wrestle a full-grown steer to the ground, and sleep standing up in a rainstorm. Ask him to do anything inside a house except eat or sleep, and you'll find he's as helpless as a child."

"Are you similarly handicapped?"

Nate's grin broadened. "I grew up a businessman's son. I can do any number of things that would make a true Texan balk."

"Oh, really? You'll have to tell me about that someday." Roberta was beginning to realize she didn't know anything about this man named Nate Dolan. She had also come to the conclusion that she wanted to know more. A lot more. After all, he thought she was beautiful.

❦

Nate settled back against his pillows after Roberta bid him goodnight. She was a confusing woman. At one end of the spectrum, she had shot him and faced down the ranchers. At the other end, she said she would never shoot any man if she weren't too upset to think straight. Nate suspected she had always been capable of the first two. She believed the second only because she'd never been put in a situation where she had to choose. He had probably felt much the same before the war, before his brother's death, but he could never go back to being that boy again. He wondered if the same might hold true for Roberta.

He was certain of one thing, however. She was a beautiful woman. The way that rosy blush spread up her neck and into her cheeks made him think no one had ever told her that before. Why hadn't Boone

Riggins told her she was beautiful at least once a day? He would have if he'd been in love with her. Didn't every man think the woman he loved was beautiful? Wasn't that part of being in love?

He didn't know why he'd never noticed her lovely figure during the several visits he'd paid to her father. How could he have been so interested in dams, crops, and cows that he'd never noticed a beautiful woman?

Probably because she'd stayed out of sight. Probably because he'd been so focused on defusing the friction between Robert Tryon and the ranchers he didn't think of much else. Probably because he'd been so obsessed with finding Laveau diViere, there hadn't been any room in his head or heart for a woman.

Being shot had shifted things around a bit.

He was still concerned about the friction between Roberta and the ranchers. He was still obsessed with finding Laveau, especially since Laveau was in the area, but now Roberta filled his thoughts, too.

Heck, she was even making her way into his dreams, and not as a Florence Nightingale stand-in. She was more like Delilah, a temptress to test the resolve of a stronger man than he. But in his dreams he hadn't resisted at all. Parts of his fantasy made it difficult to meet Roberta's gaze without embarrassment—or showing naked desire. This was something new for him. Up until now, no woman had managed to hold his interest for more than a few days. He'd have to wait to know if Roberta was different.

Roberta placed Nate's supper on the stove. The cowhand Russ sent over could feed him. Starting tomorrow, Russ had promised he would supply Nate's meals. A guard would be present at all times so there wouldn't be any need for her to do more than check on him briefly just to make sure he didn't have a fever or that his wound hadn't become infected. Since the doctor would come by at least once a day, she didn't really have to do that. She could ignore him, forget he was there.

Ignore him, maybe. Forget he was there, impossible. In the few hours she'd been around him, Roberta had learned that Nate wasn't the kind of man a woman forgot. Refuse to talk to him, look at him, or build unreasonable daydreams, that was all possible. Refuse to remember his voice, forget his smile, or be unaware of the physical magnetism that emanated from him, that was impossible.

She wasn't sure what exactly it was about him that intrigued her so much. Sure, he was handsome, but she was discovering there was more to him than he let people see. The biggest question was: would he ever want a normal life enough to give up his obsession with Laveau diViere?

She couldn't respect someone who would dedicate his life to the pursuit and death of another man. But the fact remained that Nate Dolan had unsettled her life, and it wasn't merely because he was occupying her father's bedroom.

Feeling confined in the house, Roberta left the kitchen and went out the back. The sun had set, but the sky was a deep blue. The coming darkness settled over the tomatoes, corn, and other vegetables, concealing much of the damage done by the attackers. A few more days and she and Joe would have done all they could to save her father's crops. Her body ached from the bending and twisting. Her skin was tender from the vigorous scrubbing required to remove all traces of dirt and stains. Her nails were chipped and cracked, her skin dry and tight, but she felt good. She had worked hard, but her reward was in front of her. Now the farm's survival depended on whether she could sell everything before it rotted in the field.

Boone Riggins was her father's best customer, but people from Slender Creek, as well as the ranchers, had bought their produce in the past. She didn't know if they would buy from her this year.

She wondered if Nate would help by buying to feed his own crew and encouraging others to buy from her. She had shot him. She had virtually accused him of being a killer. What had she done to encourage him to support her?

Nothing.

She walked to the well less than ten feet from the back door. Had Joe remembered to water the mules, cow, and chickens? She lifted the bucket from its hook and lowered it into the well. When she heard it splash bottom, she waited a few seconds then pulled it up. It always amazed her that a full bucket of water could weigh so much. By the time she reached the temporary pen Joe had built, she was out of breath. The quickness with which the animals thrust their noses into the trough after she poured the water told her Joe hadn't watered them. By the time she had taken a second bucket to the mules and cow and one to the chickens, she was exhausted.

The chicken coop showed little damage from the attack, but half of the barn would have to be pulled down. Its charred timbers, some silhouetted against the evening sky at angles never intended by its builder, were like skeletal remains. The acrid smell of smoke permeated the light evening breeze. Gazing at the barn, she felt like she was attending a wake. She didn't know where she'd find the money to replace it. She'd probably have to be satisfied with the remnant that was left.

She wouldn't worry about that tonight. She was tired and ready for bed. She hoped Nate's guard would arrive soon. She didn't want to sit up late, and she didn't want to wake up to let him in. She took her time walking back to the house, but he still hadn't arrived by the time she'd locked up, washed up the kitchen, and gone to her bedroom. She changed into her nightgown and put on a robe, but he still hadn't arrived. She'd have to talk to Russ and make him understand that the guards had to arrive at times convenient for her. Probably mealtimes. That way Nate's food wouldn't get cold.

She was trying to decide whether to leave the chicken on the stove or put it away when she heard a gunshot in the distance. Normally that wouldn't have bothered her. Ranchers were constantly hunting coyotes and wolves. But because of the attack, she was instantly alarmed. She rushed to the parlor window but couldn't see anyone. A second shot. Was it closer, or was it just her imagination?

She hurried to Nate's bedroom and slowly opened the door. He stirred but seemed to be sleeping. He spoke when she turned to leave.

"Probably some cowhand hunting coyotes."

"That's what I thought. Go back to sleep. Your guard should be here soon."

She closed the door, but before she reached her bedroom, she heard the distant sound of a galloping horse. And it was a hard gallop, the kind that implied real danger. The rider was headed toward her farm. Unsure of what to do, she got her father's shotgun down from its pegs and positioned herself at the window.

Moments later a rider materialized out of the night. He rode straight for the house, leapt off his horse, ran up the steps, and pounded on the door.

"Let me in," he called. "Russ McCoy sent me. I'm the boss's guard for the night."

Roberta unlocked the door then stepped back. "The door is open, but you'd better be who you say you are. I'm holding a shotgun." The man didn't have to know she'd never fired one.

A young man burst through the door, slammed it shut, and locked it.

"Why were you in such a hurry?" Roberta asked. "Did it have anything to do with the shots I heard?"

"You're damned right it did. Someone was trying to kill me."

Chapter Six

"ARE YOU SURE?" ROBERTA ASKED.

"I thought the first shot might have been an accident." He removed his hat and poked a finger through a small hole in the crown. "When the second went through my hat, I knew it was no mistake."

"Why would anyone want to kill you?"

"Beats me. But I ain't stepping outside that door until my relief comes with the boss's breakfast. And I ain't coming here again unless it's broad daylight." He looked a little embarrassed. "Sorry for forgetting my manners, ma'am, but I ain't used to being shot at. My name's Grady. I'll be taking the night shift 'cause Russ says I can never go to sleep anyways." Now that he had time to notice Roberta was holding a shotgun pointed at him, he turned skittish. "You mind putting that up? I don't hold with shotguns since my uncle dropped his and nearly took my Pappy's head off."

"Sorry." Roberta had forgotten all about the shotgun. "I didn't dare open the door without being able to protect myself."

"I'm glad to hear you're taking good care of the boss. Where's his room?"

She pointed to the far end of the parlor. "It's over there. You can talk to him, feed him some more supper if he wants, but the doctor said you had to sleep out here. He doesn't want anything to disturb Nate's rest."

Grady looked around. "I don't see no bed."

"That's because there isn't one. You'll have to sleep on the sofa or use your bedroll."

Grady didn't look pleased.

"You'd better let Nate know you're here. Tell him the chicken is still warm if he wants some."

"Where do you sleep?"

"In the bedroom at this end of the parlor." It took only a few minutes to acquaint Grady with the layout of the house. Roberta pointed to a bowl on the back of the stove. "This is the chicken soup."

Grady looked inside the bowl. "There's not much left. What if he wants more?"

"Tell him he can't have it."

Grady's eyes grew wide, and he backed up a step, like someone had tossed a snake at his feet. "I ain't telling the boss he can't have nothing."

"It's doctor's orders."

"Then the doctor can tell him."

"The doctor's not here."

"Then you tell him. He can't fire you."

"Is he that difficult to work for?"

"He's a great boss," Grady assured her. "He pays more than anybody else, we get decent food, and he built a new bunkhouse last year. He never shouts, cusses, or expects us to do things he can't do. But he doesn't like anyone telling him what to do."

Roberta picked up the bowl. "I'll go with you,

but you'll have to wash up the dish when he's done. I'm going to bed."

Nate was dozing when she and Grady entered his bedroom. He opened his eyes, and a slow grin appeared when he saw Grady. "I figured Russ would send you. He's our night owl," he said to Roberta.

"How're you feeling, boss? You don't look so terrible."

Nate's grin grew. "It's a relief to know I look only moderately terrible. I guess there's still hope for my recovery."

Grady fell all over himself trying to apologize but succeeded only in making it worse.

"He's kidding you," Roberta said.

"The boss never kids," Grady assured her. "He has no sense of humor." The words were barely out of his mouth before a look of horror indicated he realized what he'd just said. His efforts to explain his way out of that had Roberta turning away to hide her smiles. Nate wasn't so amused.

"I've never been shot when I was trying to help or been forced to stay in a stranger's house with the window boarded up and a watchman on duty because Laveau diViere is trying to kill me. I'm liable to do all sorts of things, but develop a sense of humor is hardly likely to be one of them."

"He doesn't mean half of what he says," Roberta advised Grady. "He's just bored and irritable."

"What makes you say that?" Nate demanded.

"You've forgiven me for shooting you. Only a kind and thoughtful person could do that."

"I never said I've forgiven you."

"Not in so many words, but I can tell."

Nate eyed her much as he would a puzzle whose solution had eluded him. "I'm not kind and thoughtful. I don't even want to be."

"That's something you can't hide. Why do you think your cowhands are so faithful?"

"Because I pay better than the other ranchers."

"You give them better food and have built a new bunkhouse. You never shout, curse, or expect them to do anything you won't do."

Nate eyed Grady. "That may change if a certain young cowhand doesn't learn to keep his mouth shut."

"Don't blame Grady. It's hard to know what to say when someone has just tried to kill you."

Nate turned to Grady. "What's she talking about?"

"Someone took a couple shots at me on my way over here. I got a hole in my hat to prove he wasn't hunting coyotes."

"Why would anyone want to shoot you?"

"Could it be diViere?" Roberta asked.

"He wants me dead, but I can't think of a reason why he should want to kill Grady."

"Then who could it be?"

"Are you sure you didn't get in the way of someone hunting coyotes?" Nate asked Grady.

"As sure as I can be without stopping to ask," Grady said. "I took out after that first shot 'cause I figured I was in some hunter's way, but whoever it was followed me. That second shot came from behind."

"Somebody shot Roberta's father, diViere wants me dead, and somebody tried to shoot you," Nate pointed out. "There can't be three separate killers all of a sudden."

"Do you think they're connected?" Roberta asked.

"If they are, I don't see how. I don't see why Laveau should care about your farm or Grady."

"So who else could it be?"

"I have no idea."

"I don't either," Roberta admitted, "but we're not going to figure it out tonight. I need to get to bed, and you need to rest." She handed the bowl of soup to Grady. "You can eat it all if you want, but you can't have anything else until breakfast."

"What are you going to fix?" Nate asked.

"Russ is sending breakfast with Carlin," Grady said. "Miss Tryon don't need to fix nothing."

Roberta wasn't positive, but she thought Nate looked disappointed.

Grady's brow creased. "Can't say I understand why Russ thinks she might poison you. She seemed pretty protective of you when she held a shotgun on me. "

"For all I knew," Roberta said, "you could have been working for diViere, pretending to have been shot. It'd be a clever way of getting into the house. After I was in bed, you'd be free to smother your boss in his sleep and disappear long before I knew what had happened."

Grady looked as though he'd walked into a house of horrors and didn't know how to find his way out.

"Right now, though, the most important thing is for your boss to get as much rest as possible. That way he can get well so Russ can take him home and stop worrying that I'll poison him."

"And you won't have to worry about taking care of me," Nate added.

"I haven't *worried* about taking care of you," Roberta said, "but since I shot you, it's my responsibility to care for you."

"Is that all you feel, a sense of responsibility?"

Nate's question was completely unexpected. What else was she supposed to feel? She hardly knew the man. She had seen him only a few times and then only when he was arguing with her father.

"I feel guilt as well," she said.

"That's not what I meant. Do you still hate me?"

"I never hated you. At least not after I stopped thinking you shot my father."

"Whoa! You thought the boss killed your father?" Grady asked. "He'd never do anything like that."

Roberta didn't have the energy to explain the past two days to Grady. "Let Nate eat as much as he wants, then you stay in the parlor so he can sleep."

She left before either man could object, but she knew she wouldn't be able to sleep for a while yet. Why should Nate want her to like him? He hadn't done anything to make her think he liked her or cared how she felt about him. She found him attractive, but the idea of liking him in any but the most casual way had never crossed her mind. He was a rich rancher and she the daughter of a poor farmer. That difference alone should have been enough to keep them apart.

She should put all thoughts of this out of her mind. It was ridiculous, far-fetched, not even in the realm of possibility, but she knew she would think about it half the night. She groaned. She would be exhausted by morning.

❧

"Are you absolutely sure those shots were meant to kill you?" Nate asked Grady when Roberta had left.

"I can't think of a reason why, but I'm sure that's what he meant to do."

Nate was puzzled. He understood Laveau's apparent attempt to kill him, but he couldn't think of anyone who would want to kill Grady. It didn't make sense.

"You going to eat any of this chicken?" Grady asked.

Nate glanced at the bowl Grady was holding out to him. "I don't think so. You can have it."

Grady eyed the food and wrinkled his nose.

The boy's reaction amused Nate. "Are you afraid it's poisoned?"

Grady reacted like he'd been caught in a guilty secret. "No, boss. That lady don't seem like the kind to go around murdering people."

"Even though she shot me?"

"Well, that does seem like a mighty big exception."

"You ought to stop listening to Russ. I don't know where he got the notion Roberta would try to poison me."

"Maybe because she thought you killed her pa?"

"She doesn't think that anymore."

"Still, females can be mighty vengeful," Grady said. "There was this time back home when—"

"I'm sure we all know some woman who's gone after her husband with a pot or broom handle."

"It was a butcher knife. She carved him up like a slaughtered pig."

"Roberta isn't going to carve me up. She's too anxious to get me well and out of her house."

"If I was in your place, I wouldn't be too anxious to leave," Grady confessed a little sheepishly. "She's a mighty fine looking woman."

"That's what I told her, but she wouldn't believe me. Said Boone Riggins never told her she was beautiful. And that's the man who claims he wants to marry her."

Grady stared at the closed door. "I'd marry her in a heartbeat."

"And spend the rest of your life planting corn and digging potatoes?"

"Some sacrifices are worth it."

"I'll warn you now her opinion of cowhands is no higher than her opinion of ranchers."

Grady turned his gaze on Nate. "You aiming to change her mind?"

Nate had barely acknowledged the thought to himself, so he was shocked when the question was flung at him like that. "What makes you say that?"

"You telling her she's beautiful."

"You don't think she's beautiful?"

"Sure do, but I wouldn't tell her."

"Why not?"

"She might think I was up to something."

"Like what?"

Grady squirmed under Nate's gaze. "You know. *Something.*"

Nate did know. "I'm sure Roberta could stand

being told she was beautiful without thinking you had designs on her virtue."

"Maybe by you." Grady hurried to add, "No woman would be afraid of a man who can't sit up by himself."

He looked so uncomfortable Nate knew that wasn't the reason he had in mind. "Do you think there's something wrong with me?"

Grady squirmed, avoided Nate's gaze, then his words came out in a rush. "Everybody knows you got no interest in women."

Nate could have anticipated several answers, but that wasn't one of them. "Who said that?"

Grady looked at the bowl of chicken like he had no idea how it got in his hands. "Nobody in particular."

"How is it nobody in particular said it, but everybody knows it?"

Grady became so fascinated with the contents of the bowl he couldn't stop staring down at it.

"There are no answers in that bowl, so you might as well look at me. What have I done to make people think I don't like women?"

"You haven't *done* anything," Grady said.

"Come on. Out with it."

Grady finally wrenched his gaze from the bowl of chicken. "Are you going to fire me, boss?"

"Why should I do that?"

"I've never seen you look at anybody like that."

Nate was annoyed. He didn't know why anyone should assume he wasn't interested in women. Neither did he know what he'd done to make the boy so afraid of him. "I'm not going to fire you, and

I'm not looking at you like that. I just want to know why everybody thinks I'm not interested in women."

"You don't talk about women," Grady finally said. "You never go with the men when they go to the saloon for a bit of company. None of us has ever seen you buy a drink for one of the gals or eat supper with her. You never go to the dances in town. There's one next week, and you haven't even mentioned it. At first we thought you were gone so much because you were seeing some married woman, but Russ told us you was chasing the man who killed your brother. He said you was so bitter he didn't expect you'd ever get married."

Nate didn't know what surprised him more, that everybody was watching his activities so keenly or their interpretation of them. He hadn't shown any attention to women in Slender Creek because none of them attracted him. He'd been so preoccupied with his search for Laveau he hadn't had time to do much else.

"You can tell Russ I'm not so bitter I'm incapable of considering marriage. You can tell everyone else I'll show plenty of interest in a woman when I meet one I find attractive. On second thought, don't bother. I'll tell them myself. Now take that chicken to the kitchen unless you intend to eat it. I don't need anything now, so you can get your bedroll and go to sleep, that is if your horse hasn't wandered off. I gather you didn't have time to tether him. And try not to break anything in the parlor. I've imposed on Miss Tryon enough as it is."

Grady practically stumbled over his feet getting out of the bedroom. Nate felt a little guilty for having spoken so severely to the boy, but he was shocked by what he'd been told. It was true that he'd been focused on his efforts to find Laveau, but it wasn't true that he was uninterested in women. He had the same needs as any man his age, and he'd managed to take care of them in the same way millions of other young men did. That didn't mean he was incapable of developing a romantic interest in a woman. It just meant he hadn't found the one who could make him want to spend more than a few hours—or minutes—in her company.

He hadn't been *looking* for love, but did one have to look? Didn't love find you instead of the other way around? That was the way it happened with Cade and the rest of his friends in the Night Riders. He'd never thought much about it, but he believed a person who was looking too hard ran the risk of seeing something that wasn't there. Best for love to find you and wrestle you to the ground. That way you knew you had found the real thing.

But what if love spoke in a whisper rather than a shout? Had he been so unaware that he would have missed a soft-spoken approach?

Why was he even thinking about this? He wasn't ready to get married. He was only thirty-one. He had plenty of time to find the right woman to love, and who would love him in return. Roberta was attractive. Hell, she was beautiful. He even liked her. He wasn't in love with her, but she was the kind of woman he'd want for a wife. When he was ready. After he'd brought Laveau to justice.

❧

"Are you trying to kill him?"

Carlin looked at Roberta in utter confusion. "This is his breakfast."

"Nate can't eat that without throwing up."

"The cook made it especially for him. Russ said if I didn't get it over here while it was still hot, he'd fire me."

"Russ is the one who ought to be fired." Roberta shook her head at the food spread out on her table. "Black coffee strong enough to dissolve a horseshoe, sausage spicy enough to bring tears to his eyes, potatoes fried in beef fat, and hot bread that will sit in his stomach like a lead weight. If that's the kind of breakfast he usually eats, I'm surprised he's lived this long."

Carlin didn't answer.

"You and Grady can eat that stuff. I suppose you're healthy enough it won't kill you," Roberta said, her voice laced with disgust. "I'll fix Nate something that won't have him in a fever by the time the doctor gets here."

"Russ was most particular," Carlin said. "He said you wasn't to fix anything else for the boss to eat, that the cook would do it, and we'd bring it over."

"When you bring something edible, Nate can have it." She turned to the stove.

"What are you going to make?" Carlin asked.

"A couple of eggs on dry toast. If that goes down well, I'll let him have some stewed peaches."

"What am I going to tell Russ?"

"Nothing. I'll talk to him. Now go wake Grady. That boy may have trouble getting to sleep, but he has even more trouble waking up."

Roberta should have known that a man who cooked for a ranch staffed only by men wouldn't have any idea what to feed a sick person. How could she let Nate go home when they'd probably kill him with food anyone with half a grain of sense would know was practically indigestible?

She sliced some bread and put it on the stove to toast. It took only a moment to soft scramble two eggs. The food was ready before Carlin pushed a sleep-eyed Grady into the kitchen.

"Sorry to sleep so late, ma'am," Grady said to Roberta. "The boss was in a mood to talk last night. I didn't get to my bed until late."

"I hope you didn't keep him up too late. He needs his rest."

"It's not a problem for him. He gets to sleep all day."

"You do remember that he was shot, don't you?"

Grady looked abashed. "Yes, ma'am."

"I think that entitles him to some extra sleep, not to mention a night guard who doesn't sleep like the dead. Half a dozen Laveau diViere's could have walked through that parlor, and you wouldn't have known."

"Begging your pardon, ma'am, but I hooked my spurs over the door handle. Nobody could open that door without the jingle waking me."

Roberta doubted a mere *jingle* would have woken Grady, but she gave him credit for good intentions. "Eat your breakfast. When you're done, come find me. I want to make sure Russ sends something Nate can eat next time."

Grady looked at the food on the table. "Ain't that the boss's breakfast?"

"No." Roberta picked up the plate with the eggs and toast. "This is. In about ten minutes, one of you bring me a bowl of those peaches."

She didn't know what tale Grady would carry to Russ, but she was sure it would send the foreman galloping over to the farm as fast as possible. She knew the doctor would second her opinion, so she was actually looking forward to the encounter. Somebody needed to take Russ down a notch, and she was feeling in the mood to do it.

She knocked lightly on the bedroom door.

"Come in."

Roberta entered the room but left the door open. "I've got your breakfast."

Nate had propped himself up in bed. He looked surprised, but not displeased, to see Roberta. "Russ is supposed to be sending my meals. What happened?"

"He sent food, all right, but it was indigestible."

"What was it?"

Roberta recited the menu.

"I like all those things."

"I have no intention of letting the doctor arrive to find you can't keep down your food or have developed a fever. I brought you something that's nourishing and will sit well on your stomach."

Nate eyed the eggs on toast with disfavor. "That looks like food for a sick child."

"It's suitable for a sick man as well. Now stop scowling and eat."

Nate transferred his gaze from his breakfast to Roberta. "For an unmarried woman, you're awfully bossy."

"I guess it's a good thing I'm not looking for a husband."

"You like yourself the way you are?"

Roberta set the plate of food in Nate's lap, seated herself in the chair next to his bed, and fixed her gaze on him. "I can't think of anything that would make me more perfect."

"You're serious, aren't you?"

"Do you like yourself the way you are?"

From Nate's reaction, she guessed he'd never been asked that question. "I guess so. Yes," he added as though his answer was unexpected.

"Then there's no reason I can't like myself. I don't spend half the year trying to kill anyone."

"Laveau deserves to die."

"Succeeding will make you a killer. Is your revenge worth that?"

"You don't understand."

"No, I don't. And I won't, even if you try to explain it, so let's not talk about it." She picked up the plate of food. "Do you feel up to feeding yourself today?"

Nate looked at the eggs. "Not if I have to eat that."

"Will it taste better if I feed you?"

Nate's grin was teasing. "Of course. Being fed by a beautiful woman would make any food taste better."

Roberta forked some eggs and toast into Nate's mouth. "You've got to stop telling me I'm beautiful. I might start to believe you. Then where would I be?"

Nate started to answer, but Roberta fed him another mouthful.

"It's not becoming for a woman to go around

thinking she's beautiful. Outside of it being stupid to ignore the evidence of her mirror, she would arouse the scorn of other women of superior attractions and the envy of those less blessed by the caprice of Nature."

She prevented Nate's response with another mouthful.

"Any woman so caught up in herself is likely to believe all sorts of things said to her. That could lead to very unfortunate circumstances. Some men will say anything to win a woman's favors."

Nate pushed aside the next mouthful.

"I've never heard such nonsense. Do you always talk like that?"

"Only when attractive men try to fill my head with empty flattery."

Nate held the hovering fork at a distance. "Saying you're beautiful is *not* empty flattery. It's only a statement of fact. By the way, thanks for saying I'm attractive." He pulled the fork toward him and took the food.

"This whole conversation is ridiculous," Roberta said. "I'm not beautiful, and you know you're attractive."

"Not half as attractive as my brother. I have that on the best authority. My mother's."

"That was a cruel thing to say. I'm surprised it didn't make you dislike your brother."

"No one could dislike Caleb. He was always spilling over with fun. It was all our captain could do to keep him quiet when we made a raid. We would be in camp hardly five minutes, and already a group would be gathered around him."

Roberta forked another spoonful into Nate's mouth. "I'm sure he was wonderful, but you don't have to keep walking in his shadow."

Nate looked shocked by her words. "Is that what you think I'm doing?"

"Aren't you? He's all you talk about unless it's getting revenge on Laveau diViere. And that's only because you hold him responsible for Caleb's death. You spend most of your time away from your ranch, you have no social life, and virtually no friends. You have money, looks, and youth, yet you're wasting all three."

Nate swallowed and fixed her with an irritated frown. "Is that the complete list of my faults, or did you cut it short to spare my feelings?"

Roberta couldn't repress a smile. "I'm certain there are more, but I know very little about you."

"But if you knew me better, you wouldn't hesitate to bring them to my attention."

"Not unless you gave me reason. I'm not a cruel person."

"Are they that bad?"

Nate looked so genuinely concerned, Roberta couldn't hold back a laugh. "I'm sure they're not, but you are a man, and in anything involving a man, a woman is well advised to assume the worst. That way she will never be disappointed."

Nate's brows knitted together, but there was a hint of laughter in his eyes. "You're something of a minx. I can't wait to see the man you marry."

"That won't happen."

"Why?"

"I don't plan to marry until I go back to Virginia."

"There are plenty of men in Texas."

"Not for me. Now that you've finished your eggs and toast, would you like some stewed peaches?"

"Anything to get the taste of eggs out of my mouth."

"I'll be back in a moment."

She turned toward the door but was nearly knocked down when an enraged Russ McCoy burst through it. He held a bowl of peaches in his left hand.

"What the hell do you mean by giving the boss's breakfast to Grady and Carlin while you feed him mush like this?"

Chapter Seven

NATE HAD NEVER SEEN RUSS SO UPSET, NOT EVEN when a bull they were attempting to castrate broke loose and gored his favorite horse. "Stop waving that bowl of peaches around before you spill it all over me."

"How do you know it's peaches?" Russ wanted to know. "I can't tell what it is, and I'm looking at it."

"Roberta was about to feed me some stewed peaches. I assumed they'd look a lot like mush."

"You'd eat this?"

"She assures me it will put me in the pink of health by the time the doctor gets here."

Roberta didn't waste time setting Russ straight. "I said no such thing. I *did* tell him the food you sent over was unsuitable. I didn't expect you to know anything about caring for a sick man, but I thought your cook would have had more sense."

Nate should have felt guilty letting Roberta and Russ argue over him, but he was enjoying it too much. Roberta hardly knew him, didn't appear to like him much, but she was looking out for his welfare with a vehemence he had previously associated only with mothers of small children. His own mother wouldn't have defended him with such vigor.

As long as he could remember, everything had always been about Caleb. From the time his little brother could walk, there had been a litany of things Nate had to do to make sure nothing happened to him. *Never* let him out of your sight. Make sure he doesn't run too fast. Keep him from picking up anything that could hurt him. Protect him from bullies and rough games. If their father hadn't intervened, Caleb might not have been allowed to leave the house until it was time to go to school. At the end of every list came the same threat. *I'll never forgive you if anything happens to him.*

She had been true to her word. When Nate told her of his brother's death, he feared she would go insane with grief. For weeks she roamed the house, crying hysterically and cursing him for being the one to survive. After she regained her senses, she refused to speak to him, look at him, or stay in the same room with him. She died less than five months later.

The weight of guilt was suffocating. It was made worse when his father died, and he inherited everything. Knowing he couldn't return to a home filled with so many painful memories, he'd sold everything and bought a Texas ranch. Despite being rich enough to sit back and let others work for him, he'd devoted himself to bringing Laveau to justice. But that hadn't brought relief. He was still pursued by the knowledge that his parents wouldn't have hesitated to exchange his life for Caleb's.

A particularly loud outburst from Russ drew his attention back to the discussion of what constituted suitable food for a man convalescing from a gunshot wound. He was relieved from having to intervene by the entrance of the doctor.

"If you can't learn to speak like a sensible man, you can wait outside," the doctor said to Russ.

Russ pointed an accusing finger at Roberta. "She's the one who's not sensible. Do you know what she fed the boss for breakfast? Eggs on toast. Now she wants to feed him a mush she says is peaches."

"I suppose your idea of a good breakfast is what those two boys in the kitchen are eating."

"I ordered it especially for the boss."

The doctor pushed past Russ to get to Nate. "Then it's a good thing Roberta has some sense. He'll get well much faster with her feeding him. You can poison him after you get him home."

"I'd just as soon not be poisoned at all," Nate said.

"Then you had best let this young lady order your meals even after you go home. Now let me look at you." After a brief examination, the doctor stood back, a satisfied look on his face. "Youth is a wonderful thing. If I'd been shot like you, it would take me a month to recover. You ought to be as good as new in a week. I could let you go home today, but I think I'll keep you here another day."

Nate didn't want to admit he was relieved. As much as he disliked being confined to the bed, he enjoyed having Roberta take care of him. And there was no disputing that she could hold her own against Russ. He admired her determination to save her father's crops. He could only imagine how much backbreaking work that required.

"You want to go home today, don't you, boss?"

Nate didn't know quite what to make of Russ's distrust of Roberta.

"I don't like to impose on Roberta, but if she's willing to put up with me, I'll stay here another day. I'm not looking forward to the ride home."

"Sensible man," the doctor said before turning to Roberta. "What do you say?"

Nate thought Roberta looked slightly uncomfortable at being addressed so directly. Could it be that she really didn't want him here a minute longer than necessary?

"Nate can stay here as long as necessary. With one of his men here to look after him, there's not much I have to do. However, I do have one condition. Well, maybe two."

"What are they?" Nate felt a tightening in the pit of his stomach.

Roberta turned to Russ. "I have to be the one who decides what Nate eats. If he's going to have a relapse, it's not going to happen in my house."

"What's the second?" Nate asked.

"That Russ not set foot in my house again. Grady, Carlin, and any other cowhand he wants to send are fine, but I will not be bullied and shouted at in my own house."

Russ apparently had a lot he wanted to say, but Nate cut him short. "Your requests seem reasonable considering all the trouble I'm putting you to."

"You're damned lucky this woman has good

common sense," the doctor said. "You don't know how rare that is."

"What am I supposed to do about food?" Russ asked. "Our cook would quit if I asked him to fix eggs on toast."

"Talk to Roberta," the doctor said. "I'm sure she can tell you what to have your cook fix."

"And if you're still afraid I'll poison your boss, you can have one of your men feed him."

"I'm not afraid you're going to poison me," Nate said. The boys would be so uncomfortable they were likely to get more food on his clothes than in his mouth. Besides, he'd be so embarrassed to have one of them feed him he'd end up doing it himself.

"If that's all you want me for, I'm needed in the fields," Roberta said. "I expect Joe is out there already."

"I don't trust that man," Russ told Roberta. "He's not called Crazy Joe for nothing."

"I'd trust him with my life. Now I'll write out some instructions for your cook and leave them by the front door. Tell him to follow them exactly. If he doesn't, I'll throw it out."

"I don't know how you can stand that woman," Russ said to Nate after Roberta left.

Nate chuckled. "She's a lot prettier to look at than you."

The doctor wrinkled his nose. "Smells a mite better, too. Go talk to your horse while I finish checking out your boss. And don't forget the list for your cook. It may not seem like it to you, but her breakfast was the best choice for your boss."

Russ had several things to say about a self-respecting

man being run over by a high-and-mighty female, but he finally took himself off.

The doctor changed the bandage, remarking once again on how quickly Nate was healing. He placed the last pin in the new bandage, leaned back, and looked Nate in the eye. "When are you going to ask that woman to marry you? If would be a shame if she ended up wasting herself on Boone Riggins."

❧

Roberta straightened up, putting her hand to her back to ease the pain. She looked over the fields she'd worked so hard to save. Some of the plants were standing tall again. Others had started to put out new leaves. She had never wanted to be a farmer, but she was proud of what she'd accomplished. "That's about all we can do for today," she said to Joe.

"Joe can work more."

"You've done more than enough already. You need to get back to town so you can clean up and eat your dinner before going to the saloon."

"Mr. Boone says Joe can work here as long as you want. Mr. Boone says you're more important to him than the saloon."

Roberta had doubts about that, but Boone had been a persistent suitor. There were rumors he was on a very friendly footing with one of the women who worked in the saloon, but Roberta had given Boone no reason to think he was pledged to her.

"You need some rest," she told Joe. "You're out here first thing in the morning, and you work in the saloon until late at night."

"Joe rests at the saloon. As long as Joe's there, nobody causes trouble."

"Giving you a job was the smartest thing Boone ever did."

"Miss Prudence says Joe is smarter than people think."

"She's right. Now come with me. You can wash up at the house." She hoped Nate's cook had sent the beef and vegetable stew she'd requested. She didn't feel up to cooking tonight.

"Miss Prudence said she would see Joe today," Joe said. "Miss Prudence says she likes to check on Joe to make sure he's doing all right."

Almost as though she'd been conjured up by the sound of her name, Prudence drove up the lane toward the house. By the time Roberta reached her, Prudence had already alighted from a wagon.

"Glad I caught you before you went home," Prudence said to Joe. "I need you to unload."

"What have you got?" Roberta asked.

"Your hogs," Prudence said.

"What do you mean *my hogs*?"

"People in town processed the hogs killed in the attack. They kept some, and I brought you the rest."

The wagon was nearly full. "I can't use all of this."

"Then sell it. That's what your father meant to do."

"I gave those hogs to anyone who wanted them."

"Everybody's grateful, but they thought they ought to give you some back."

It looked like a lot more than *some*. Roberta had a strong suspicion Prudence had demanded people give back just about everything.

"Is your smokehouse still standing?" Prudence asked.

"It's hardly big enough for all of this."

The front door to the house opened, and Carlin stuck his head out. "Is Webb here yet?"

At the sound of an unknown male voice, Prudence pivoted, lanced a baleful glare at Carlin, and demanded in a fearsome voice, "Who is that man, and what is he doing here?"

Roberta started to remind Prudence of the reason for Carlin's presence in her home, but it appeared she now felt the threat from diViere wasn't sufficient reason for such a young, healthy man to have the run of Roberta's house.

"This man is not bedridden."

"Nothing can happen to me as long as Joe's here," Roberta reminded Prudence.

"I only stay during the day," Carlin said. "Webb will be here this evening and Grady back for the night."

"It sounds like Sodom and Gomorrah!"

Roberta couldn't repress a laugh. "Don't be ridiculous, Prudence. These are boys. What harm can they do?"

"They may be boys, but they're boys in men's bodies."

"I have a shotgun, a rifle, a pistol, and a lock on my bedroom door. I'm as safe as anyone in Slender Creek."

"The boss would fire us on the spot if we did anything to upset Miss Tryon," Carlin told Prudence. "He won't even let Russ come here anymore because he argues with her."

"It's only for one more night," Roberta said. "The doctor said he can go home tomorrow."

"I should think it's about time. No respectable man would impose himself on a woman."

"I shot him, Prudence. He didn't exactly impose himself on me."

"Where do you want Joe to put this?"

While they'd been talking, Joe had emptied the wagon and placed everything on the front porch.

"Part of it has to go in the smokehouse and the rest in the storeroom," Roberta told him. "Let me divide it up."

Roberta was glad to have something to distract her from Prudence's homily on the inherent immorality of men. With Joe and Carlin's help, she was able to get everything put away by the time Webb rode up with Nate's supper.

"You'd better hurry back to the ranch, or you'll miss your supper," she said to Carlin. "Joe, I want you to escort Prudence back to town."

"Joe will take care of Miss Prudence."

Much to everyone else's amusement, Joe picked Prudence up like she was nothing more than a doll and placed her in the wagon. Ignoring her indignation at his treatment, he climbed onto the seat next to her, picked up the reins, and turned the wagon toward town.

Webb's gaze followed them, his jaw slack. "I never thought I'd see the day any man laid a hand on Miss Prudence," he said. "And it was Crazy Joe."

"Joe is *not* crazy, and he idolizes Prudence. He'd tear apart anybody who tried to touch her."

"Nobody's crazy enough to do that," Carlin said.

"I won't have either of you criticizing Prudence

within my hearing," Roberta informed the boys. "She's done more for me since my father's death than everyone in Slender Creek put together. She has a heart of gold."

"And the hide of a cactus," Carlin added. "That woman scares me."

"She wouldn't hurt a flea."

"I'm not a flea. I'm a man, and she definitely hates men."

Roberta decided there was no point in trying to convince either man of Prudence's finer attributes. "I'll heat the stew," she said to Webb. "Carlin can explain what you have to do and where you sleep."

The beef stew was richer than she wanted, but there were enough vegetables to ward off indigestion. The cook had made enough for half a dozen people, so she assumed it was meant to be her supper as well as Webb's. She'd have to thank him as soon as she had the opportunity. About the time the stew was ready, Webb walked in.

"The stew's supposed to be my supper as well as Carlin's." He looked unsure, like he expected Roberta to tell him he couldn't have any.

"I'll just take enough for Nate and me. You and Carlin can have the rest. Eat all the sourdough bread. Nate shouldn't have anything that heavy yet."

"Russ had the cook make that especially for the boss."

"That's exactly what I'd expect Russ to do."

Leaving Webb to take that remark any way he wanted, she put two bowls on a platter and headed to Nate's bedroom. Carlin was inside when she entered.

"Your supper's in the kitchen," she told him. "Eat it while it's still warm."

"I was just giving him a few instructions," Nate said. "You will remember what I said?" Nate asked Carlin. "You won't forget anything?"

"No, boss. I won't forget anything."

"Good. Now leave. Miss Tryon is about to treat me like a helpless child, and I'd be embarrassed for you to see."

"Do you always talk nonsense?" Roberta asked as Carlin hurried to leave the room.

"Only when I'm about to be fed by a beautiful woman."

"You're definitely better. I hope Russ is here early tomorrow."

Nate sniffed the air. "What is that heavenly aroma? I know it's not eggs or chicken soup."

"It's beef stew. I figured you were strong enough to eat beef as long as it was well-cooked and seasoned with plenty of vegetables."

She picked up her bowl from the platter and set it aside. Then she placed the platter with the other bowl on Nate's lap.

"You don't intend to feed me?"

"You're strong enough to feed yourself. You only let me feed you because you liked being spoiled. I only fed you because I knew you wouldn't eat what was good for you if I didn't."

Nate shook his head in mock despair. "I think I'd better warn all those Virginia men before you go back."

"What would you tell them?"

"Hmm. How does one warn of great danger when it's clothed in such beauty?"

"If you don't stop talking about me being beautiful, people are going to think you were shot in the head rather than the chest."

"Sharp-tongued *and* bossy. We'd better keep you in Texas. It would be cruel to let you loose among those unsuspecting Virginians."

The stew was quite good. Maybe the cook would provide better meals when Nate was there to make his own requests. "Do you think there's any man in Texas capable of handling a sharp-tongued, bossy female like me?"

"Texans always rise to a challenge."

"You're not from Texas."

"Ma'am, if you had to be born in Texas to be a Texan, this state would just about be empty."

"So how would you describe Texans? A bunch of misfits looking for a place to land?"

"I'd never be so rude as to call you a misfit."

Roberta didn't try to prevent her lips from curving into a smile. "I believe you have the nerve to do just about anything." Her humor abruptly changed to confusion. "Why are you wasting your time chasing after diViere when you could stay here and become a part of this community? You could do something important with your life."

The laughter disappeared from Nate's eyes. "I am doing something important."

"Murdering diViere won't bring your brother back. It'll just end with you going to jail."

Nate's eyes turned hard. "So you think I should

leave him free to continue spreading evil wherever he goes?"

"If he's so evil, he'll come to a just end on his own. I don't want him to carry you down with him."

"But you hate ranchers, remember? Why would you care what happens to me?"

She hadn't known she did, but now that he raised the question, the answer wasn't in doubt. She just wasn't sure she could explain it. "You have so much to offer it would be a shame to throw your life away."

"And what exactly is it you think I have to offer?"

"I don't know you well enough to—"

Using his arms to push himself off the pillows, he leaned toward her. "Don't turn squeamish on me now. What happened to the sharp-tongued, bossy female who was here just a minute ago?"

"She's still here. She's just trying to avoid saying something she doesn't mean."

"Tell me what you do mean—even if it's only one thing."

Roberta was tempted to return a sharp response, but she sensed that her answer would be important. She really *didn't* know him well, but she could see the tension in him, sense that something inside him might be altered or changed by her answer. Odd that a man she'd barely seen until two days ago would place so much importance on what she thought.

"Well, you've got brains. I also think you're fair. You didn't agree with my father, but you had the courtesy to explain your reasons in person, without condemning him for not accepting your advice. You care for others. You didn't hesitate to come to my father's aid when you thought he was in trouble. You don't hold grudges. You've forgiven me for shooting you and for thinking you were one of the attackers. You must be a wonderful boss because all the men who work for you practically fall over themselves to do whatever you want."

She paused, but Nate didn't respond. He just looked at her. Yet she got the feeling he wasn't seeing her, that he was seeing something from another time or place, something that had caused great pain and unhappiness.

"I find you very likeable," she continued.

That seemed to surprise him so much it brought him out of his abstraction. "Why? Nobody likes me."

"How can you say that? Your cowhands can't wait to—"

"They're afraid of losing their jobs. I pay better than the other ranchers, feed and house them better, and provide their outfits. The other ranchers don't trust me. Even my best friends say I get on their nerves."

"You don't pay me, feed me, or house me, so I can say what I think. I trust you, and you haven't gotten on my nerves, though you will if you continue telling me I'm beautiful."

Some of the anxiety left Nate's face. "I'll make you a deal. I'll try to believe I'm likeable if you try to believe you're beautiful."

"But it's not true. I'm—"

The strain was back. "I don't believe I'm likeable. But if you believe it, I'm willing to try."

"Okay, I'll try, but that means I have to avoid my mirror."

His expression eased. "You must consult your mirror constantly. Staring back at you will be the face I see, the face I find beautiful. Will you do that for me?"

Roberta suddenly felt an inexplicable urge to cry. There was something terribly sad behind that request, something so full of pain Nate didn't feel he could face it alone. Of all the people he knew, he'd turned to her, a virtual stranger he had no reason to like or trust, to give him the hope he couldn't give himself. "I will, but I can't promise that my mirror won't break."

Nate leaned back against his pillows and picked up his spoon. "I'll buy you another. Now tell me what I can have for breakfast tomorrow. I particularly like this stew."

"I haven't decided yet, but it won't be eggs on toast."

"Good. I'd hate to have to go back on my promise to buy all those mirrors."

He favored her with a slow smile then went back to eating his stew as if a crack in his soul hadn't opened long enough for her to see the pain hidden inside. Nate Dolan wasn't a revenge-obsessed zealot. Some deep hurt, some searing pain, was driving him. She didn't know what it was or why it had such a stronghold over him, but she hoped she could find a way to ease it. There weren't enough good men in the world to waste one like Nate.

࿇

"You're here mighty early this morning," Roberta said to Carlin when she entered the kitchen to find him laying out Nate's breakfast.

"Grady needs to get some sleep before Russ puts him to work. He did stay awake last night, didn't he?"

"I don't know. I followed Prudence's orders and locked my door."

Carlin's laugh was self-conscious. "You know Grady wouldn't do nothing."

"Of course, but Prudence says it's the only way to preserve my reputation. Let's see what the cook has sent."

"The boss is not going to like it."

"He will if it was made like I asked." Roberta had requested a gruel made of ground hominy and ham, cooked with milk, and accompanied by buttered toast.

"Will you take it to him?"

Roberta laughed at his reluctance to face his boss. "Sure. He's used to turning up his nose at what I take him."

"It makes a difference when a beautiful woman is the one bringing it."

Roberta froze. "You said I was beautiful."

Carlin looked uncertain. "I didn't mean to be disrespectful."

"Never mind."

Roberta left Carlin looking as puzzled as she felt.

Nate was sitting up when she entered his bedroom. "What have you got for me this morning?" His dark mood of last evening seemed to have passed. His smile was welcoming, even inviting.

"Something Carlin is so afraid you'll hate he insisted I bring it to you." Grady moved the chair against the wall next to the bed for Roberta.

"Should I be afraid to taste it?" Nate asked.

"No, but you should close your eyes. I want you to taste it before you make a judgment."

"That means it looks so horrible I'd hate it no matter what it tastes like."

"It means no such thing. I just want an unprejudiced opinion."

"Oh, lord. You sound like my mother, my aunts, and my grandmothers all rolled into one. I definitely can't let you go back to Virginia. You'll scare every man in the state."

Roberta couldn't imagine why Nate thought he was unlikeable. When he was like this, he was charming as well as funny. And his smile was powerful enough to cause any female heart to flutter. "But naturally I won't intimidate a *real* Texan, even if he wasn't born in Texas."

"Not at all. We outsiders acclimate real fast."

"You certainly learn to talk nonsense real fast. Now close your eyes and eat your breakfast."

"Should I say my prayers first?"

"If you don't stop talking, not even prayers will save you."

"I'm just trying to postpone the fatal moment."

"What have you done to him?"

"Nothing." Roberta had almost forgotten Grady was still in the room. His look of troubled disbelief bewildered her. "Even the doctor says he's getting well exceptionally fast."

"I don't mean that. He's making jokes. Laughing. Talking to a woman like he enjoys it. The boss has never done that."

"She hasn't done anything to me," Nate told Grady. "We've just made a game out of her giving me baby food and trying to disguise it so I'll eat it."

"You never play games. If you go back to the ranch acting like this, the boys will swear she put something in your food."

"If the breakfast Russ sent yesterday is an example of what he's been eating, no wonder he's grumpy," Roberta said. "Who makes up the menus?"

"Russ," Nate told her.

"I should have guessed. Now, enough talk. It's time to eat."

Like a small child, Nate closed his eyes tightly and opened his mouth wide. Roberta was tempted to make a scathing remark but limited herself to putting a spoonful of the gruel in his mouth.

Nate appeared to roll it around on his tongue before swallowing. Then he opened his eyes. "That's good. What is it?"

"Ground hominy seasoned with pork and cooked with milk."

"You can't fool me. That's cornmeal mush with ham. I had it growing up in Arkansas. I liked it then, and I like it now."

"Then I'll leave you to enjoy your breakfast."

"What about lunch?" he called after her.

"We'll see," she called back without turning around.

"Did he eat it?" Carlin asked when she entered the kitchen.

"It's one of his favorite childhood foods." She forgot what she intended to say next because through the kitchen window she saw Russ McCoy ride by. "What is he doing here?" She started toward the door.

"He's probably here to show the men what to do."

Roberta turned back to Carlin. "What men to do what?"

"The boss wants us to tear down your barn."

Chapter Eight

ROBERTA'S IMMEDIATE REACTION WAS TO TELL THEM to leave. She didn't like strangers on her property, and no matter how familiar these men were to Nate, they were strangers to her. But it was Joe who concerned her most. Even from a distance, she could tell there was tension between him and Nate's men. She had no doubt Russ's presence would make it worse.

She had tried not to dislike Russ, but his opposition to everything she did made that impossible. Now he'd ignored Nate's promise that he wouldn't set foot on her land again. By the time she reached the barn, Nate's men were lined up behind Russ, who was yelling at Joe. When she heard Russ call Joe an imbecile and a moron, her temper snapped. Walking as fast she could, she thrust herself between the two men.

"Stop this instant! Not another word," she ordered when Russ opened his mouth to speak. "You will *never again* refer to Joe in those terms. Not only are they untrue, they are cruel and hateful."

"He tried to stop—"

"Joe is here at my request doing what I've asked

him to do. *You* are not. If you had even a nodding acquaintance with basic courtesy, you'd have stopped at the house to let me know you were here and told me what you wanted to do."

"The boss told me what to do. He said—"

"I doubt he told you to arrive without warning or to abuse the only person helping me. He also promised you wouldn't come here again."

"I'm here to make sure the boys know what to do."

"I'm perfectly capable of doing that."

"These men don't know how to take orders from a woman."

"I'll make it easy. I'll use *little* words."

"They *won't* take orders from a woman."

"Then they'd better go back because I'm the only one who gives orders here."

Russ's face turned red, and he seemed to swell up. "You don't know what's good for you any more than your father did. You're nothing but a foolish, stubborn female who thinks she knows as much as a man."

"You're wrong there. I'm positive I know *more* than most men. Most particularly you." Roberta was certain Russ heard the snickers behind him.

"I'm not leaving here without the boss," he shouted.

"You're welcome to take him home as soon as the doctor says he's well enough to travel."

"I expect he's at the house now. I see a buckboard."

But it was Prudence who came striding toward them with a look of determination guaranteed to strike terror in any male heart.

"What's that woman doing here?" Russ demanded.

"She's a friend who is free to come anytime she wishes." That wasn't quite the truth, but Roberta was too angry to quibble at a small inaccuracy.

"I don't like her. She can't mind her own business."

"Is it just women you dislike, or is it anybody who disagrees with you?"

Russ was prevented from answering by Prudence's demand to know who these men were and what they were doing here.

"Nate sent them to tear down the barn," Roberta told her, "but I'm sending them home."

"I should think so. Much more of this, and people will be thinking the road to your house is the path to sin and perdition."

Nothing like Prudence's outrage to take the edge off Roberta's anger. She was still upset, but she was no longer seeing red. "Well, they can stop thinking it. Russ is taking Mr. Dolan home as soon as the doctor gives the okay."

"I passed the doctor on my way here," Prudence said. "He should be at the house anytime now." Prudence might be a hidebound spinster, but she drove like youngsters with their first buggy.

"He's coming up the lane now," Russ said.

"You go up to the house," Prudence said to Roberta. "I'll make sure these men leave. There'll be no hiding in what's left of that barn, or anywhere else, as long as I'm here."

Roberta was sure the men's only thought was getting away. "You stay here," she told Russ. "I won't have you in the house. Carlin can tell you everything you need to know."

"You can't keep me out of that house as long as the boss is there."

"I can, and I will."

"Now look here—"

Russ didn't get to finish the sentence. Joe thrust himself between them and grabbed two handfuls of Russ's shirt.

"Miss Roberta doesn't want you in her house. Joe takes care of Miss Roberta."

"Let go of me, you crazy fool."

Russ was a big man, but Joe was bigger and stronger. He picked Russ up and shook him. "Miss Prudence says Joe is not crazy. Joe doesn't like it when people disagree with Miss Prudence."

"Put me down." Russ sounded more humiliated than angry.

"Joe is not crazy."

"Okay, you're not crazy. Now put me down."

Joe released Russ so abruptly he nearly lost his balance. Certain Joe and Prudence had the situation under control, Roberta headed to the house.

"I was wondering where you were," the doctor said when she entered the bedroom.

"Is Nate strong enough to go home today?"

The abruptness of the question and the tone in which it was delivered caused both men to look at her with puzzled expressions.

"I know you had good intentions when you asked Russ to send some men to help Joe," Roberta said to Nate, "but I wish you'd talked to me first. The men had trouble making Joe understand they were here to help. And when Prudence arrived, Joe thought Russ was threatening us. He lifted Russ off the ground and shook him like a rag doll."

"I wish I'd seen that," the doctor mused.

Roberta ignored his interruption. "If the doctor says it's okay, I think it's best for you to leave as soon as possible."

Neither man spoke.

"I can't have anybody upsetting Joe. I can't manage this farm without him. And I don't want anyone getting hurt."

As she spoke, Nate drew inside himself, but not before Roberta saw sadness deep in his eyes, the kind of sadness that made her feel like she'd taken something important from him, something he wished for very much. She was tempted to tell him she didn't want him to go, but that would have implied something she didn't feel. He had never expected to stay once he was strong enough to go home.

"What about it, Doc?" Nate asked in a falsely cheerful voice. "Am I strong enough to survive the ride home?"

"Thanks to your excellent nurse, you're more than strong enough. Just make sure Carlin doesn't drive too fast."

Roberta couldn't think of anything to say except, "I'll let you get dressed."

She was more confounded by her reaction than Nate's. It felt like she was losing a friend. Worse, it felt like she was sending him away. She hadn't realized, until now, how much she enjoyed the time she spent with him. Feeding him wasn't a chore. She wouldn't have minded preparing his meals if she hadn't been nearly exhausted at the end of the day. Yet somehow she didn't feel so tired when she sat with him. They disagreed on some things, argued over a few, but without heat. He was better about accepting her criticisms than she was about accepting his. Not that she expected him to change. Texas men didn't, even those born in Arkansas. Maybe *especially* those born in Arkansas because they thought they had something to prove.

He definitely had something to prove to himself, but she was certain it had to do with diViere and what happened during the war. She was just as certain the problem wouldn't be solved by killing diViere. She couldn't believe Nate was a killer by nature. She wanted to help him, but she didn't know how.

More importantly, she didn't have the right to interfere.

When she reached the kitchen, Carlin was cleaning up the breakfast dishes in preparation for taking them back to the ranch. He looked up from his work to smile at Roberta. "The boss is looking real good this morning, isn't he?"

"So good he's going home."

The trace of a frown clouded Carlin's countenance. "He seems really happy here."

"Maybe, but he can't stay here forever."

"I guess not."

"I'd have thought you'd be relieved not to be coming here and standing guard all day."

Carlin's expression remained cloudy. "I don't mind. The boss has been different since he's been here. Grady and Webb said the same thing."

"You three seem to stick together."

"I guess we do. We're the only ones the boss hired. We feel a special allegiance to him for keeping us on since Russ doesn't like us much."

"Why not?"

"I don't think he trusts us, but we've never done anything except what he tells us."

"As far as I'm concerned, Russ not liking you is a point in your favor."

Carlin smiled shyly. "Thank you, ma'am. We appreciate you taking such good care of the boss."

"It'll be your responsibility to take care of him once he's home. He's not to do too much until he regains more of his strength, and don't let Russ order his meals."

Carlin looked uneasy. "I can't do that. Nobody will listen to me."

"You can threaten them by saying I'm planning to check on him. If need be, I'll bring Prudence. Nothing will scare a bachelor more than the threat of having a fire-breathing spinster invade his home."

Carlin brightened. "Will you really?"

His eagerness was unexpected. "You think I should?"

"He's never happy when he's at the ranch, not like he's been here." He looked unsure then proceeded resolutely. "I'm sure it's having a pretty face to look at rather than our ugly mugs."

"Nonsense. I think you and Grady are quite handsome. Webb would be, too, if he'd get rid of that ridiculous beard he's trying to grow."

Carlin laughed. "Grady's been telling him the same thing, but he's a year younger than me and Grady. He thinks it makes him look older."

Roberta wondered why Nate would hire such young boys, but movement in the front of the house told her Nate had left his bedroom. He was standing between Grady and the doctor when she reached the parlor. She was surprised to see how strong he looked now that he was standing up and wearing proper clothes. A faint whiteness around the mouth told her he was still far from fully recovered.

"Thank you for your good care the past four days." He spoke with a rigid formality he had never used with her. "The doctor assures me I wouldn't be doing so well otherwise."

"I'm sure anyone could have done as well."

"But would they?"

There seemed to be a question behind his question, but she didn't know what it might be and was afraid to ask. "Of course they would. I've been giving Carlin instructions on what you're to do to take care of yourself. I've promised to check on you so you'd better do as he says."

Nate's whole being underwent a change. "I doubt he can remember anything that complicated for more than a few hours. You'd better check with him every day to make sure he hasn't forgotten anything."

The change surprised Roberta. "I have a lot of work to do here."

"You don't have to worry about those boys forgetting things." Russ had entered the house despite her telling him not to. "I can take care of the boss."

Nate continued as if Russ hadn't spoken, "Even one day of neglect could bring about a relapse."

The doctor looked from one to the other. He

showed no reaction beyond the slight widening of his eyes and a suspicious turning up at the corners of his mouth.

Roberta's gaze hadn't left Nate. "I'll see what I can do, but I can't guarantee anything."

"You'd better write out some instructions for the cook."

"It won't take but a minute. Webb, would you come with me?"

They left the room to the accompaniment of Russ's complaints that they were wasting time waiting for instructions the cook wouldn't follow.

Once they'd left the parlor, she said to Carlin, "I want you, Webb, and Grady to keep an eye on your boss. I'm not saying Russ would do anything to hurt him, but he might decide not do something just because I recommended it."

"I don't know why he gets so angry at you."

"Neither do I, but it doesn't matter. I won't be seeing him again."

"But you said you were coming to the ranch to check on the boss."

"The three of you can take care of him for me. Besides, my being there will just cause trouble with Russ."

"I don't think the boss would care how much you upset Russ as long as you come."

Roberta finished writing her instructions and folded the piece of paper. "You think so?"

"I've never seen him as happy as he's been here. He's not happy about going home, either. He asked the doctor if he shouldn't stay one more day, but the doc said the boss was plenty strong, and it was about time he stopped parading a bunch of men through your house."

"What did Nate say?"

"He said he guessed it was time he stopped being selfish."

"I'll see if I can get over, but there's so much to be done here."

Carlin said he understood, but she knew he didn't. She didn't know what he thought she could do for Nate that they couldn't do as well. Until she shot Nate, she had rarely seen him. It was time things returned to normal. Farmers and ranchers would always be at odds.

Russ was still complaining when she returned to the parlor. He reached for the paper, but she handed it to Nate.

"I didn't write much, just a few guidelines, but I'm sure your cook will have no trouble understanding them. You may want to talk to him yourself."

"If you don't, I will," the doctor said, forestalling a protest from Russ. "I'm not driving all the way out to that ranch if you're not going to follow instructions."

Nate looked down at the paper, then looked at Roberta. His gaze connected directly with her, closing out everyone in the room. "I wouldn't dare ignore instructions with both of you checking on me each day."

Roberta started to remind him that she hadn't promised to see him every day, but something about the way he was looking at her changed her mind.

"Let's go," Russ said to Nate. "I want to get you home before it gets too hot."

"Why don't you come early tomorrow?" Nate said to Roberta. "You can talk to the cook yourself."

"I have to be here when Joe arrives."

Nate seemed to conclude that she was turning him down, and the warmth in his eyes faded. "Thanks for everything. I'll let you get back to your work."

Roberta watched as four men gave Nate directions on how to get in the buckboard without injuring himself. Whoever he listened to, if he listened to anyone at all, he climbed into the buckboard without any trouble. He waved to her as Carlin drove away, then he turned his back and saw her no more.

Roberta stood in the doorway, watching the four men disappear in the distance. She had expected to feel relief, not loss. She hadn't anticipated the emptiness that settled over her. She felt cut off, separated, left behind. Shaking her head to dispel the disquieting feelings, she turned and entered the house. She should put all thoughts of Nate behind her because she had work to do. She would probably visit to see how he was progressing, but it would be a visit like she would make to an ailing friend or neighbor. Nate Dolan had not needed her for the first thirty-one years of his life.

Nothing had changed.

∽❧∽

"I don't see why you won't work for Boone," Blossom McCrevy said to Roberta. "It's easier than working in these fields. Look at you. You're covered with dirt, you're exhausted, and it's not even quitting time."

After Nate left, Roberta had spent most of her day

digging potatoes, the one crop that had suffered the least damage in the attack. She'd never realized what a backbreaking job it was. Her father had chosen a hard way to make a living. Nate had suggested that he raise blooded bulls and sell them to the ranchers to upgrade their herds. After several days of working in the fields, she wondered why her father hadn't accepted Nate's suggestion.

She hefted the basket of potatoes and headed toward the house.

"I'd offer to help carry those," Blossom said, "but I can't afford to ruin this dress."

"I have a string of reasons for not working for Boone, most of which you wouldn't understand or agree with."

"I understand Boone's crazy about you and would marry you even looking like you do now."

If Boone was as crazy about her as he said, why had he never told her she was beautiful? "I'm not ready to get married."

"Why not? You're practically an old maid."

"I'm only nineteen. You're three years older. You've never been married, and I know you've been asked."

The potatoes were getting heavy. She wished she'd asked Joe to carry them up to the house, but she didn't want to stop him from working in the corn.

"I don't have the kind of reputation that would attract a man like Boone or Nate Dolan."

Roberta wondered why Blossom mentioned Nate. "So what are you going to do? Be an old maid with me?"

Blossom's laugh wasn't wholehearted. "One of these days a decent man will come along who's so desperate he'll overlook a bit of tarnish, and I'll snap him up before he has time to think twice."

"Don't you want to love the man you marry?"

"Love is for women who look like you. Women like me marry a man who'll have us, one we hope we can stand until he goes looking for amusement elsewhere."

"I'd rather stay single."

"What are you going to do when you get old? Crazy Joe can't work for you forever."

Roberta was relieved to reach the house and set the potatoes down on the porch. "I don't know what I'm going to do about a lot of things, but right now I want to wash up and have some coffee."

"You wash up, and I'll make the coffee. And don't think I'm done trying to make you see sense. It's not likely that another man half as good as Boone will come along and want to marry you."

She was sure a better man was close at hand, but two obstacles stood in the way of anything developing between them. He was determined on a revenge that could put a noose around his neck. And she was going back to Virginia. She couldn't live in a state where people killed each other just because they couldn't agree.

❧

Nate surveyed the men gathered in his house but failed to believe any of them capable of murdering Robert Tryon. He had owned his ranch slightly more than three years, but he had been away at least half of the time, so he didn't know any of them well. He sensed a simmering resentment that money had enabled him to purchase what they hadn't been able to achieve by hard work.

They had gathered at his house on an errand liable to ratchet up the resentment if not turn it into outright anger. It was foolish to think he had any influence over Roberta merely because he'd spent four days recovering at her home.

When they fell silent, he could tell they had gotten past the preliminaries of asking how he was doing and hoping his recovery would be rapid. Their gazes shifted from one to another, all of them waiting for someone to start. It didn't surprise him that Frank Porter was the one to break the silence. The pompous little man believed he spoke for all the ranchers.

"You know why we're here," he said.

"I can guess, but I won't know until you tell me."

"Has Roberta said anything about rebuilding the dam?"

"She intends to continue with the farm, so she'll need water to do that."

"You've got to talk to her. We can't let her rebuild that dam."

It annoyed him that they expected him to deliver their complaint to Roberta. If they had anything to say, they ought to say it to her. "If she does build it, will you blow it up a third time?"

"We didn't blow it up the second time," Ezra Kemp said.

"Then who did?"

"I don't know."

"Who else would have a reason?"

Ezra turned red in the face. "Are you calling me a liar?"

"I merely asked a question. You blew it up the first time."

"I didn't do it by myself," Ezra protested.

"It doesn't matter which one of you lit the dynamite. You're all responsible. How about the raid on her farm?"

Three men spoke at once. "We had nothing to do with that."

Nate studied the men one by one. He believed them, yet who else would have a reason to destroy the crops and the dam? "Somebody ordered an attack that killed Robert Tryon. The sheriff is going to be looking for the culprit. Roberta has said she won't stop until she knows who killed her father. *I'm* going to be looking as well."

"I helped blow up that dam the first time," Ches Hale admitted, "but I'd blow up a hundred dams before I'd even think of shooting a man in cold blood."

"Somebody did, and unless the sheriff finds a reason to go after somebody else, the four of you are going to be the prime suspects. I would go so far as to say the *only* suspects."

All four men voiced vigorous protests, but eventually they fell silent.

"We came here in hopes of persuading you to talk Roberta out of rebuilding that dam."

"You're the only one she'll listen to," Mead Ryan added.

"What makes you think she'll listen to me?"

"She knows you weren't involved in blowing up the dam the first time."

He had been in Colorado searching for Laveau at the time. "I'm not going to try to talk her into or out of anything. In fact, I'm sending some of my men to help rebuild the barn."

"We don't give a damn about the barn or the crops," Mead said. "We just can't let her rebuild that dam."

"If you're smart, all of you will keep far away from Roberta Tryon. You'll stop making threats and start trying to find who's responsible for the attack. Maybe you got together and hired someone to do it for you. Maybe one of you lost patience and decided to act on your own."

"You start spreading that kind of talk around town, and you'll be the one in trouble," Mead threatened.

"Don't be a bigger fool than you are," Ezra said to Mead. "Don't you understand what Nate is saying?"

"He's saying one of us killed Robert Tryon."

"He's saying everybody believes one or all of us are responsible because we destroyed the first dam, and we've been telling everybody what we intended to do if Tryon rebuilt the dam. Well he did, and somebody blew it up *just like we said we would*. Only that somebody killed Robert Tryon. I know I didn't do it, but I can't vouch for anyone else."

"I was at my ranch that night. My hands will vouch for me."

"Of course your hands will vouch for you. If they don't, it means they were involved."

The argument that followed got so heated the men

might have come to blows if Nate hadn't spoken up. "Standing around accusing each other won't do any good. If no one in this room is responsible, you need to come up with some information, supported by facts, that point to someone else."

"But who?" Frank asked. "Where do we start looking?"

"Why should we do anything?" Mead asked. "That's the sheriff's job."

"I don't like being suspected of murder," Ezra said.

Ches Hale and Frank Porter agreed.

"Do it very quietly, but talk to everyone in the county. Somebody must have seen something. Somebody around here had to be involved. There were eight men in that attack. They didn't materialize out of nowhere."

"There's got to be two hundred men in and around Slender Creek," Mead pointed out.

"Counting your families and the men working for you, you've got more than two dozen people who can start asking questions. Somewhere, somehow, somebody knows something."

"What if it's one of us?" Ezra asked.

"Then I'll do everything I can to make sure he hangs."

❧

Roberta didn't want to get up. It didn't matter that birds were chirping, or that the sun was already over the horizon. The world wouldn't stop if she stayed in bed a little longer. If Joe wasn't here already, he soon would be. He could feed the animals just as easily as she could. Probably better. He liked doing it. He was patient, even talked to the mules and the cow. He had named the pigs and knew exactly how many chickens she had. She was impatient of anything to do with the livestock. Watching corn waving in the breeze or seeing tomato vines heavy with fruit didn't cause her heart to beat faster. Neither did it fill her with a desire to rush out and plant more rows of corn and tomatoes. She didn't have strong feelings either way about beans, but she could live happily without ever seeing another potato unless it was cooked and on her plate.

But her parents had bred into her a sense of responsibility, had instilled in her a strong work ethic. It didn't matter that her body ached, or that she had lain awake half the night wondering if the boys were taking proper care of Nate. She had work to do, and she couldn't do it lying in bed. Groaning in frustration and from the muscle aches in virtually every part of her body, she sat up and swung her feet to the floor. She was tempted to put on a housecoat over her nightgown, but that would only encourage her to take longer to leave the house. Stepping out of her night-gown, she reached for a clean work dress and pulled it on over her head. She pulled on a pair of slippers. She wouldn't put on her boots until after breakfast.

She went to the kitchen and was about to make coffee when she heard shouting in the distance. She couldn't remember that Joe had ever raised his voice, but a sudden outburst from two more voices convinced her something was wrong. She hurried out of the house and toward the lane that led to the barn. There was a tangle of men on the ground. Breaking into a run, she arrived to find Joe fighting Grady, Webb, and Carlin. A badly bruised Webb flew through the air and landed at her feet. He scrambled up and would have plunged back into the fray if Roberta hadn't stopped him.

"What is going on?"

"The boss sent us to help fix your barn, but Crazy Joe won't let us. He said Miss Prudence told him not to let anybody set foot on your farm."

Chapter Nine

NATE SAW HER COMING WHEN SHE WAS A SMALL FIGURE in the distance. He knew it was Roberta even before he knew the men with her were Webb, Grady, and Carlin.

"Benny," he called. "Get in here." His Italian cook's name was Benito, but he preferred Benny. He said it made him feel more American.

"What's wrong, boss?" He was of medium height and build with light olive skin and an unruly shock of black hair.

"I'm going to have a guest. A lady. Fix something for her."

"I never cooked for a lady. What should I fix?"

"I don't know." Nate tried to remember some of the things Pilar had fixed when she and Cade had guests. "How about some cakes? Maybe a custard. Do we have tea?"

"This is a cow ranch," Benny replied. "The men would dump me in the horse trough if I tried to serve them tea. What day is the lady coming?"

"She'll be here in less than ten minutes."

Benny's skin went pale. "I can't get the stove going that fast."

"I don't care what you do, but do something."

Benny turned and fled, his mane of hair bobbing behind him.

Nate hoisted himself out of his chair. He was nervous about Roberta's reaction to his house. Having never had a female guest, he'd never really looked at it. It was just like any other with furniture, pictures on the walls, and rugs here and there. There was nothing distinctive about any of it. It was just *there*. He'd bought the ranch from a man who'd lost his wife early in life and had given the house a thoroughly male atmosphere. Leather and wood dominated, giving every room a dark if restful feeling that was only partially relieved by the light from the windows. He wondered when he'd become so aware of his home's appearance. It must have been the four days he'd spent in Roberta's house.

A picture flashed in his mind of the hacienda where Cade and Pilar lived, the home he'd shared with them for four years. It reflected the people who lived there. The heavy Spanish elements had been diluted by the Texas openness with both being refined by French elegance. He wondered why he'd never realized his house had none of that. He'd brought nothing from Arkansas. That home was tainted by bitter memories he wanted to forget.

But he had no memories to put in their places. When he worked with Cade, he'd been absorbed into Cade's family. After he bought his ranch, his life had been dominated by his search for Laveau. There was nothing of him anywhere. Who was he? What was unique to him? He wasn't sure he'd recognize himself if he met himself coming down the street. He had a name, a body, a place to live, but none of that had given him a sense of self. So here he was, eager to meet a woman who appealed to him as no other had, and he didn't even know who he was. She was bringing her buggy to a stop in front of the house. He went out to greet her.

"I hadn't expected to see you here so soon."

Grady helped her down from her buggy while Carlin tied her horse to the hitching post.

"I hadn't planned to come so soon, but we ran into some trouble this morning."

He figured that when he saw the boys with her, but she looked okay, and that was all that mattered. "Come in. We can't stand talking with the sun bearing down on us. I'm pleased you were concerned enough to check on me. I'm sure you have plenty of work to keep you busy."

"That's what I came to talk about," Roberta said.

He didn't know why he should be so excited to see Roberta and so disappointed that she hadn't come purely because of her interest in him. Nothing of a romantic nature had passed between them.

"Have a seat," he said. "You boys go see if Benny needs any help."

"I'd like them to stay. They need to hear what I have to say."

Any eagerness he'd had to see Roberta slipped away with the elusiveness of a daydream. He settled back in his chair and waited for her to tell him she didn't want his help. After the ruckus Russ kicked up, he wasn't sure he could blame her.

"I appreciate you sending the boys to help with the barn. You know I like them and would have been glad of their help."

"Did they do something wrong?"

"It's Prudence. I didn't know this, but after the trouble yesterday, she told Joe not to allow any man on the place. When the boys showed up this morning, Joe tried to make them leave. When they wouldn't, he fought them."

"All three of us," Grady told Nate.

"He tossed us about like we were children," Carlin added.

"Now I see why nobody causes trouble in Riggins's saloon," Webb said.

"I tried to convince him it was all right for the boys to be there, but Joe worships Prudence. She's always looked out for him. He'll do whatever she says. He won't let the boys be anywhere, except at the house, until Prudence tells him it's okay."

It was probably foolish of him, but Nate felt better. Roberta hadn't rejected his help. What's more, she'd been concerned enough to explain the problem in person. It might not seem like much to someone else, but it made a big difference to him. He turned to Grady.

"Ride into Slender Creek and find Miss Prudence. Ask her to go out to Miss Tryon's farm and tell Crazy Joe it's okay for the three of you to be there."

"If you call him Crazy Joe, she won't lift a finger to help you," Roberta warned. "She's more likely to run you off herself."

"All three of you go," Nate said. "That way you

can look over the damage to the barn and make a list of what you need to begin work tomorrow."

"There must be work here you need them to do."

"Russ has taken the rest of the men to make a count of the steers that are ready for market. I wouldn't know where to tell them to find him."

The boys were gone in a matter of minutes, and he was alone with Roberta. He wondered if she was as on edge as he felt.

"Are you feeling better?" she asked.

"Yes. Benny has kept so close to your recommendations Russ swears I'll die of starvation. The doctor has filled Benny's head with so much praise he wouldn't fix me a steak if I asked for it. It doesn't matter. I've never had much of an appetite."

"Considering what Russ thinks is suitable food, I'm not surprised." She seemed to relax a little. "I don't know how you survived. If I were cooking your meals, you wouldn't be so thin."

She looked as though she feared he might consider her remarks too personal, but it pleased him that she'd been interested enough to notice. "What would you feed me?"

"I'd have to find out what you like, what agrees with you, what is good for you."

"That sounds like it might take a long time. Possibly years."

"I could probably do it in a few months. Maybe even a few weeks."

"When can you start?" He hadn't meant to say that. He certainly hadn't wanted to cause Roberta to look for a way to escape. He forced a laugh that he hoped would dispel the tension. "It would be nice, but I couldn't get rid of Benny. Besides, Prudence would have to move in. The thought of you being on a ranch with nearly a dozen men would give her nightmares."

Roberta's laugh wasn't entirely spontaneous. "I shouldn't laugh. She has the best intentions. She just doesn't trust any man."

"She trusts Joe."

"I do, too. He would defend me with his life."

He wondered if she trusted him half that much.

"How long does the doctor expect you'll be laid up?"

"That depends on what I want to do." He was well enough to talk to her as long as she would let him.

"Do you think you'll be well enough in a week to attend a dance?"

She couldn't be inviting him to go to the dance with her. Everybody knew she'd been keeping company with Boone Riggins. "I never go to dances."

"That's not what I asked."

"I expect I'll be well enough to dance some of the slower numbers, but I won't be there." He'd never been good in social situations. When he was growing up, attention had always centered on Caleb. It didn't matter that Nate was bigger, stronger, and more of a leader. Caleb was better looking, more outgoing, and possessed that magic something that made him the center of attention wherever he went.

"Why not?"

"I don't know anybody, and I don't dance." That was something else Caleb did better.

"If every bowlegged cowboy in three counties

can dance, so can you. The best way to get to know people is to go to church or a dance."

"Or a hanging."

She laughed. "I wouldn't know. We haven't had one of those. One of the boys said you never went into town with them. Are you that busy, or do you dislike people that much?"

How did he explain that even though he liked Grady, Webb, and Carlin, he really had nothing in common with boys who were more than ten years younger? Nor did he have any interest in drinking too much or talking with women whose job it was to flirt with the customers so they'd spend more money. "I like those boys. They're good cowhands, but they have few interests beyond doing their work, getting their pay, and spending it as quickly as they can. I have to think of the dozen people depending on this ranch for a living. If that weren't enough, I spent four years fighting a terrible war and losing my family as a consequence. I wouldn't be good company."

Roberta studied him for a moment. "What happens when you find diViere, assuming he doesn't kill you, or you don't end up in jail? Are you going to stay here, or will you go somewhere else and avoid becoming part of that community?"

He knew Roberta didn't approve of his pursuit of Laveau, but he hadn't realized she disapproved of everything. "I don't see any reason why I shouldn't stay here, assuming I have the choice." But he hadn't thought about the future, not about the ranch, not about the people of Slender Creek, not even the rest of his life. Everything had been focused on Laveau.

What *would* he do when the search was over? "I expect I'll stay here. Slender Creek seems like a nice little town."

"Then you'd better come to the dance. You should consider going to church, too. There are several pleasant young women in Slender Creek. That would give you a chance to meet them. There are some nice young couples I'm sure you could make friends with."

He didn't have to ask why she thought he ought to meet eligible young women. Everyone thought a man should be married, especially a rich one. "How about you? How many of the *nice young men* have you met? Sorry. I forgot you're engaged to Boone Riggins."

She reacted like something had stung her. "I'm *not* engaged to Boone."

"I heard he'd asked you to marry him."

"You haven't heard that I've said *yes*."

"Is that because you're going back to Virginia?" He had no right to ask that question, but he had to know the answer.

She didn't meet his gaze, but she was quick with her answer. "No, but it would have been sufficient reason."

She wasn't in love with Boone. That shouldn't have made him happy, but it did. "How about the other nice young men?"

"Why would I get involved with anyone when I'm going back to Virginia?"

"You might change your mind."

"I'd have to change my mind about Texas first."

"What's so terrible about Texas?"

"What's so good about it? Why did you come here instead of going back to Arkansas?"

Not even Cade knew what happened when he went home after the war. "There were too many unhappy memories in Arkansas. I came to Texas because my captain during the war offered me a job on his ranch."

"Why did you buy a ranch here? You must have had the money to go anywhere you wanted."

"Laveau and Cade grew up on neighboring ranches. Laveau's family lost their land during the war, and Cade's father took advantage of it. After the war, Cade married Laveau's sister and took over the diViere ranch. Laveau hates the seven of us who survived the war, but he hates Cade most of all. I knew he'd come back sooner or later."

"So every decision you've made is based on your hatred of one man."

That wasn't entirely true, but it was uncomfortably close to the truth. "He's responsible for my brother's death. I can't forget that."

"What if you don't find him? What if he leaves Texas for good? Are you going to spend the rest of your life looking for him?"

He hadn't thought about that. When he was at the ranch, he corresponded with several agents he employed to help trace Laveau. When he wasn't at the ranch, his focus was on the chase. When that was over, he'd figure out what to do next. "Why do you care what happens to me? I'm a rancher, and you don't trust ranchers. I don't think you should rebuild the dam, and you don't approve of anything I do.

You never would have done more than speak to me in passing if you hadn't shot me. You were relieved when I was well enough to leave, and you wouldn't be here now if Prudence had kept her mouth shut." He regretted the words as soon as they left his lips. "I'm sorry. I shouldn't have said that. I have a temper that is made worse by my confinement."

Roberta didn't flinch, and she didn't look away. "No need to apologize. I probably wouldn't have gotten to know you if I hadn't shot you, but I did. And now that I know you better, it bothers me to see you wasting your life. I know you don't see it that way, but I do."

She was interrupted by the entrance of Benny bearing a tray with coffee and a slice of pie.

"You didn't have to go to so much trouble," she said to Benny.

"The boss said I had to do *something*." He sounded aggrieved. "I didn't have time to make anything, so I cut the pie I made for supper."

"You'll spoil my lunch," she said to Nate.

"After all the trouble I caused you, I couldn't think of not offering you something."

"Do you need anything for your coffee?" Benny inquired.

"No. I like it black."

"Then I'll leave you to enjoy your visit with the boss."

"I don't think you're enjoying it very much," Roberta said after Benny left, "not with me criticizing you all the time."

"It's not a problem." He was used to it. His mother found even less to like.

"Can I pour you some coffee?"

"Thank you, but my nurse says I can't have coffee until I'm completely well."

What was it about Roberta's smile that made him want to touch her? It wasn't welcoming or inviting, yet it made him feel like a special friend, one close to her in a way she allowed no others. It wasn't true, but it was how he felt.

"You really should stay away from coffee, but you can have some if you put a little milk in it."

"Bite your tongue! I'd be run out of Texas."

Her laugh caused him to laugh. That was something else that didn't happen with anybody else. Why did it happen with Roberta?

"My father felt the same way, but my mother put cream and sugar in her coffee."

"I wouldn't think that was drinkable."

"It's not bad, but I prefer the way people drink it here."

"So there *is* something you like about Texas," he teased.

"They drink coffee black in Virginia, too."

"But I distinctly heard you say *I prefer the way people drink it here*."

Roberta's laugh was easy, her smile genuine. "Okay, you caught me. I like other things about Texas, but I'm not going to tell you. You'll probably make a list and remind me every time you see me."

His spirits soared. She expected they would see each other again. Surely *every time* meant more than once. "I would hope your list would be long enough that you wouldn't go back to Virginia."

"Why do you care if I leave Texas?"

"I'll answer that if you finish answering my question. You got distracted when Benny brought the coffee."

She took a bite of pie. Nate wondered if she did that to give her time to come up with a meaningless answer.

"I pretty much said all I had to say. I think you're wasting your life."

"What should I do?"

She put her plate down and fixed her gaze on him. "The first thing I'd do is quit looking for diViere."

"I'm not sure I can do that since he appears to be looking for me."

"I don't mean that you should ignore his being here. You must defend yourself, but don't spend months looking for him. Killing him, or whatever you need to do to satisfy your need for vengeance, won't bring your brother back. You have a fine ranch. You must also have money in reserve since you didn't sell any steers last year. Invest in your ranch by improving your stock. Invest in the town. There must be several businesses that could use money to expand."

"That takes care of my business. What about me?"

Roberta didn't look quite as confident now. "It's impossible to answer for another person, but young men usually get married and settle down to raise a family."

"That requires a wife."

"There are several unattached women in Slender Creek."

"I'm acquainted only with Prudence Goodfellow. I can hardly imagine a worse fate."

Roberta laughed so hard tears streamed from her eyes. "I shouldn't laugh, but the images that called to mind hardly bear thinking of."

"Since you think that's so funny, tell me what kind of woman you think I *should* marry?"

Roberta sat bolt upright. "I can't possibly answer that question."

"Why not?"

"I hardly know you. Besides, people fall in love for all kinds of reasons. Sometimes the most unsuitable people marry and are perfectly happy. At other times, what looks like a perfect match ends up a miserable mess."

"Do you think I would be happy if I married a woman like you?"

"Absolutely not. You'd end up killing each other."

He smiled despite himself. "Even though you shot me, I never thought of you as a violent person."

"I'm not under normal circumstances."

"But being married to a man like me wouldn't be normal circumstances."

"You're twisting my words." She set her coffee down. "I'd better be going. I can't leave Joe to work by himself all day."

"I didn't mean to make you uncomfortable. I just wanted to know what kind of woman you thought could put up with me."

"It's not a *kind* of woman. It's a *who*. The woman who falls in love with you."

"Do you think there is such a woman?"

"Certainly. You just have to give people a chance to get to know you."

"And I can do that by going to the dance and to church?"

"That's a beginning, but there are lots of other things you can do."

"Will you come back tomorrow?"

Apparently she hadn't expected that request. "You're doing very well, and I have a lot of work to do."

"If the boys can convince Prudence to let them help Crazy Joe, you'll have time to make sure I'm still progressing."

She fixed him with a stern look. "I will accept your offer on one condition."

"What is that?"

"That you stop referring to Joe by the name *Crazy Joe*. He's slow, but he's not crazy."

"You shouldn't be alone at that farm. Would you like one of the boys to stay with you at night?"

"Thanks for the offer, but I don't think Prudence could stand it."

"I don't care what she thinks," he snapped. "I'm asking you." He hadn't meant to let his temper get the best of him, but he wasn't used to putting up with all kinds of silly social etiquette. Prudence would have to be an idiot to think one of the boys would harm Roberta.

"Prudence means well. I sometimes lose patience with her, but she's often right. Thanks for your offer, but I don't need a guard. Now I really must go."

Unable to think of any reason to postpone her departure, Nate accompanied her outside. "I'm counting on a visit tomorrow. I want to know what

Prudence said, how Cr— er, Joe reacted, and how the boys are doing. They're good kids, but I don't know how much experience they have working on a farm." He followed her down the steps.

"You don't have to help me into the buggy."

"I can't lift you, but I can help you keep your balance."

"Thanks." She climbed onto the seat and gathered the reins. "I'm not sure I can come tomorrow, but I'll try."

He didn't reply, just watched while she turned the buckboard and drove away. There was no longer any question in his mind that he was powerfully attracted to Roberta Tryon. What's more, he liked her. She had backbone. She wasn't ready to admit she had a vengeful streak, but she was kind. A less patient and understanding woman would have been ready to murder Prudence Goodfellow. He hoped she would return tomorrow. He had to know if there was any chance she could learn to like him.

❧

"Is everyone incompetent?" Travis shouted. "Can't anyone get to this man?"

"I can't kill him in his own home. One of those boys is always around him."

"Send in some of the other men."

"Dolan isn't stupid. If he sees the new men hired since he was here last, he's going to know some- thing's wrong."

Travis eyed him in a way that made him wish he'd never gotten involved with this man.

"You'd better start thinking of a way to get to him. If Dolan finds the calves you're branding before you figure out how to get rid of him, your neck will end up in a noose. I expect better news when I get back. If I don't get it, there are a few tidbits of information I think the sheriff might like to know."

Just like the bastard to throw the blame on someone else, but Travis wasn't going to throw it on him. No amount of money was worth a stretched neck.

"Did you convince Prudence to tell Crazy Joe—damn! I've got to remember not to call him crazy—to tell *Joe* to let the three of you work for Roberta?"

"We tried, boss, but she wouldn't change her mind," Carlin said.

"Damn that woman! Why does she have to interfere in everything Roberta does?"

"I can't answer that," Grady said, "but Miss Roberta came into town when we were still there, and she convinced Miss Prudence to tell Crazy Joe not to run us off tomorrow."

"You'd better get used to calling him Joe. If Roberta hears you say Crazy Joe, she's liable to send you packing. I want one of you at that ranch at all times."

"How are we supposed to do that?"

"Work with Joe two at a time. The other one can stay here and sleep. Then when two come home, the third goes to stand guard through the night. You can work out a schedule among yourselves."

"Is somebody threatening Miss Roberta?"

"I don't know. All of the local ranchers swear they had nothing to do with the attack. If that's true, I have no idea who's behind this or what they're after. Until I have the answers to those questions, I don't want her without a guard."

"If we sleep in the house, she's going to know we're there."

"Take your bedroll and sleep behind the house or in a nearby field, but make sure it's close enough that you can hear anything that goes on."

"Wouldn't it be easier to bring her here?"

"And have Prudence Goodfellow on my doorstep preaching fire and brimstone within the hour?"

The boys laughed. "We hadn't thought of that."

"I doubt Roberta would come if I asked. She's very independent and remarkably unafraid."

"True. Mr. Riggins did everything but tie her up when she was in town today."

"She refused Riggins?"

"She did more than that," Grady told him with a grin. "She said if he didn't stop plaguing her, she wouldn't go to the dance with him. She was right put out with him, if you ask me."

Nate doubted he was successful in hiding his smile. He wasn't happy Roberta was going to the dance with Boone, but he was delighted she had turned down Boone's offer to help yet had accepted his. It was a small but significant point in his favor.

❧

Nate heard the rattle of the buckboard from his office. "She's here," he called to Benny on his way to the front of the house. "You can bring the coffee in ten minutes."

"Sure thing, boss. I got fresh apple cake today."

"Good. Everybody in Virginia eats apples." Only they had fresh apples, not the dried kind you got in Texas. He didn't care about the apples, only that Roberta had come a second day in a row. He was waiting on the porch when she drove up.

"Don't fuss," she called. "I can get down by myself."

He came down the steps and offered her a hand. "The doctor says I'm a miracle patient."

"Don't push your miracle too far." Roberta reached in the buckboard and took out a hat.

"What are you doing with my hat?" he asked.

"You left it at my house."

"No, I didn't. I distinctly remember wearing my hat home. Russ said it was so badly battered I could never wear it again."

"I found this in the yard the night of the attack."

"I never carry two hats. Are you sure it's mine?"

"Your name is printed on the lining."

Nate took the hat and placed it on his head. It fit perfectly. "I have my hats custom-made. The hatmaker always writes my name inside."

"If this is your hat but you didn't wear it, how did it get in my yard the night of the attack?"

Chapter Ten

"A BETTER QUESTION IS WHO PUT IT THERE AND WHY?"

Nate ushered Roberta into the house. She had hardly removed her bonnet and settled into a chair when Benny came hurrying in with a tray loaded with several kinds of sweets.

"Are those macaroons?" she asked, pointing to a cookie that appeared to be festooned with toasted coconut.

"Do you like macaroons?" Benny asked.

"What sane person doesn't?" She turned to Nate, who was seated opposite. "Are you trying to lure me here with sweets?"

"Would it work?" he asked with a laugh. He was feeling much better today. He'd been able to get out of the house for a couple hours. Having Roberta show up made everything better.

"It just might," she said eyeing the macaroons. "I've been working so hard I haven't had any desire to cook, and not much more to eat."

Roberta helped herself to a macaroon while Benny left with a promise to return with coffee as soon as it was ready.

"I was hoping the boys would pick up part of the load," Nate said.

"They're working on the barn. I think Prudence has been meddling again. My other cow has returned, and the pigs have been showing up one at a time."

"How is Prudence responsible for that?"

"I think she has shamed people into looking for my lost animals."

"Maybe she threatened to read a list of their misdeeds from the middle of the street."

Roberta almost choked on her macaroon. "Not even Prudence would do that," she said once she'd recovered sufficiently to talk.

"How is Joe getting along with the boys?"

"He's okay as long as they don't come near the house. They had to eat their lunch inside what's left of the barn."

Nate thought blind loyalty in a man of limited understanding could be dangerous even when he acted out of the best intentions. He considered warning Roberta about Crazy Joe's fanatical adherence to anything Prudence told him, but he figured Roberta wouldn't listen to him. In her eyes, Crazy Joe was perfectly safe and his loyalty admirable.

Benny's return with the coffee was a welcome diversion from his troubling thoughts. He watched with amusement as Benny preened under Roberta's compliments. Was there ever a man who didn't respond immediately to attention from a beautiful woman?

"Can I hire you to cook for me?" Roberta asked Benny.

Benny was staring at her as though hypnotized. "It would be an honor."

"An empty one," Roberta said with a laugh. "At least Nate can pay you."

Benny didn't take his eyes off Roberta. "The boss is very generous."

"So I've found out. I've been trying to convince him to spend more time here. I'm sure people would enjoy getting to know him."

Benny assumed a confidential tone. "I've been telling him the same thing."

"You can stop talking about me like I'm not here," Nate said. "You'd better get back to the kitchen. Russ and the rest of the crew will be here soon, and they'll be expecting their supper."

"I do not like the men he hired, boss."

"Well, you don't have to see much of them. Now back to work. Miss Tryon and I have serious matters to discuss."

"You tell him he ought to stay here at the ranch," Benny said to Roberta. "That is a serious matter, too."

"You have some very loyal hands," Roberta told Nate after Benny left, "who obviously respect you and care about you—and not just because you pay them well."

"I'll take that into consideration. Right now I'd rather know more about why you found my hat at your place. Maybe it's one I lost and somebody was wearing it."

"Everybody except you was wearing a mask," Roberta said.

"Then that means somebody put it there to implicate me."

"You were the only rancher who didn't threaten to blow up my father's dam. Could it have been one of the other ranchers trying to throw suspicion on you?"

"I know you'll find this hard to accept," Nate explained, "but I don't believe any of the local ranchers are capable of murder. If it had been just the destruction of the dam, I'd have been certain they were behind it."

"For argument's sake, let's say you're right. That means somebody we don't know was behind the attack and wanted to implicate you. What reason would a stranger have to kill my father, destroy his crops, and blow up his dam?"

"I don't know."

"And why would he want to frame you?" Roberta asked.

"Laveau has already tried to kill two Night Riders. I see no reason to suppose he would hesitate to shoot a third, but I don't know why he would attack your farm. As far as anybody knew, I was nowhere near Slender Creek. There's still another question that needs answering."

"What?"

"Even if Laveau was behind it, who actually carried out the raid?"

"There are lots of cowhands on the local ranches," Roberta noted.

"They all swear they were in their beds when the attack took place."

"Somebody is lying. Eight men couldn't appear and disappear without somebody knowing or seeing something."

"I agree, but if we can find who left my hat there and why, we might be able to unravel the rest. No one knew when I was coming back. I didn't even know until I decided at the last minute to change my plans."

"So we're back where we started." Roberta sighed, exasperated. "I think the ranchers were behind the attack, but you don't. I think they tried to implicate you, but you think diViere is the only one who would have done that. However, you don't see any reason for diViere to bother when he was willing to kill you himself. So where does that leave us?"

"With a mystery that doesn't make any sense. I'm going to start from the standpoint that Laveau is behind it even though I don't know why or how."

"And I'm going to assume the ranchers are behind it. They're the only ones with a reason."

"But you don't believe I had anything to do with it?" He had to be sure of the answer to this question, and he had to believe she was sincere. If not, there was no reason to keep thinking any of the thoughts that kept popping into his head.

"No."

"Why? You think I'm practically a killer."

"You want to bring diViere to justice, but I don't believe you really want to kill him. You're not a killer."

"How can you tell? As you said, you know nothing about me."

"I don't know a lot of *facts*, but I've learned a lot about your character. You aren't angry at me for shooting you. You don't agree with what I intend to do with the farm, but you've sent your men to help me.

Just as important is the devotion you've inspired in your men. No cold-blooded killer could have done that."

Nate felt uncomfortable with that kind of praise. He'd never made any attempt to instill devotion in his men. As far as he knew, they weren't capable of it. Russ took care of him, but he would never call Russ devoted to him. Grady, Webb, and Carlin were little more than overgrown boys who reveled in being given responsibility and being paid for it. Benny liked him because he noticed what Benny cooked. He didn't know the rest of the crew because Russ had hired them while he was gone. Beyond that, he couldn't say anybody except the Night Riders gave a hoot whether he lived or died.

"You give me too much credit. I give an honest wage for honest work, but I don't expect anything beyond that."

"Why are you trying to avoid all relationships, even ordinary friendship?"

Her question unsettled him. To answer it would force him to look at a part of him he'd tried to ignore, to remember things he wanted to forget. "I'm not trying to avoid them. I just haven't had time for them."

"If I hadn't shot you, you wouldn't have had time for me, either."

He had known Robert Tryon had a daughter. He'd seen her when they talked about the dam, but he'd never exchanged more than a few sentences with her. After that, he'd dismissed her from his thoughts the way he dismissed most people, especially young, single females. "I suppose that means I ought to be grateful you shot me."

Roberta's laugh was charming and genuine. "If you're trying to make me believe getting to know me was worth being shot, you're wasting your time. My father didn't raise a half-witted child."

"Let's just say it was an unexpected benefit."

Roberta took a swallow of her coffee and rose. "It's time for me to go. Much more, and you're going to have me thinking too highly of myself."

"I doubt that's possible."

"That's exactly what I mean. If I didn't know better, I'd think I shot you in the head and addled your brains."

"Instead, you shot me in the heart and woke it up."

Roberta's smile vanished. "Now you're talking nonsense. Thank Benny for the coffee and the macaroons. If I were to come here often, he'd spoil me for my own cooking."

"Come as often as you like."

"I have too much work to do to come here every day and listen to your foolish talk. Besides, from what I can see, you're practically well."

"You never know when I might have a relapse," he said with a rakish grin. "Wouldn't your conscience bother you if I were struggling to stay alive, and you went blithely along with your work in ignorance of my suffering?"

"Do you always talk such nonsense when you've been shot?"

"I don't know. I've never been shot."

"Well, don't let it happen again. Other people might think it has affected your brain."

"I don't care as long as you don't think that."

"That's exactly what I *do* think. Now, I'm going to leave, and you ought to go to bed. Maybe some extra rest would restore you to your senses."

"Nothing will ever restore them to what they were."

"Then you ought to send Benny for the doctor."

"I'll go to the doctor right now if you'll go with me."

Rather than go out the front door as Nate expected, Roberta turned and walked across the room to the door Benny had used to enter the room. She opened it, went through, and called the cook's name. Benny appeared almost immediately.

"Your boss is suffering from a fever of the brain. Do you have any herbs you can use to brew a tea to restore his mind?"

Benny regarded her with a blank expression.

"Dried plants, flowers, or bark with medicinal properties. They grow wild."

"I come from Italy," Benny said. "We don't eat weeds."

Nate was eager to hear how Roberta would explain that certain weeds weren't considered *weeds*, but she disappointed him.

"Warm some milk and have him drink it. If you can lay your hands on any vervain or passion flower—you can ask around the next time you go into town—make a tincture for him."

She might as well have asked him to put rotten eggs in his cakes.

"Send for the doctor. He'll know what to tell you. You," she said, turning to Nate, "should go straight to bed and not get up until the doctor says you've recovered your senses."

"I'll go to bed if you'll sit with me." Nate knew he was acting rather silly for a grown man, but he couldn't resist teasing Roberta. He liked the flush on her cheeks when she was exasperated. He adored the way she would throw her head back and roll her eyes when she was really trying not to laugh. Best of all, he liked it when she looked at him in a way that let him know she was looking only at him, as though at that moment, no one else mattered. He'd never had that response from a woman, at least not from a woman he cared about.

Roberta threw her hands up. "You're impossible." She started for the front door with such purposeful strides he had to run so he could help her into her buckboard.

"You'll come back tomorrow?" Nate asked as Roberta gathered the reins.

"I have a farm to run. I'm sure Benny can do anything that needs doing."

She couldn't have been more wrong, but this wasn't the time to tell her.

"Thanks for sending the boys to help. I shouldn't need them more than a few days."

Watching her drive off, Nate felt something had been taken away. Everything was different with Roberta. He was like a starving man who couldn't stop thinking about how sweet she'd taste. She was rapidly becoming an obsession, and he didn't like that. Nor did he trust it. His parents had felt that way about Caleb.

One's life should be a web woven so intricately that the loss of any one strand couldn't destroy it.

That hadn't been true for his parents. Was he in danger of depending too much on his search for Laveau? Was it really about Laveau at all? Wasn't it more about trying to make up for his failure to protect his brother?

What did that have to do with his feelings for Roberta? At the moment, all he knew for certain was that he had to know more about her, see her more often. He wanted her to know more about him, too. He was certain she liked him. Could her feelings grow stronger? Would they match his?

One thing he knew for sure: he wouldn't let the past deprive him of a future.

❧

Roberta told herself she had to get her emotions under control. She was a grown woman. She was responsible for a farm. She couldn't let one man overturn her ability to think clearly and logically.

Okay, he *had* overturned her ability to think clearly and logically, so what was she going to do about it? In her agitation, she had urged her mule into a fast trot that threatened to bounce her out of the buggy. She pulled back on the reins until she had achieved a more comfortable pace. Nate had upset her so much she couldn't even drive sensibly. What was it about this man that made him so different from all others? He was certainly full of contradictions. He had shown no interest in becoming part of the community, yet he had sent three of his cowhands to help rebuild her barn. She had shot him, but he appeared to hold no resentment. He had ignored her up until four days ago. Now he wanted her to visit every day. Despite that, she wondered if he would ever have room in his life for anything but his hatred of Laveau diViere.

She found herself hopeful, even if it went against every rational part of her being. Her mother had always said she was too logical, too practical. She wasn't the type to fall in love with a man just because he was handsome, likeable, and she had shot him by mistake.

She didn't think she'd fallen in love. But she very much wanted to know more about him, wanted to discover what made him think so little of himself, needed to know why bringing diViere to justice seemed more important than his own future.

She'd been so deep in thought she hadn't been aware that the mule had wandered off the trail onto a grassy area that had been covered in Texas bluebonnets a few months earlier. Now lantana and Indian blanket clustered around prickly pear cactus. The straggly heads of a few Mexican hats were visible among the grass. She pulled back on the reins.

"You'll find plenty to eat at home without the chance of getting a thorn in your mouth," she told the mule when he resisted her efforts to pull him back to the trail. A final tug reminded the animal of his duty, and she was soon on her way home. Things were worse than she thought when she was so preoccupied she hadn't even known the buggy had come to a stop. She wouldn't see Nate again. He didn't need her, and she needed to get him out of her system before it was too late.

❧

Boone was waiting for her when she got home.

"What are those men doing here?" he asked before she had alighted from the buggy.

"What men?" She knew who he meant, but she resented his tone.

"Those cowhands. They're Nate Dolan's men, aren't they?"

She allowed him to help her down from the buggy. She immediately started leading the mule toward the barn. "If you've been here long enough to know who they are, then you know what they're doing."

"I told you I'd hire someone who knew what he was doing. Between those bumblers and Crazy Joe, you're liable to have a jerry-built mess that will blow down in the first wind."

"Joe is not crazy. And I doubt Nate would have sent those boys if he didn't believe they knew enough to rebuild the barn."

"Why would he do that? You shot him."

"He wanted to help."

"I wanted to help."

"You wanted to do everything for me. That's different."

"I don't see how."

When they drew near the barn, Joe came to meet her. "Joe will unharness the mule," he said.

"Thank you. How have things gone today?"

"Everything is torn down. Joe will get wood tomorrow."

Roberta looked at what was left of the barn. About two thirds had been pulled down. "I don't know that I have enough money to pay for that much wood."

"I'll buy the wood," Boone offered.

"I couldn't let you do that."

"Why not? Nate is practically a stranger, but you let him send his men to help you. I want to marry you, yet you've refused my help."

She could understand why Boone would feel slighted, but he didn't understand that he was crowding her. She had never said she loved him and had repeatedly told him she was going back to Virginia. In spite of that, he'd pursued her doggedly. He refused to take any of her objections seriously. He seemed to think all he had to do was keep asking, and she'd eventually relent. He hadn't been backward in pointing out that marriage to him would be very advantageous. He was an important man in Slender Creek, owned two thriving businesses, and was said to be the most eligible bachelor within a hundred miles.

"Okay. I'll let you buy the wood, but I'll pay you back."

"I don't need your money."

"Maybe not, but I don't want to be in debt to you."

"Why don't you mind being in debt to Nate?"

"It's not the same. If you had offered to work with Joe, I wouldn't have felt obliged to pay you."

"I have more money than free time. Letting me hire someone to rebuild your barn would have been better for both of us."

"You are bothering Miss Roberta," Joe said to Boone. "Joe wants you to go away."

"I'm not bothering Roberta," Boone objected. "I'm trying to help her."

"Miss Prudence said Joe was not to let anybody upset Miss Roberta."

"You'd better go," Roberta said to Boone.

"He works for me. He knows I wouldn't hurt you."

"He'll do what Prudence says regardless of what either you or I say. I'll let you buy the wood, but I will pay you back as soon as I can."

Boone wanted to argue, but he knew Joe well enough to understand what Roberta said was true. "I sometimes wonder if Prudence and Crazy Joe aren't more trouble than they're worth."

"I wouldn't have survived the attack without them."

"If you'd married me, you wouldn't have to worry about any of this."

"But I didn't. Now you'd better go before Joe gets upset."

"I can't believe I'm being driven away so a half-wit won't get upset."

"If you keep talking about Joe like that, *I'm* going to get upset."

"I'll see that the lumber is here tomorrow, and I'll make damned sure Prudence puts me on the list of men *Joe* is supposed to allow on your land. I suppose it's too much to ask for a kiss."

❦

Nate rode on a loose rein. He was going to see Roberta because she hadn't come to see him. Common sense told him he should stay home and work on getting better, get to know more about his ranch and the work Russ and the other men were doing, but neither seemed as important as seeing Roberta. He had several reasons to offer if she wanted to know why he was visiting when he shouldn't yet be in the saddle. He expected she'd know they were excuses, but that didn't stop him. This attraction was something new for him. For the first time his parents' rejection didn't hurt quite so much. Finding Laveau didn't seem absolutely essential. Logic said a rancher should have nothing to do with a farmer, especially one who disliked Texans. His responsibility for his ranch and his duty to his neighbors would be best served by convincing her to abandon the farm. Her marriage to Boone Riggins would be better for her and for the whole community. The last thing she needed was to fall in love with a man who couldn't escape his past.

Rather than dissuade him, every obstacle seemed to encourage him to persist. He didn't have to remind himself it wasn't logical, that it wasn't smart. He already knew that and didn't care. For once he was going to do something he wanted to do despite a list of reasons why it was the one thing he *shouldn't* do. Just knowing that made him feel good. It made him feel better than good. He felt the best he had in years, the most hopeful he could remember. The hole in his shoulder was an inconvenience that would soon disappear. Everything else was a matter of perspective. Change the way he looked at things, and obstacles could suddenly become opportunities. Even the brittle summer landscape—the lush flowers of spring supplanted by less vibrant colors—seemed to be nature resting rather than defeated by heat.

It was with that hopeful frame of mind that he brought his horse to a stop in front of Roberta's farmhouse. It was a modest building, but just seeing it generated a warmth in him that his own home didn't. It wasn't particularly attractive or well-appointed, but there was a friendliness about it that brought a smile to his face. It was comfortable with itself, unpretentious, unambitious.

He laughed softly, shook his head. He must be crazy talking about a house like it was a person. He dismounted carefully to avoid putting any strain on his wound. He hitched his horse, climbed the steps, and knocked on the door. He wasn't surprised when he got no answer. Knowing Roberta, she would be in the fields until she was too tired to work any longer. He could hear the sound of hammering coming from the direction of the barn, so he decided to see how the boys were getting along with Crazy Joe.

Leaving his horse at the house, he headed down the lane toward the barn. He was pleased to see that many of the tomato plants were showing signs of recovery. The beans and peas looked like they'd been through a tornado, leaves shredded and stems twisted or ripped off. He could only imagine the many hours of backbreaking work it had taken to go through the fields, working on one plant at a time. Even though he still thought trying to farm in this part of Texas was foolhardy, he had to admire her determination.

When he reached the barn, he was surprised to see they were building, rather than tearing down.

The fresh-cut lumber formed a stark contrast to the weathered or smoke-blackened wood that survived the fire. He wondered where Roberta had gotten the money to pay for the new lumber. Had Otis Parker changed his mind about giving her a loan?

Carlin and Webb were standing on the skeleton of the barn framing the roof. Crazy Joe was passing up pieces of lumber with ease that the boys handled with difficulty. As Nate reached the corner to the barn, a voice called out to him.

"What are you doing here? You ought to be home in bed."

Chapter Eleven

ROBERTA DIDN'T WANT TO ACKNOWLEDGE THE abrupt lift in her spirits or the smile she couldn't keep from her lips. She could make her words sound severe, but she was sure her eyes sparkled with welcome. It was no use. She was beguiled by Nate Dolan. She could only hope it was no more than that.

Yesterday had been one of the most difficult days of her life. It seemed that staying away from Nate had only served to anchor him more firmly in her thoughts. He was in the beans she picked and delivered to Boone's restaurant. He was in the butter she churned, in the eggs she collected, even in the ham she fried for supper. His spirit pervaded her father's bedroom so thoroughly he might as well have been there in person. Today had been so much worse she'd given up working alone and had joined Joe and the boys, hoping their presence would distract her. How far she'd fallen short of her goal could be measured by the joy she felt that he'd apparently missed her as well.

She hadn't realized how much she missed his

smile. It wasn't a big grin or the kind of smile accompanied by a hearty laugh. She didn't know whether he was constrained by the presence of the others or if he always restrained his emotions, but there was only a barely perceptible turning up at the corners of his mouth. The real smile was in his slate-blue eyes. They widened slightly and seemed to sparkle from within. Given the way she looked right now, she'd have forgiven him if he'd turned and made a rapid retreat. She wasn't covered with dirt, but she could hardly have looked worse if she'd tried.

"Doc said I'm so ornery that staying inside would probably slow my recovery."

He didn't look like a man who'd been shot a week ago. He appeared to be in blooming health. She didn't know how she'd managed to be virtually unaware of his existence until he ended up in her father's bed.

"He's probably right." She tried to put her dress in order but gave up. She pulled her bonnet from her head and smoothed her hair. She was sure she looked a fright, but at least she could see him. "Still, you shouldn't be riding this far."

"I'm used to riding much farther. I wanted to see how the boys were doing."

"We're doing okay, boss," Carlin called from his perch above. "It takes both of us to keep up with Joe. If we were half as strong, Russ wouldn't keep us at the ranch all the time."

Roberta was pleased that Carlin didn't stumble over Joe's name. It had taken two days, but none of the boys called him Crazy Joe anymore.

"I didn't realize you were rebuilding already," Nate said to Roberta.

"With the boys helping Joe, they were able to clear away the rubble quickly. I'm planning on having a big bonfire to celebrate the completion of the barn."

"I'm glad Otis changed his mind about giving you a loan."

She had expected he would wonder how she managed to purchase the wood. Everyone knew Otis had refused to give her a loan.

"Mr. Riggins gave it to her, boss," Carlin volunteered. "I think we got enough extra to build a chicken coop and a cowshed."

"Otis didn't change his mind," Roberta told Nate. "Boone insisted on buying the lumber now so I wouldn't have to wait. I'll repay him as soon as I'm able." It annoyed her that she should feel uncomfortable telling him Boone had paid for the lumber. Knowing that she had accepted the lumber only on the condition that she would repay him didn't make it any easier.

"That was generous of him," Nate said.

"Not as much as you'd think," Carlin said. "He's been trying to get Miss Roberta to marry him. He said if she married him, she wouldn't have to worry about anything."

"Mr. Riggins is a successful businessman," Nate said. "I'm sure he'll provide quite amply for the woman who becomes his wife."

Roberta made a mental note to tell Carlin he didn't have to blab everything he knew. She doubted the boy could see the change in Nate, but the slight stiffening of his body, along with the dimming of the light in his eyes, was easily visible to her.

"I'm sure he will," Roberta said. "But at the moment, he hasn't found a willing candidate for that honor. I'm about to go up to the house. Would you like some coffee?"

"I was hoping you'd give us a hand," Carlin called down to Nate. "With three of us working, we might be able to keep up with Joe."

"Not until he's a lot stronger," Roberta said. "I'm not going to be responsible for him breaking that wound open."

"Doc says there's no danger in that happening," Nate said as he followed Roberta to the house. "He said I was well enough to come see you."

"You shouldn't have."

"Why? Does that bother you?"

It worried and excited her, but she couldn't say that. It would make her sound weak-minded. "I'm not sure." She took advantage of walking toward the house to avoid looking at him. "I felt so guilty about shooting you I would have done anything to make sure you got well. In the process, I discovered you weren't at all like what I had thought." She looked up at him briefly before glancing away. "I like you very much, but I still feel guilty."

"Don't."

They had reached the house. "I'm going to clean up. You can wait for me in the parlor."

"You look fine as you are."

"I look like I've been working in the fields all day.

Don't make it hard for me to believe what you say by making exaggerated statements."

Nate's smile reappeared. "I stand chastised."

She smiled despite herself. "No such thing. You're about the most audacious man I've ever met."

He looked so astonished, even unbelieving, she laughed.

"Don't tell me you've never heard that before."

"As a matter of fact, I haven't."

"What kind of women have you met?"

"Apparently not the right kind."

"Go inside before you cause me to say something that will embarrass me."

"Could I?" He appeared to have asked the question in all seriousness.

"Too easily."

She hurried around the side of the house to the kitchen before he could respond. She didn't know quite what to make of that exchange. It was those contradictions again. One moment he would be smiling and a little outrageous, and the next he would act like he didn't recognize himself. She wondered what had happened to cause that conflict? He had never appeared to lack self-confidence, yet there was something that seemed to be eating away at its foundation.

There were some questions for which she'd probably never receive answers. Still, she couldn't help but wonder. She hurried inside to wash up and change. She was sure Nate wouldn't leave regardless of how long she took, but she wasn't willing to put it to the test.

༄

Nate had never studied Roberta's house to learn what it said about its owner, what made it a home rather than just a house. Cade and Pilar's home spoke more of Pilar's grandmother, more of her heritage and how she wanted to be seen, rather than who she was. His father's success had enabled him to buy a house much bigger than they needed and had allowed his mother to furnish it in a style dictated by her social aspirations rather than the character and needs of the people who lived there.

Roberta's home wasn't like that. Her father's bedroom was simply furnished. Clothes hung on hooks on the wall and the back of the door. The heavily decorated wallpaper was free of pictures, but two handmade quilts were stacked on a shelf in a clothes chest. The curtains at the window were white. A water basin and a kerosene lamp sat on a table next to the bed. It was the room of a man who had no need or desire for decoration. It was where he slept. The rest of his life was spent elsewhere.

The parlor was different. The furniture was sturdy and practical, but the decorative touches were definitely feminine. A cabinet in the corner contained small figurines of shepherdesses and lambs, birds, various baby animals, and a golden-haired angel. A small bookcase spilled over with books. Kerosene lamps stood on tables at either end of the sofa. Pictures of pastoral scenes adorned walls covered by flowered wallpaper. Curtains decorated with tiny knots of roses fluttered at the window. Clearly a room decorated by a woman but not so overpowering a man would feel uncomfortable.

Rather the opposite. Nate felt welcomed. Almost embraced. This was a place where a man's spirit could find peace and solace, a place where the cares of the world could be kept at bay. It was a place where he could be happy.

The door at one end of the parlor opened, and Roberta entered. "I'm sorry I took so long, but my mother would turn in her grave if she knew I met company looking like I'd come in from the fields."

Roberta had changed into a white blouse and gray skirt. Rather than pin her hair up as was her habit, she had allowed her abundant, chestnut curls to fall over her shoulders. Nate thought that made her look especially feminine. She was beautiful.

"I'm sure your mother would forgive you, knowing how hard it is to farm in Texas."

"Sit down. You shouldn't be standing."

She sat on the sofa. He chose a rocking chair with a leather-covered seat and a floral pattern on the back.

"My mother would never have agreed to come to Texas. My father and I moved here after she died."

"Is that why you want to move back to Virginia?"

Apparently unsatisfied with her position, Roberta moved over. Nate thought she was using the time to gather her thoughts.

"The only family I have left is in Virginia."

"That wouldn't be true if you were to marry."

The sofa must have been uncomfortable because she moved again. "I haven't yet found a man I wish to marry."

"Have you decided against every man in Texas, or might you find one who could change your mind?"

She still looked uncomfortable, but she didn't move. "I'm sure there are lots of nice men I've never met. I only got to know you in the last week."

"Could I change your mind?"

His question galvanized her, vanquished her uneasiness, turned her back into the direct and open woman he had come to know. "You've been asking questions like that for several days now. I find them confusing. You can't be asking me to marry you. We barely know each other, so what are you trying to say?"

"I'm falling in love with you."

Roberta stared at him like he'd lost his mind. "I shot you. I don't trust ranchers, and I don't like Texas men. Why on earth would you want to fall in love with me?"

"I didn't want to. It just happened."

"Well, make it stop."

Then Nate did something untypical of himself. He got up from his chair, moved to the sofa, and sat next to Roberta. When she tried to move back, he took both her hands. "I don't want to stop. I've never felt as good as I have since I was shot."

"You had a hole in your chest. How could that feel good?"

"Because it let me meet you."

Roberta tried rather halfheartedly to pull her hands from his grasp. "Either you have a fever, or your mind has become deranged."

Nate chuckled and gripped her hands more firmly. "I don't have a fever, and I'm not deranged."

"Then how do you explain your actions?"

"I don't even try. I just know I want to see you,

to be around you, to talk with you, to get to know everything about you. When I'm not with you, I spend half my time wondering what you're doing."

"I'm a farmer. I'm boring."

"You fascinate me. I've never seen your hair down. It makes you look different, more approachable. Prettier."

She pulled her hands from his grasp and scooted back. "Stop talking nonsense."

Nate closed the distance between them. "Boone must see you the same way. Why can't you believe us?"

"Boone doesn't talk about my hair or tell me how pretty I am."

"Then he's a fool."

"He's a successful businessman."

"I know several successful businessmen who are fools. I'm a successful rancher, and I'm a fool."

"Why?"

"Because I never really saw you until now."

Roberta met his gaze. "Are you trying to court me?"

"I hope I'm doing better than *trying*."

She didn't answer.

"You said you didn't dislike me."

"I don't."

"You find me attractive."

"I do."

"Then you don't object?"

"I can't figure out why you'd think of marrying someone like me. You think it's stupid to try to farm in this part of Texas, and you hated the dam."

"I'm not interested in your tomatoes or the dam. Just you."

"I don't see why."

"There doesn't have to be any *why*, but I've got a list of reasons."

"If you're going to start telling me again that I'm beautiful, you can stop right now. I won't believe you."

"Maybe you can believe this."

He reached for Roberta, drew her to him, and kissed her. His experience with other women had led him to expect so little from a kiss he probably wouldn't have tried to kiss Roberta if he'd had time to think about it. But he didn't think, and he got the biggest surprise of his life.

A barrage of sensations poured through him. The kiss was sweet and gentle, but it jolted him down to his toes. Her lips were soft and giving, but her mouth was firm. He wanted to melt into the embrace, yet energy surged through him with the force of a raging mountain stream. He felt like shouting for joy, but he wanted to prolong the kiss until neither of them could breathe.

It was Roberta who broke the kiss.

"I shouldn't have let you do that."

Nate was encouraged to believe she hadn't disliked it when she didn't move away or avert her gaze. "Why not?"

"Because I *wanted* you to kiss me."

The situation was changing almost too fast for Nate to follow. "I thought you didn't like me."

"I didn't." The way she said it made it sound like she meant to say *she did*.

"What caused you to change your mind?"

"You."

"I didn't do anything."

"That's what I thought at first, but I was too busy thinking you were one of the attackers. After I decided you weren't, I couldn't stop wanting you out of my house because I thought I could then stop feeling guilty. It was only after you left that I realized how much my feelings had changed."

"I knew before I left, but I thought you were going to marry Boone Riggins. When you said you hadn't refused his proposal solely because you were returning to Virginia, I had hope."

"My going back to Virginia didn't discourage you?"

"Yes, but it didn't change my feelings. Not even moving to Arkansas could do that." He moved a bit closer. "I'm not any good at being in love. It's never happened before. I'm not very good with women, either. I've been too interested in other things, but that's changed. Do you think we have a chance?"

She smiled and his heart turned over. "I do enjoy spending time with you, but I hope you'll stop falling in love with me. We're too different. We even want to live in different places. You want to bring diViere to justice, but I don't know how I could love a man who would hunt down another. I know that sounds hypocritical coming from the woman who shot you, but that brought home the horror of what it means to kill someone. I couldn't live with myself if I'd killed you."

That was a lot to swallow at once, but it didn't discourage Nate. She didn't love Riggins, and she did like him enough to have thought of all the reasons why they shouldn't fall in love. She was still sitting next to him, her hands in his, her gaze locked with his. She had accepted his help willingly, Riggins's help reluctantly. This wasn't all he wanted, but it was enough for a beginning. He didn't know what he would do about Laveau—he couldn't live with the knowledge that, after all the evil that man had spawned, he would be left free to keep doing it—but somehow he would find an answer. As for living in Virginia, being a farmer couldn't be all that bad.

❦

"Was that Nate Dolan I saw leaving here?"

Blossom McCrevy had arrived before Roberta had time to get over Nate's declaration that he was falling in love with her. She desperately wanted time to think, but Blossom was Roberta's best friend and had an insatiable curiosity. Fortunately, she was discreet.

"You know it was, so don't try to be clever. Sit down, and take off your bonnet. I'm surprised you aren't getting ready for work."

Blossom settled in the rocking chair Nate had so recently vacated. "I've been meaning to come see how you're getting on, but you're always in the field."

"So why are you here now?"

"I'm not supposed to tell you, but Boone thinks you're angry at him. I'm supposed to find out why."

"I'm not angry at him."

Blossom's look was skeptical. "That's not the way it looks to me."

"He keeps trying to do everything for me."

"What is a husband supposed to do but take care of you?"

"He's not my husband, and I don't want *anybody* to take care of me. I can do it myself."

"By working in the fields like a hired hand?"

"If necessary."

Blossom studied Roberta for a minute. "I heard a couple of Nate Dolan's men have been working on your barn. You seem awfully friendly with him. The other ranchers think you hate them."

"Nate was the only one who talked to my father about the dam without threatening him. The night I shot Nate, he had seen the fire and was coming to help."

"Is that what he told you?"

"No. He was delirious that first night. He talked in his sleep."

"You sat up with him all night?"

"The doctor said he couldn't be moved, and I had Russ McCoy here swearing I was going to poison him. I was determined to do everything I could to make sure he got well enough to go home. If anything happened to him after that, it wasn't my fault."

"Yet you went to his ranch to see him. Twice."

"Have you been spying on me?"

Blossom laughed. "I didn't need to spy. You're Slender Creek's most intriguing citizen at the moment. Nate Dolan is close behind."

Roberta was horrified to know her movements were so well known. "I went the first time to make sure he was getting food that wouldn't set his recovery back a week. I went the second time to explain why Joe threw his men off the farm."

"Prudence is still not happy about that. If she weren't

so busy taking care of old lady Gilbert, I expect she'd camp on your front door until the barn was finished."

"I would never wish anyone ill, but I can only hope Mrs. Gilbert's recovery isn't rapid."

Both women laughed, but the tension didn't ease.

"You know, the generally held belief is that Boone Riggins is the best husband you could hope to find, and that you're a fool for not snapping him up before he gets tired of waiting and looks around for someone else."

"If there's ever a time when a woman *should* make up her mind by herself, it's when it comes to choosing her husband."

"There are no other single men around here but cowhands and drifters. There's no *choosing* to be done. Boone is the *only* choice."

"I'd stay single before I married a man I didn't love."

"No woman in her right mind stays single, not when she can marry a man like Boone Riggins. Do you know how rich he is?"

"I'd never marry a man just because he was rich."

"Boone isn't just rich. He's handsome, virile, and as nice as any man can be and still be a man. What's more, he's in love with you."

"He's never said he loves me."

Blossom sat up in her chair. "Of course he has."

"That's something a woman remembers. He hasn't said I'm beautiful, either. I know I'm *not* beautiful, but wouldn't I be beautiful to a man who was in love with me?"

Blossom's gaze narrowed. "Who've you been talking to? I know it's not Prudence. She doesn't believe in love, and a man would have to be blind to think she's beautiful."

"Why do you think I've talked to anyone?"

"I don't know how they do things in Virginia, but in Texas, if a man wants to marry you and he's got enough money to put a roof over your head and is thoughtful enough not to beat you in public, you marry him and hope he doesn't die on you after he's given you six kids. Then you'd *have* to marry any man who'd have you."

"All the more reason to stay single."

Blossom nearly shouted, "Not when you could marry Boone."

Roberta had a sudden revelation. "You're in love with him, aren't you?"

Blossom looked away. "Don't be ridiculous. What would a man like Boone Riggins see in a woman like me?"

"He'd see a fine, lovely woman who'd make him a better wife than I ever could be."

Blossom's eyes swam with tears. "I'm not a *fine, lovely* woman. I have a past. No man like Boone would have anything to do with me. And if he did, half the women in town would close their doors to him."

"That would be a decision for Boone to make."

"Well, he doesn't love me. He loves you, so the only decision to make is for you to agree to marry him. If you go to Virginia, Boone swears he'll follow you or kidnap you."

"He's just being melodramatic. Boone's used to getting what he wants."

"What do you want? And don't tell me you want

to go back to Virginia and be single for the rest of your life."

"I want to find out who killed my father. And I want to put this farm back on its feet to show the ranchers that killing my father didn't change anything."

"And after you've done that, what then?"

"I don't know."

Blossom got her to her feet. "While you're making up your mind, remember you've promised to go to the dance with Boone. He'll pick you up early."

"I'll be ready."

Blossom studied Roberta for a moment. "You don't *want* to go to the dance with Boone, do you?"

"Why do you say that?"

"Because you said *I'll be ready* like you were being told you had to be up before dawn to dig forty rows of potatoes."

"I'm just tired."

"No, you're interested in someone else."

"Don't be ridiculous."

Blossom crossed to Roberta, pulled her down on the sofa, and sat next to her. "I'm your best friend. You can't lie to me even if you can to yourself. You're falling in love with Nate Dolan, and there's no use denying it."

Rather than make the denial that sprang to her lips, Roberta burst into tears.

❧

"You don't have to worry that I'll betray myself." Roberta had spent the better part of an hour trying to convince Blossom. "Nate said he never goes to dances."

Blossom had insisted on helping Roberta dress for the dance. Roberta wasn't sure if Blossom was there to give her moral support or to keep her from standing up Boone at the last minute. Considering what she'd confessed a few days ago, she couldn't blame her.

She *was* falling in love with Nate, and she couldn't come up with a single good reason why it should be happening. He was likeable, attractive, young, and rich, all wonderful attributes in their own right, but they weren't reasons to fall in love. Perfect reasons *to marry,* according to Blossom, but Blossom hadn't been talking about love, either.

Roberta hadn't wanted to come to Texas. She'd only come because it was her father's dream. She didn't want to fall in love with a Texas rancher. They acted like they could take the law into their own hands whenever they wanted. Worse, she didn't want to fall in love with a man determined to chase Laveau diViere until one of them killed the other.

Blossom was working on Roberta's hair. She had wanted to leave it down—she couldn't forget what Nate had said about it—but Blossom insisted it had to be pinned up to be truly elegant. Roberta didn't care what her hair looked like. Nate wouldn't be there.

"Boone is really looking forward to this evening," Blossom said.

"You've told me that a dozen times. I'll do everything I can to help him enjoy himself, but I won't promise to marry him."

"You know he's going to ask you."

Roberta sighed. "Yes, I know."

"And you're going to refuse him because you're falling in love with Nate Dolan."

"Try to remember I refused him *before* I shot Nate."

"Everybody thought you were just being coy."

"Why would people believe that? I've never been coy."

"People don't know much about you."

"That's because they were too afraid of going against the ranchers to show any interest or sympathy for me and my father. Now stop messing with my hair. Unless I'm mistaken, that's the sound of Boone's buggy coming up the lane."

Boone wasn't happy about having Blossom ride with them to the dance, but it was a short ride.

It was a lovely night. The moon was full, the stars had been flung across the sky with a prodigal hand, and an invigorating breeze swept down from the hills to the west making it a perfect night for a dance.

A dance floor had been set up in the middle of the street that ran through the center of town. Lanterns hung from ropes tied to posts on opposite sides of the street, streamers from clotheslines strung between roofs. Light poured from half the buildings in town, but the brightest light came from Boone's saloon. The dancers would need refreshment, and like the good businessman he was, Boone was ready to provide it.

Everyone would be at the dance. Families coming from a distance would camp outside of town. Cowhands from as far away as twenty-five miles would sleep up to three in a bed in the hotel—if they bothered to sleep at all. Boone let Roberta and Blossom down on the boardwalk in front of his restaurant before taking his buggy to the livery stable.

The dancing hadn't begun, but the streets were filled. Even though many of the people saw each other every day, a dance was a festive occasion not to be missed.

"Come on," Blossom said. "Let's get some lemonade before it's all gone."

Roberta wasn't interested in lemonade, but she had made up her mind to be as agreeable as possible. She allowed Blossom to lead her to a table operated by two little girls who didn't appear to be more than ten.

Boone returned just as they were handed their lemonade. "Patronizing the competition?"

"If you started selling lemonade, we wouldn't have to," Roberta told him.

"If I started selling lemonade, I'd be out of business in a week," Boone told her.

"And me out of a job," Blossom added. "Can you imagine our customers giving up whiskey and beer for lemonade? You'd be more likely to find them in church on Sunday morning."

"If that happened, I'd have to take up preaching to make a living," Boone said. "I'm going to ask the fellas to strike up a tune. I hope you have your dancing shoes on. I feel like I could dance all night."

After the first three dances, Roberta was convinced Boone meant what he said. "If I'm going to last the rest of the evening, I've got to rest," she told him. "My body hasn't gotten used to working in the fields all day."

"If you'd marry me, you wouldn't have to work in the fields at all."

"I'm doing this for my father."

"He's dead. You're not."

Roberta thought that was a particularly insensitive remark, but she only said, "You should get something to drink. You've got to be thirsty by now."

"I am a little."

"You don't have to hurry back. I'll sit with Blossom."

Blossom was seated on a bench in front of the mercantile talking to a young man wearing a wide-brimmed hat, a checkered shirt, and a pair of boots guaranteed to do more damage to his feet than that of his partners.

"Thanks for the dance," he was saying when Roberta walked up. "I'll be back for another."

Blossom gave him a broad smile. "You know where to find me."

"Capturing another cowboy heart?" Roberta teased.

"Lord, no." Blossom fanned herself. "Just trying to keep a customer happy."

"You're not working now."

"I'm *always* working when it comes to customers." Blossom made a face. "At least your tomatoes don't want to dance with you."

"Or wear boots that will bloody his toes before midnight."

Both women laughed, but Blossom's ended in a gasp.

"Look who just showed up."

Chapter Twelve

ROBERTA'S BREATH CAUGHT IN HER THROAT. NATE Dolan was coming down the boardwalk in their direction.

"Did you know he was coming?" Blossom asked.

"No. I asked him if he would—I was telling him he ought to go to dances and to church, if he wanted to become a part of the community—but he said he never went to dances."

"Either he changed his mind, or he's come for a drink. I've never seen him in the saloon, so I guess he's come because of you."

Blossom looked positively eaten up with curiosity. And excitement. Her eyes were like those of a little girl about to open her birthday presents.

"He's coming this way," Blossom whispered.

"Probably because the boardwalk comes this way," Roberta pointed out.

"He could have walked down the boardwalk on the other side of the street. He could even have walked down the street itself."

"Nobody in his right mind would walk down the middle of that street, and you know it."

Blossom's confidence wasn't shaken. "He's coming to see you. I know it."

At that moment, Nate looked in her direction and smiled.

Blossom jumped to her feet. "I'll stall Boone, but I won't be able to keep him away for long."

"That's unnecessary," Roberta protested. "Nate won't—"

"Don't waste time pretending. It's just not fair that you have Boone and Nate Dolan chasing after you when I can't hold the interest of anyone fancier than a broom-tailed cowhand."

It wouldn't have done any good for Roberta to protest that Nate wasn't *chasing* after her because Blossom was already gone.

A rancher coming out of Boone's saloon nearly bumped into Nate. Apparently surprised to see him, Frank Porter buttonholed him. Knowing Frank's habit of talking for fifteen minutes when three would have been enough, Roberta started to turn away. Much to her surprise, Nate cut Frank off and continued toward her. He was stopped twice more, but each time he paused only briefly. In what seemed like much too short a time, he was standing before her. She could think of only one thing to say.

"You said you never went to dances. What changed your mind?"

"You."

Roberta was relieved Blossom wasn't here. If Nate was going to be that direct with his first word to her, there couldn't be any doubt about his feelings. Nor, if the way her heart was beating was any indication, about her feelings for him.

"I'm here with Boone."

"I know."

"I can't dance with you."

"That's okay. I can't dance with anybody."

She didn't want it to be okay. Perversely, she wanted him to have come for the sole purpose of dancing with her, of spending as much time as possible with her. She wanted him to be angry he couldn't. "Then why did you come?"

"To see you. May I sit down?"

"It's a public bench. You don't have to ask me."

"But I did."

"Of course you may sit. You probably shouldn't be standing. You certainly shouldn't have ridden into town. Does the doctor know what you're doing?"

Nate settled on the bench a safe distance from Roberta. His slow smile appeared. "I'm pleased to know you're still concerned about me."

Roberta didn't know why she was acting like a snappish spinster, but worrying that Boone would appear any minute wasn't making her feel less on edge. "I suppose I will be until you're completely well."

"Could you manage a bit longer?"

"How long?" What a stupid question. She knew the answer without asking. That's what made the situation so impossible. "Don't answer that."

"Why? Does sixty years seem too long?"

"An eternity."

"An eternity is much longer. Sixty years is only a beginning."

"This conversation is absurd. You must think I'm an idiot."

"No. Just unsure of what you want. I should say I'm sorry to put pressure on you, but I can't. I know what I want."

"Very few people get what they want. When they do, they often find it's not good for them."

"Then I will have to be careful to want the right thing."

Roberta didn't know what to say next. Her head was in a whirl, and it shouldn't have been. She knew Nate was falling in love with her because he'd told her. She hadn't been sure he knew what he was talking about, but apparently he had, or he wouldn't be here tonight saying the things he was saying.

"I'm glad you took my advice to take a more active part in the community."

"I have little interest in the community. I'm here because you're here."

"Why would you want to be at a dance with me when you can't dance?"

"I'd be happy to be anywhere with you. It doesn't matter that I can't dance. We could talk. I always looked forward to our talks when I was at your house."

She hadn't known that. If she had, would she have spent less time with him? She didn't think she'd spent that much. After working in the fields all day, she didn't have the energy to stay up late talking. "I'm still determined to move back to Virginia."

"I spent most of the war in Virginia. I wouldn't mind living there."

Roberta was shocked Nate would consider leaving

Texas, but she reminded herself that he'd only moved here after the war. "But not until after you've killed diViere."

"Bringing Laveau to justice doesn't mean I have to kill him."

"It doesn't mean he won't kill you first. We've had this discussion before, and it ended the same way. This is a dance. We're supposed to put aside our worries and have fun."

"I'll enjoy watching you have fun."

How was she supposed to have fun knowing he was watching everything she did? Would he be wondering what Boone was saying to her, what she was saying to Boone? Would he wonder if Boone would kiss her when he took her home? Would he wonder if she wanted Boone to kiss her? It wouldn't matter what he was thinking. It's what *she* would be thinking that would make this evening more of a trial than it was already.

She didn't know whether to be relieved or worried when Boone and Blossom emerged from the saloon and headed her way.

Nate's gaze narrowed when he saw Boone wasn't alone. "I thought you were with Boone."

"That's Blossom. She works for Boone."

"She appears to like him as more than just a boss."

Roberta wondered how a man like Nate could see at a glance that Blossom was in love with Boone. "Boone is a good boss."

"Would you say I'm a good boss?"

"The boys seem to think so. Russ fusses over you like a mother hen, so I guess he thinks so as well."

"I have a half-dozen cowhands I've never seen. I wonder if they'd agree."

She didn't have a chance to respond because Boone and Blossom had reached them. Nate stood to greet Blossom. Roberta had to give him credit for good manners.

"I'm glad to see you're strong enough to be out of bed," Boone said to Nate. "Now Roberta can stop feeling guilty for shooting you."

He wrung Nate's hand in a way that must have put a strain on his wound. Boone was a fine man, but sensitivity wasn't one of his strong points.

"Roberta has been telling me I need to make more of an effort to be part of the community. She suggested I start with the dance and follow up with church."

"The dance is a good idea. You can get a drink in my saloon if you get bored, but I'd stay away from church. The preacher will tell you you're going to hell, and every unmarried woman will be trying to figure how she can be the one to go with you."

Nate turned to Roberta with the slow smile she was beginning to like far too much. "I think that's what Roberta had in mind."

"Marriage is a good thing," Boone said, looking at Roberta with a glance that had too much pride of ownership in it. "I've been trying to convince Roberta to marry me, but she's holding out." He winked. "I'm hoping she'll give me a different answer after tonight."

If Roberta could have kicked Boone in his shins without anyone noticing, she'd have beaten a tattoo on them. There were some things you just didn't say in front of anyone who would listen.

"I'll make you a trade," Boone said to Nate. "Roberta for Blossom. The next dance is about to start."

"I'd be pleased to get to know you," Nate said to Blossom, "but I don't dance."

Blossom's smile was broad and genuine. "That's okay. I've already danced enough for two lifetimes."

Roberta was shocked by the upsurge of jealousy that claimed her the moment Blossom sat next to Nate. It was as ridiculous as it was unexpected, but it was also undeniable. She could protest all she wanted that any relationship between her and Nate was impossible, but a part of her refused to listen to reason, ignored facts, and wouldn't be bullied into submission.

"It's good to see Dolan up and about. Now you can stop worrying about him."

But that's exactly what she *couldn't* do. It was more than she could do not to look to where Nate and Blossom were sitting. She couldn't pretend she wasn't irritated Blossom was sitting with Nate, and she wasn't, that Blossom was smiling, laughing, and appeared thoroughly charmed while she was unhappy and feeling ill-used. She was even more annoyed that Nate didn't appear to miss her. As far as she could tell, he hadn't once glanced in her direction.

Boone had his arms around her—they were dancing—but she couldn't remember how she got there. Was her infatuation with Nate so powerful she could be oblivious to her surroundings, to her actions? Boone held her closer, bent down until his cheek brushed against hers. Her instinctive reaction was to pull back, but it was a slow dance, and most couples were dancing cheek to cheek. "Marry me, Roberta. I've been asking you for months, and I'm going to keep asking until you say yes."

Roberta struggled to find the words that would convince him to stop proposing at every opportunity. What could she say tonight that she hadn't said already?

Boone whispered in her ear, "You can invite the whole town to the wedding. In fact, I *want* you to. I want everybody to see I'm marrying the most beautiful woman in Slender Creek."

Roberta came to a halt right there on the dance floor even though couples continued to swirl around her. She stepped back and looked Boone full in the face. "That's the first time you've ever said that."

"That I want you to invite the whole town to the wedding?"

"No. That you think I'm beautiful."

"Of course I think you're beautiful. I've told you a hundred times."

"You've never said it."

Boone put his arms around her and resumed dancing. "If I haven't said it, I thought it. I wouldn't propose if you weren't the very best."

She was sure Boone intended his remark to be a compliment, but that wasn't the effect it had on her. What if a more attractive woman moved to Slender Creek? Would he lose interest when she grew older and lost her looks? What qualities other than looks made her *the very best*? He didn't value her loyalty to her father or her allegiance to her principles. He certainly didn't value her independence, resourcefulness, or willingness to work in the fields herself. How could she believe he thought she was beautiful when it had taken him so long to say it?

Rather than feel flattered or pleased, she felt depressed.

"We can have any kind of wedding you want, but we ought to go to San Antonio for your dress. There's nothing in town good enough for my future wife."

Not for *her*. For his *future wife*. Did Boone think of her as an individual, or would she be just another prize for him? She wouldn't have thought to ask that question, if it hadn't been for Nate. His interest in her had changed everything. She couldn't marry Nate either, of course—he was too focused on vengeance—but at least Nate valued her for herself.

"We can go to San Antonio any day you want." Boone seemed intent on pressing his case despite her repeated refusals. "As long as you have Crazy Joe and Nate's cowhands working for you, you don't have to feel guilty about leaving."

She refused to ask him *again* to stop calling Joe crazy. "I'm flattered by your offer, and I appreciate your help with the farm, but I don't think we'd suit as husband and wife."

Boone's eyes hardened for a moment before his well-practiced smile came back into place. "Well, I will just have to do whatever it takes to convince you otherwise."

Roberta was doing all she could to remain polite, but she couldn't endure one more strained dance with Boone and his incessant planning for a wedding she would never agree to. "I'm sorry to cut our evening short, but I'm afraid I have a headache that's getting worse. Could you please take me home?"

As Boone led her back to the carriage, she could feel Nate's heated gaze following their every move.

~∞~

Roberta had been stretching a point when she told Boone she had a headache, but by the time he brought her home, it was very real. As soon as she closed the door behind him, she could feel the muscles in her body start to release their tension. It was like being unbound, one rope at a time, until there was nothing left to hold her together beyond willpower. Unwilling to face the ordeal of undressing just yet, she sank down in the chair her father had occupied most evenings. Her world was falling apart. What was she going to do?

The problem wasn't the farm. She wasn't deluding herself. It was all about Nate.

Until she shot him, he hardly knew she existed. Not a conventional way of starting a courtship. She would have thought it was the perfect way to end one. Yet she'd gone from being a woman he barely remembered to one he couldn't forget. Boone wanted to marry her because he wanted *only the best*, whatever that meant. Could Nate want to marry her simply because she'd nursed him back to health? Were all men so illogical?

Frustrated and restless, she picked up her lamp and went to the kitchen, but she couldn't decide whether to fix coffee, have something to eat, or both. She'd left the dance before eating anything. Rather than dither, she stepped onto the back porch. The air was soft and cool. The breeze was just strong enough to make itself felt against her cheek. She leaned against the porch rail, looking at the night sky beyond the fig tree and grape arbor that skirted the backyard. It was so quiet it was almost eerie. Puffy clouds floated by with barely perceptible movement. A thin veil of high clouds nearly obscured the pulsing stars. On such a serene night, how could everything be so out of kilter?

Maybe she was the one who was out of step. It was time she stopped trying to understand Nate and accept him at face value. It was also time she looked to herself. Why was she falling in love with Nate when it was the last thing she wanted to do?

Much to her dismay, she didn't have an answer. Saying he was attractive and likeable weren't reasons an intelligent woman could accept. What was it about Nate that made him different from any man she'd ever met?

Everybody liked him. The other ranchers put a lot of weight in his opinion even though they didn't agree with him. Her father had liked him even though they'd argued every time they met. It was more than being a rich man who could afford to pay his cowhands well and treat them fairly. It was more than the sense of humor that occasionally peeked out from behind his somber facade. It was more than his half-smile that had etched itself in her memory. It was more than his courage and forbearance in facing his injury. It was more than the secret in his past that drove him to hunt diViere at the expense of his personal happiness.

That was not a lot to know about a man when she looked at it objectively, but it had been enough to reach out to something inside her that up until now had lain dormant. She could argue as long as she wanted, but she was falling in love with Nate, and there was nothing she could do to stop it. All that she could do was decide on a course of action and take it regardless of the emotional cost.

The night wasn't looking so beautiful anymore. Coming to Texas against her wishes had been a snap compared to what she faced now. This time she didn't have her father to make the decision for her. She would have to do it all alone.

Suddenly, she was aware of the sound of a horse walking by her house. That wasn't unusual, but its gait was. Either the horse had escaped, or its rider had a reason for wanting his presence to go unnoticed. Deciding to leave her lamp in the kitchen where it wasn't visible from the road, she walked to the end of the porch and entered the parlor. She hurried to the window and looked out in time to see a horse and rider go out of her line of sight, down the lane that led to the barn, the dam and the low hills beyond. She was certain the rider didn't intend to go that far. She raced to her room, threw on a cloak over her pale yellow dress, and grabbed her father's shotgun on the way out. She meant to find out who the rider was and what he was doing on her land when every other man within twenty miles was at the dance.

Once outside, she hurried down the lane. Sounds coming from the other side of the barn indicated the man had gone inside. Moving as quickly as she could without giving her presence away, she reached the corner of the barn and peered around. His horse was not in sight. She didn't know what the man was doing there, but she figured he wasn't going to destroy the barn as long as his horse was inside. She decided to wait.

A few minutes later, the man left the barn, a bedroll over his shoulder, and turned toward the cornfield.

"What are you doing here?" Roberta demanded.

When the figure turned around, she could see it was Webb. At the sound of her voice, he must have jumped a foot. His bedroll went flying as he dropped to a crouch and drew his gun. Roberta could see his body relax and the thunderstruck expression fade from his face when he recognized her. "What are you doing out here this time of night?"

"I live here. What are you doing in my cornfield?"

The explanation was slow coming. "The boss doesn't want you to be here by yourself, so the three of us take turns sleeping here each night."

"I'm not in any danger. The attackers were after the dam."

Webb holstered his gun and picked up his bedroll. "Begging your pardon, ma'am, but you don't pay our salary. As long as the boss wants us here, we'll stay. You ought to be in bed. The boss said you had a headache."

"Did he tell you to leave the dance?"

"No, ma'am. It was my turn."

So she'd ruined another person's night. "You can't be comfortable with just a bedroll. Let me bring you something from the house."

"I don't want to get too comfortable, ma'am. I might not hear something I ought to hear."

"What if it rains?"

"I can sleep in the barn."

"The ground is damp."

Webb grinned. "My bedroll will keep me dry even if it rains."

There didn't seem to be anything more to say, but she intended to speak to Nate as soon as she got a chance. "I don't want to get you in trouble with your boss, but come up to the house for breakfast."

"Thanks, ma'am, but one of the boys brings me breakfast."

"Which will be cold by the time it gets here. Come up to the house, or I'll take it to you in the cornfield. That ought to give your boss something to think about."

"It sure would. About how quick I could clear off after he fired me."

❧

Nate had no doubt he'd been responsible for Roberta's headache. He'd left the dance shortly after she did. It had been a struggle to wait until morning to speak to her and make sure she was okay.

"Sure would be nice if you would help us." Grady rode alongside his boss. "We'd get done a lot faster. I'm surprised Russ isn't raising a fuss because we can't help him."

Nate had wondered, too, but he didn't worry about Russ as long as the man did his work. "I've got business in town."

When Nate pulled his horse to a stop in front of the house and dismounted, the boys continued toward the barn. The door opened before he could knock.

"I had a feeling I'd be seeing you this morning." Roberta didn't look like she'd had a lot of sleep, but she was smiling at him.

"I was worried about you."

"I'm fine, but I know you won't take my word for it, mount your horse, and ride away."

He smiled back. "It'll take more convincing than that."

"I have time for one cup of coffee. Then I have to go to work."

He followed her into the kitchen. It amused as well as heartened him to see two cups set out on the table. She had not only expected him. She'd prepared for him.

Roberta reached the coffee pot and started to pour. "I was afraid you'd come by last night. I'm grateful you didn't."

Nate tasted his coffee while he decided whether it was wise to be honest. He decided against employing pretense. "I did come by. When I saw you come back to the house after stalking Webb with a shotgun, I figured it would be best to wait until morning to see you."

"Why are you telling me this?" She raised an eyebrow. "How did you know I wouldn't be angry?"

"I didn't, but I'll never lie to you, not even about little things. Between two people who love each other, no lie is little."

Roberta returned the coffeepot to the stove and

sat down opposite Nate. Her mood was darker. "I haven't said I loved you."

"I know, but I don't want to give you a reason not to."

She didn't look any happier. "Are you sure you love me, that it's not some reaction to me having taken care of you?"

"My old boss's wife would have done the same, and I've never had a single romantic thought about her. And, in case you're wondering, she's almost as beautiful as you."

Roberta opened her mouth to speak, but a vigorous pounding on the front door interrupted her. "I wonder what the boys want."

But it wasn't one of the boys who strode into the house when Roberta opened the door. It was Prudence, and she wasn't happy to find Nate ensconced in the kitchen.

"What are you doing here?" she demanded.

"Pretty much what you're doing here." Nate made no attempt to hide his irritation. "Making sure Roberta is okay."

"I'm here now, so you don't need to stay."

"But I want to stay."

"Then you can go help with the barn."

"The doctor won't let me lift anything heavier than a coffee cup for at least another week."

Prudence eyed him with dislike as well as distrust. "I don't believe Dr. Danforth would say such a thing."

"Would you believe he asked me when I was going to propose to Roberta?"

Prudence looked scandalized. "Certainly not!"

"Well, he did. You can ask him."

Nate was more anxious to see Roberta's reaction than he was to hear Prudence's response, but she had left the kitchen to respond to another series of knocks. He was disgusted, but not surprised, when Boone Riggins followed her into the kitchen.

"What are you doing here?" Boone demanded.

Nate thought it was obvious. "The same as you and Prudence."

"But you aren't engaged to marry her."

"Neither are you." Nate got to his feet. There was nothing he could accomplish with Prudence and Boone regarding him like an interloper. "I'm glad to know you're feeling better," he said to Roberta. "I'd like to stay longer, but I have business in town."

"I'll see you out," Roberta volunteered.

"I'm sure he can find the door on his own." Roberta ignored Boone's remark.

"Thanks for worrying about me," Roberta said when they reached the front door, "but I really am fine today."

"I hope you'll be able to say the same after those two finish arguing over you."

Roberta laughed. "I'll retreat to the fields. I doubt they'll follow me there."

Nate's answering laugh disappeared. "Are you *really* okay? I didn't mean to upset you."

"Then why did you come to the dance?" The look he gave her said more than words ever could. "I think you already know the answer." He bent down and kissed her lightly on the mouth. "And it won't change."

Roberta stayed in the doorway while Nate mounted his horse and rode away. She didn't want to go back to the kitchen and the inevitable questions. She was at a crossroads and didn't know which way to turn. Of one thing she was certain. Neither Prudence nor Boone could give her the answers she needed.

Nate told himself he was an idiot to be riding around in the middle of the night. Nothing was going to happen to Roberta just because he'd had a bad dream. Still, he couldn't lie in bed for the next several hours, waiting for dawn, while trying to think of a new excuse to ride over to her farm for the fifth day in a row. This way he could see for himself that she was alright and be back in bed without anyone knowing he'd gone slightly crazy over this woman.

Nothing was sillier than trying to sneak out of the house, saddle his horse, and ride away without anyone hearing him. *It was his ranch!* He could do anything he wanted without having to justify it. Still, he was surprised he'd succeeded. If he hadn't known better, he'd have sworn the cowhands were away on a drive.

Maybe he would check on whichever one of the boys was sleeping out at Roberta's tonight. *Stop trying to think up excuses. You're not responsible for getting Caleb out of scrapes, so you don't have to explain everything you do.* Odd how difficult it was to change the pattern of a lifetime. From his parents, to his commander during the war, he had had to provide an explanation for his actions. At least Cade gave him credit for being able to think for himself. His parents never had whenever it involved Caleb. And since Caleb clung to Nate like a second skin, everything he did involved his brother. That had never felt like a burden while Caleb was alive. Since then it had weighed on him like a death sentence.

Nate liked riding at night. It had been one of the reasons he had volunteered for the Night Riders. There was a peace and serenity about the night that couldn't be found during daylight. It gave a man time to think about himself and how he fit into the world around him. To think about what he wanted. What he didn't want. What he must do, and what he must avoid at all costs.

And when he decided he *must* do what he knew he should not, he had time to calculate the costs.

Many years earlier he had calculated the cost of chasing Laveau and had decided that his death would be an acceptable price to pay. It would avenge his brother's death, it would fulfill his promise to his mother, and relieve him of the burden of failure.

Now he'd fallen in love with Roberta, and the price for bringing down Laveau seemed too great. How could he look toward a future with Roberta knowing his past would destroy it?

His horse shied when a jackrabbit crossed the trail quickly followed by a gray fox. How easy it was for the quiet to lull him into thinking the rest of the world was asleep.

The air felt cool and dry against his skin. Limited light from the tiny slice of moon cast the surrounding prairie in shades of gray and silver. Occasional pinpoints of brownish red revealed the presence of resting cows with their calves, or small animals that preferred shadows to bright sunlight. For a long time he'd felt the same. He didn't want get to know people or let them get to know him. He felt removed from the community around him. He had liked that, but getting to know Roberta was causing that to change.

He had business to conduct at the bank. He intended to drop by Boone's saloon. He might even eat at his restaurant. And despite Boone's advice, he intended to go to church. Now that he had a reason to remain in Slender Creek, he wanted to be part of the town. His position as owner of the biggest ranch in the county gave him a—

His thoughts snapped like a thread. There was a light coming from the direction of Roberta's farm, the kind of light that could only be caused by a fire.

Chapter Thirteen

NATE SET HIS HORSE TO A HARD GALLOP, BUT THAT couldn't stop the questions from springing up like mushrooms after a rain. Who could be angry enough at Roberta to burn the barn they'd just rebuilt? That indicated a kind of hatred he found difficult to attach to any rancher he knew. Who was on duty tonight? Was it Carlin? Had he been able to make sure Roberta was safe? Had people from town seen the fire? Were they already at the farm?

Cutting the corner, Nate drove his horse from the main trail to the lane leading toward the Tryon farm. When he did, he saw a sight that nearly caused his heart to stop beating. It wasn't the barn that was on fire. It was the farmhouse itself.

Was Roberta still inside?

Unable to drive his horse any faster, Nate endured the agony of terrible visions that had their origin in the scenes of horror he'd witnessed during the war. This couldn't be happening to Roberta. He wouldn't let it.

He vaulted off his horse before the animal had come to a halt. The porch was consumed in flames, making it impossible to reach the front door. The fire had caught on the corner of the house where Roberta had her bedroom. Without breaking stride, he ran around the side of the house and circled to the kitchen at the back. The fire had taken hold on the back porch, but it hadn't started on the walls. It smelled like the fire had been started with coal oil. The flames were high but not as hot as they would have been had the wood floor of the porch started to burn.

Nate spied a bucket sitting on the ground next to the well. He drew up a full pail of water and poured it over his head. A second bucket thoroughly soaked his clothes. Taking a deep breath, Nate dashed through the flames.

The kitchen door was locked. Without hesitation, Nate threw himself against the door. It held. The contact sent a sharp pain shooting through his shoulder that was not yet fully healed. Blocking out the pain and fear of reopening the wound, Nate threw himself against the door, but it still held. The fire had not caught his water-soaked clothes, but the hot air was burning his lungs. Unable at that moment to appreciate the sturdiness of the house, he reared back and hit the door next to the lock as hard as he could with his foot. The door splintered, but it still held. Nearly exhausted and unable to breathe, Nate hit the door once again.

It gave, and he stumbled into the kitchen. Smoke had settled over the floor. For the moment, he was able to breathe, but the open door gave the fire access to a fresh supply of oxygen. He would have less than a minute before the smoldering wood burst into flame.

Nate had never been in this part of the house, but he guessed Roberta's bedroom had to lie ahead. He pushed through to the dining room and into a hall nearly choked with smoke. Opening the door in front of him, he found himself in her bedroom.

She lay in the bed without moving. Falling back on his years of combat experience, Nate pushed aside the fear that threatened to paralyze him. He wouldn't let his mind dwell on the possibility that Roberta was dead. At this moment, he had to get her to safety, or both of them would perish. He threw the covers aside and scooped Roberta into his arms. Despite the pain to his shoulder, he wrapped her in a blanket to protect her from the flames, and ran from the bedroom through the dining room to the kitchen. The heat had steamed most of the water from his clothes, but there was still enough moisture to protect him as he plunged into the flames that engulfed the back porch.

He raced away from the house and almost ran into a man who was rounding the corner of the house. "Is there anybody else inside?" the man asked.

"No." He'd given the boys strict instructions never to sleep inside. He found a patch of grass well away from the house and lay Roberta down.

"That's Roberta, isn't it?"

Nate didn't bother to answer the obvious. He was more concerned that she didn't seem to be breathing. The fire hadn't reached her room, but more people died from smoke inhalation than from the flames.

Unsure of what to do, Nate sat her up and pounded on her back, but she didn't respond.

"Is she dead?"

Desperate for a way to get smoke-free air into her lungs, he put his mouth to Roberta's and pushed air from his lungs into hers. Pulling back, he took another deep breath, placed his mouth over hers, and exhaled.

"Why are you kissing her?"

The woman sounded angry, but Nate didn't stop to explain. He pushed another lungful of air from his body to Roberta's. Much to his relief, she went into a spasm of coughing. Putting his arm under her shoulder, he lifted her into a sitting position.

"What have you done to her?" the woman demanded. "She doesn't look like she was hurt."

"I had to clear her lungs of smoke," Nate explained.

As Roberta's coughing grew less severe, her attention focused on the fire. Her expression showed shock followed by horror that turned to anger. "They tried to kill me."

"Who?" the woman asked.

"The ranchers." Roberta went into a spasm of coughing.

"I don't think a rancher would do this," Nate said. "It's too cruel."

"Then who?"

He didn't have an answer. By now more than a dozen men had arrived from town. They were doing their best to put out the fire, but Nate doubted they could save the house.

"How did the fire start?" the woman asked Nate.

"I don't know."

"You weren't here?"

It was too dark to see the woman's expression, but Nate wondered if she thought he'd spent the night in Roberta's bed. "I was out riding because I couldn't sleep."

"Did you see anyone?" Roberta asked.

"No. Once I realized the house was on fire, I couldn't think of anything else."

"Where's Carlin?"

Nate was ashamed to admit he hadn't thought about the boy.

"He would have been here in time to get me out of the house if something hadn't happened to him." Roberta struggled to her feet.

"You're not strong enough to wander around the farm."

Roberta was unsteady but determined. "There's nothing you or anybody can do to save the house. Even if there were, finding Carlin is more important. I'll show you where they bed down. "

Nate hoped nothing had happened to the boy. He was young, but he had impressed Nate by his loyalty and his readiness to tackle any task.

Nate put his arm around Roberta's waist. "Lean on me. You're still weak."

Nate wasn't so caught up in the events unfolding around him that he was beyond being affected by Roberta's nearness. The feel of Roberta in his arms was intoxicating. He didn't know why the mere presence of this woman could affect him so strongly, but he didn't waste time denying that it did. He would have given anything to sweep her into his embrace and kiss her until both of them were powerless to kiss again.

Roberta led him through a field of tomatoes into a stand of corn. "Carlin said he could watch the house from here without being seen."

It didn't take long to discover why Carlin hadn't come to Roberta's aid. He was still in his bedroll, but the position of his body made it clear he wasn't sleeping. Breaking loose from Nate's hold, Roberta stumbled forward and dropped to the ground next to Carlin.

Nate didn't have to get that close to know Carlin was dead. The gaping wound at his throat told how he'd died. Who would do something like this? What about Roberta's farm, or Roberta herself, could be so important?

"Who could do that to a boy who never hurt anyone?" Roberta's anguish was evident in every word.

Nate knelt next to Roberta and put his arm around her. "I don't know, but rest assured I will find out who did this."

"We can't leave Carlin here."

"I'll get somebody to take his body into town."

"I'll stay with him while you go make the arrangements." Roberta looked down at Carlin. "He was here to protect me. I can't leave him alone now."

Nate was uncomfortable leaving Roberta, but he knew she wouldn't be budged. "I'll be back as soon as I can. In the meantime, I'll send someone to stay with you."

"I don't need anybody to protect me."

Nate thought it was quite clear that she *did* need protection. Somebody was willing to do anything to achieve his objective.

By the time he got back to the house, it was apparent the home couldn't be saved. At that moment, a buckboard was driven into the yard with reckless speed. The horse was jerked to a halt, and Boone Riggins leapt to the ground. He rushed from one man to the next asking, "Where is Roberta?"

Nate didn't know whether Boone truly loved Roberta, or just thought he did, but he wasn't willing to see anybody suffer needlessly. He had to put himself squarely in Boone's path before he got the man's attention. "She's all right. I got her out in time."

"What are you doing here?"

Was jealousy a stronger emotion than fear? "I was taking a night ride and saw the fire."

"Where is she?"

"With Carlin's body."

"Who's Carlin?"

"A cowhand I had watching Roberta. Whoever started this fire killed him."

Boone reeled in shock. "You mean somebody intended for Roberta to die in the fire?"

"It looks that way."

"Where is she? I'm taking her to town right away."

Nate wasn't ready for a showdown with Riggins, but it was time Riggins knew his claim on Roberta was about to be questioned. "Leave her alone. She wants to stay with Carlin's body until I can make arrangements for it to be taken to town."

"You can't tell me what to do about Roberta. I'm in love with her. I'm going to marry her."

"I'm also in love with Roberta. She hasn't agreed to marry you, so I think that means I still have a chance."

"Roberta can't be in love with you. She's in love with me." Boone could hardly have looked more shocked if someone had hit him in the face with a ripe tomato.

"We'll have to leave that for Roberta to decide," Nate said. "In the meantime, could I use your buggy to take Carlin's body to town? I'd use Roberta's wagon, but your buggy is closer, and your horse is faster than her mules." Apparently Boone had gone too long without having anyone question him. He looked momentarily too discombobulated to make a decision. "Come on," Nate said. "You can help me carry Carlin's body from the cornfield."

While keeping pace with Nate, Boone advanced numerous reasons why Roberta intended to marry him even though she hadn't accepted his proposal. As far as Nate was concerned, the only reason Roberta hadn't agreed to marry Boone was because she didn't love him. That was all he needed to hope she would come to love him instead.

"Boone has offered to let us use his buggy to take Carlin's body to town."

Boone gave every indication that he was prepared to dispute that statement. But when Roberta looked up and thanked him while tears streamed down her face, not even Riggins could refuse her.

Carlin had been a tall, rangy young man. Even

though he wasn't heavy, carrying him put a strain on Nate's wound. Roberta supported his head. She said letting his head hang down made the gash in his throat look even more terrible.

Roberta enlisted the help of a couple extra men before she was happy with the way Carlin's body was positioned in the buckboard.

"Since I'm the one who has to make the funeral arrangements for Carlin, I'll drive him into town," Nate said to Boone. "You can use my horse when you're through helping the men put out the fire."

Roberta's tearful thanks put a stop to Boone's attempt to be the one to drive the buckboard. Nate didn't feel so much as a twinge of conscience for having appropriated Boone's buggy. He didn't know if Roberta would ever love him, but she deserved a better husband than a man who had picked her out just because she was the prettiest woman in Slender Creek.

"Something has changed, hasn't it?" Roberta didn't look at Nate. She just stared into the distance.

Nate had already come to that conclusion. "It looks that way."

"You don't think it's the ranchers, do you?"

"No."

"Who would have a reason to shoot my father, murder Carlin, and set my house on fire with me in it?"

"It has to be Laveau."

Nate had tried to find an explanation that didn't involve Laveau diViere, but he couldn't forget Laveau prowling outside his window or the way his hat had been found after the first attack. It looked like Laveau had tried to destroy Nate by implicating him in the raid on the farm and her father's death, but didn't account for this last attack unless it could be explained by a depth of evil he hadn't suspected even of Laveau.

"I can't believe anyone can be that pitiless. He could have knocked Carlin out, gagged him, and tied him up."

"That would be too much trouble."

At least his death had been quick. Nate knew from the war that being burned alive was unimaginably painful. Many who survived begged for death. Why would Laveau have wanted to do something like that to Roberta? Was it possible for anybody to enjoy cruelty for the sake of being cruel? That was all the more reason Nate couldn't give up his quest to find Laveau. Any man capable of such evil had to be stopped, regardless of the cost.

Roberta didn't appear ready to accept Laveau's being behind the attacks. "How would he know about Carlin? Even I wasn't supposed to know."

Nate couldn't answer that question, but Laveau had a way of knowing things other people didn't. Nate used to think it was luck, even a really good spy system. Lately he'd come to believe Laveau had an uncanny sense for ways to cause trouble. It was a lot like Cade's ability to sense impending danger. No one could explain that, either.

On reaching town, Nate turned the buckboard in the direction of the doctor's house. The town slept peacefully, most of them unaware of the tragedy of a lost life. The darkened streets were empty, the windows of most homes like sightless eyes staring into the street. Only Boone's saloon, emptied of its patrons by the fire, stood open, the light from its windows casting yellow streaks across the faded boardwalk to be swallowed up by the hungry maw of the empty street.

Conditioned to respond to calls at all hours of the night, the doctor opened his door before Nate had to knock a second time. Clad in pajamas a half-dozen sizes too large for his slender body, Dr. Danforth went directly to the body. After a brief examination, he said, "It's a blessing the boy was knocked out before his throat was cut."

The repeated strain on Nate's wound made it more difficult to move Carlin this time, but with Roberta's help they managed to get him inside the doctor's house. Once he was settled and Nate had explained what had happened, the doctor asked, "How soon can you have the funeral?"

"I'll need time to get some clothes from the ranch. I can't have him buried in his long johns."

"Can you close the wound?" Roberta asked. "He ought to look good enough to be kissed good-bye by his mama."

"I'll do what I can," the doctor said. "What about you? You don't look so good."

"I'm okay. I just breathed in a little smoke."

The doctor eyed Nate. "You seem to have a way of turning up where there's trouble."

Roberta appeared troubled by the doctor's words. "You can't think Nate had anything to do with the attacks."

"I'm only saying what others will say. So far he's the only link between the two attacks."

"They might think I wanted to get rid of the dam," Nate said, "but they'd be hard-pressed to explain why I'd want to hurt Roberta. I'm in love with her, and I intend to do everything I can to make her want to marry me." Nate enjoyed the looks of surprise on both faces. "Nor would I have any reason to murder one of my own men."

"Does Boone Riggins know of your intentions?" the doctor asked.

"I don't see any reason to tell Boone. I don't want to marry him."

The doctor choked out a laugh. "You don't mind stirring up trouble, do you?"

"I don't see why there should be any trouble. Roberta doesn't love Boone. I hope to convince her to fall in love with me. Now, if we have nothing else to do here, I've got to find a place for her to stay."

Roberta's heightened color still hadn't returned to normal. "I can find a place on my own."

"Where could you stay?" Nate asked.

"With Prudence."

The doctor cast Nate a look that seemed to ask *what do you plan to do now?* "An excellent choice."

But not as excellent as the place Nate had in mind. His ranch. "Until we know who's behind these attacks and why, you need to stay where I can make sure you're safe."

Roberta had recovered her equilibrium. "I can't move to your ranch unless you have room for Prudence as well."

"She's right," the doctor said with a grin. "She will attach herself to Roberta like a barnacle on a rock, and you won't be able to shake her loose with anything less than a marriage ceremony."

"I'm ready to do that right now."

"I'm not," Roberta declared. "I think we ought to have Carlin's funeral this afternoon. Now, before this conversation becomes any more ridiculous, I'm going to Prudence's house."

"I'll go with you," Nate offered.

Boone rode up just as they were leaving the doctor's house. He did his best to convince Roberta to let him put her up at a hotel, to rent a house for her, to give her his own home, but she held firm to her intention to stay with Prudence.

Prudence answered her door almost as quickly as the doctor. Unlike the doctor, she was fully dressed. Nate wondered if she ever undressed. "Of course you can stay with me," she said as soon as Roberta told her what had happened. "I don't understand why no one woke me."

"Boone's last customers were the only ones awake to see the fire," Roberta explained.

"I stayed open later than usual. We had two hot poker games going, and no one wanted to stop."

Prudence eyed Boone with disapproval. "I suppose sin can be useful on occasion."

Boone knew Prudence well enough not to waste time challenging that remark.

"Both of you can go away now," Prudence said to Nate and Boone. "Roberta will be safe as long as she's with me."

Nate didn't want to leave. Now that he was convinced Laveau was involved, he didn't believe Roberta would be safe anywhere except at his ranch. He just had to convince Roberta.

❧

Travis's rage was beyond description. Curses weren't enough. Travis wanted blood, and he wanted it now. Travis struck him a vicious blow with the back of his hand bringing blood to his mouth.

"I killed that stupid boy hiding in the corn. All you had to do was set the house on fire."

"I did," he protested. "How was I to know Dolan was going to show up? What kind of man rides about in the middle of the night?"

"You should have shot him," Travis shouted. "There was no one to stop you."

"I wasn't hanging around long enough to have someone recognize me. I could be hanged for what I did tonight."

"I could shoot you right now," Travis threatened.

He backed away. "You do that, and the boys will turn on you."

Travis spat. "That's what I think of your boys. You've got to do better, or you'll have to shoot him in his bed."

The money was good, but he wasn't that stupid. A thousand calves weren't worth that kind of risk.

❧

Roberta was relieved when Prudence left her alone to get what rest she could before dawn, but sleep was impossible. Too many questions roiled through her brain. Why would Laveau diViere want to kill her and her father? She'd never heard of the man before Nate came to Slender Creek. Could Laveau be after revenge because she had nursed Nate back to health? Was it possible that diViere had turned his attention to Roberta because Nate wanted to marry her? But up until less than an hour ago, only she knew that. Which brought her face to face with four questions she could no longer avoid.

What was she going to do about Nate? Was it possible the attraction she felt was love? But then what about Boone? How could she make him see that she would never marry him?

Going back to Virginia would solve everything. She wouldn't have to work so hard at the farm. She could finally send Boone a message he would be forced to understand. And as for Nate, her heart turned over at the thought of never seeing him again. But surely whatever she felt now was just a passing infatuation. She'd get over him eventually. She had always felt out of place in Slender Creek. The people here didn't like or trust her as they liked and trusted one another. She would *never* forgive any rancher who had had any part in the death of her father. DiViere might be behind the attacks, but he hadn't acted alone. She couldn't live in a community that would tolerate that kind of lawlessness.

Despite her friendships with Prudence and Blossom, she felt set apart, kept at a distance. She had aunts and uncles in Virginia, more than a dozen cousins, and a network of friendships that reached back to childhood. Going back would be like falling into the warm and welcoming arms of people as concerned for her happiness as they were for their own. Life would once more fall into familiar and comfortable patterns. People would believe as she believed, act as she acted, want what she wanted.

She would be home.

But she would be without Nate.

◦◦◦

"I never heard of anybody named Laveau diViere," the sheriff said to Nate. "Neither has anyone else in this town. Why would he be behind the attacks on Miss Tryon?"

"He's really after me. Laveau betrayed men he'd served with for three years knowing they would be slaughtered in their sleep. He stole the life savings of his best friend. He cut the throat of the man standing guard that night. In the intervening years, he's committed every crime from theft to murder, the last time by leaving a man to burn to death in his own home. Roberta saw a man fitting his description about to enter her house the day after I was wounded."

"Suppose I accept your theory that this diViere is behind the attack. How do I go about finding him?"

How could Nate expect this sheriff—a good man but a very ordinary one—to track down a man who'd eluded capture for seven years? "Laveau has the money to live anywhere he wants and the brains to succeed in almost any profession, but he's spent most of his time trying to cause as much trouble as he can for the seven of us who survived the war. I believe he hates me because I've spent the last two years trying to bring him before a Texas court that will hold him accountable for what he's done."

"You still haven't said how I'm to find him."

"He's a master at remaining out of sight. He won't hesitate to commit any crime, but he prefers to hire others to do the work for him. You have to start by looking for men in the area who helped him."

"I don't believe anybody around here was involved in that attack."

"Roberta says eight men attacked her farm the night her father died. You have to assume at least some of the same men were involved in the attack on Roberta and Carlin. Could that many strangers be in the area without anybody knowing? Where would they sleep, keep their horses, buy their supplies? Men like that aren't likely to stay away from whiskey or women for long, but no strangers have shown up at any of the saloons. What other explanation can there be?"

"Okay, suppose this diViere happens to fall into my hands. Forget, for the moment, that's about as likely as Texas turning into a tropical paradise. What am I going to present to a judge as proof? I gather you don't think he's likely to confess."

Nate didn't appreciate the sheriff's sarcasm, but he understood it. "There's sufficient evidence to bring him to trial for a murder in Overlin, Texas. It's not important which crime we use to stop him. Just that he's stopped."

The sheriff frowned at Nate before shrugging his shoulders and leaning back in his chair. "I'm going to accept your theory. Not because I believe it, but because I can't see how it could be strangers. I'm damned sure it wasn't any of the ranchers. Now I need a good description of diViere. If he's so distinctive you can identify him from Roberta's account, we ought to be able to find him if he's anywhere around."

After giving the sheriff a detailed description of Laveau, Nate was relieved to be outside again and able to release some of the tension created by the sheriff's attitude. He couldn't blame the man, but this was one more time when Laveau seemed able to remain just beyond reach. The only bright spot was that, with the end of Reconstruction in sight,, he would no longer be protected by the government.

Nate turned his thoughts to Roberta. He wouldn't do anything until after Carlin's funeral, but he was determined to convince her to move to his ranch. He would hire extra hands if necessary, but he wouldn't feel she was safe as long as she was out of his sight.

He was so preoccupied by his worries he almost missed the appearance of a man who by his clothes, shoes, and fair complexion was clearly a stranger to Slender Creek. Nate was surprised when the man walked toward him, his amiable expression appearing easy and natural.

"I hope you can help me," he said. "I'm looking for Miss Roberta Tryon."

Maybe it was instinct. Maybe it was just that he was on edge, but there had been too much trouble surrounding Roberta in the last weeks. Nate's gun appeared in his hand before he could think. "What do you want with her?"

The man appeared more surprised and confused than frightened. "I don't want to hurt her."

This stranger didn't look like a murderer, but Nate wasn't willing to take the chance. "You still haven't told me what you *do* want."

"My name's Carl Peterson. We used to be sweet on each other before she came to Texas. I've come into a considerable inheritance, and I've come to take her back to Virginia so we can get married."

Chapter Fourteen

NATE WANTED TO TAKE THE MAN BY THE THROAT AND bury him at the bottom of a ravine. He was tall, slender, handsome, and smiling. He reeked of being a tenderfoot, but it was obvious he was no fool. He was just the kind of man to appeal to a woman uncomfortable with the rough and tumble world of Texas.

"You haven't seen Roberta in five years. How do you know she wants to marry you?"

Peterson's smile was friendly and without constraint. "I don't, but I'm going to do my best to make her feel about me the way she used to."

"How was that?"

Peterson's smile tightened just a little. "Friendly enough to encourage me to come all the way from Virginia. If her father hadn't dragged her out here despite her protests, we might have been married by now. How is the old codger?"

"When did you get into town?"

"This morning. Why?"

"A lot has happened you don't know." By the time Nate finished relating the events of the last few weeks, Peterson was clearly concerned.

"I knew I should never have let her leave Virginia, but she was too young when her father moved her down here. Where is she now? I have to see her."

Nate wanted to send Peterson back to Virginia on the first horse going north, but he was certain it wouldn't help his relationship with Roberta. Of course, that didn't mean Nate was going to step back and give Peterson an open field. He intended to haunt his every step. "She's staying with a friend in town. I'll take you."

Peterson pelted Nate with questions, all having to do with Roberta's well-being. Not once did he mention himself, his recent inheritance, or Virginia. Nate ground his teeth. This was a man he could like, probably trust as well. It was too bad they wanted to marry the same woman.

"It's a shame she lost her home," Peterson said. "But I'll take her back to Virginia as soon as the funeral is over."

"If you have her best interest at heart, you won't pressure her to make a decision right away," Nate said. "She needs time to recover from the shock before she can decide what she wants to do."

"I'm here so she doesn't have to do any of that."

"I don't know what Roberta was like when she left Virginia, but I think you'll find her changed."

Peterson stopped and turned to Nate. "How do you mean?"

"She doesn't like anyone making decisions for her."

"But I want to marry her."

"You're not the only one."

Peterson's gaze narrowed. "I take it you're refer-ring to yourself."

"Not exclusively."

"There are others?" Peterson didn't seem surprised.

"The town's most successful businessman."

Peterson shook his head. "I knew I shouldn't have let her get away. If you're an example of the competition, I'm in for a rough time."

Nate was liking Peterson more and more. "The fight of your life. Now, don't let Prudence scare you off. She thinks all men ought to be banished to some place hot and uncomfortable."

"Sounds like an aunt of mine." Peterson shivered, then grinned. "Scared the wits out of me growing up."

It didn't take long to complete the short walk to Prudence's house. When she opened the door and saw Nate was accompanied by a stranger, she stepped outside and closed the door behind her. The look she gave Peterson was enough to cause a less brave man to cringe.

"Who are you, and what do you want?"

Nate was afraid that if Peterson said he was here to marry Roberta, Prudence wouldn't let him in, so he answered for him. "He's a childhood friend from Virginia." Though why he was making it easier for Peterson was beyond him.

Prudence gave Peterson a second going over before saying, "I'll see if Roberta wants to talk with you."

She then went inside and closed the door.

A few moments later, the door burst open, and Roberta came through like she'd been shot from a catapult. She uttered Peterson's name like a strangled cry, threw her arms around his neck, and burst into tears. Nate started trying to think of suitably remote canyons for burying competing swains. He'd pulled Roberta from a blazing house, and she hadn't acted like that.

Watching Peterson hold Roberta while she cried like her heart was broken taxed every bit of Nate's self-control. Just when he thought things couldn't get any worse, Boone Riggins showed up.

"What the hell is going on?" Boone demanded. An instant later, he'd torn Roberta's arms from around Peterson's neck and was preparing to deck him. Nate hoped he could score points with Roberta by stepping between the two men. He would have done it anyway, but why waste a chance to make a positive impression on Roberta? He didn't have all that many.

He deflected Boone's punch.

"This is Carl Peterson, a childhood friend of Roberta's from Virginia. Roberta hasn't seen him in five years. Starting a fight isn't a good way to welcome him to Slender Creek."

"I don't want to welcome him, dammit," Boone swore, "not when he's got his arms around Roberta."

For the first time, Nate found himself in complete agreement with Boone.

"Why don't we go inside?" Nate suggested. "It would make introductions a lot easier."

Prudence looked aghast at the sight of three men entering her parlor. She held her tongue, but her stance clearly indicated that any or all would be ejected for the slightest transgression.

When Roberta took a seat on a couch and pulled Peterson down beside her, Nate made sure he got the seat on Roberta's other side leaving Boone to seethe helplessly. When Roberta asked Peterson about friends and family in Virginia, Boone interrupted with offers to do everything from marry Roberta within the hour to buy a house for her and furnish it from top to bottom. When Peterson asked about the recent attacks, Boone dismissed them saying Roberta could depend on him to make sure nothing like that happened in the future. When Peterson asked about Roberta's future plans, Boone said she didn't have to worry about the future. He would take care of that, too. Nate wasn't sure whether Roberta was on the verge of tears or an intemperate outburst, but he *was* sure Peterson looked ready to plant his fist in Boone's face.

Nate decided he could help Roberta most by taking Boone away. "Why don't we leave Roberta and Carl to catch up on old times?" Nate said as he got to his feet. "It's not much fun listening to talk about people we don't know." Boone started to object, but Nate cut him off. "There's something I need to talk to you about. It's rather urgent."

"What's so damned urgent?" Boone asked when they were outside. "I want to get back in there. That tenderfoot is trying to steal my woman."

Nate had to stifle an impulse to plant *his* fist in Boone's face.

"Roberta is not *your woman*. She's told you that more than once. Furthermore, you're not going back inside because nobody wants you there—not Roberta, Carl, Prudence, or me."

Boone fired up. "You plan to try to stop me?"

"If necessary, but if you have an ounce of sense, you'll realize Roberta doesn't want to see either of us right now. You and I represent a Texas that murdered her father, destroyed her farm, and attempted to kill her. If you don't want her to head straight for Virginia the minute Carlin's funeral is over, you'll stay away until she's had time to get over the worst of the shock."

Boone started to speak—then stopped to think. He eyed Nate, his expression decidedly unfriendly. "Are you in love with her?"

"Yes."

"She hates ranchers."

"She doesn't hate me."

Boone's stance stiffened. "How do you know?"

"We had a lot of time to talk after I was shot. Besides, I pulled her out of the fire."

Boone's expression turned black. "If I ever find out who set her house on fire, I'll kill him. If she'd married me, none of this would have happened."

"If you want to protect Roberta, you can start by keeping an eye out for anything that doesn't seem right, for anybody doing something unusual. I've told the sheriff I think an old enemy of mine is behind the attacks, but I'm sure he's using local people for the actual dirty work."

Anger flared in Boone's eyes. "You come in my saloon talking like that, and you'll end up with a broken head. You haven't stayed home long enough to know that nobody around here would do a thing like that. Anyway, why would your enemy want to hurt Roberta? That doesn't make any sense."

"It would if you knew Laveau diViere."

"Well I don't, and it doesn't. Now before you go spouting any more outlandish theories, I'm going back into that house. I'm not letting that city slicker get a march on me."

Nate didn't have any choice but to knock Boone down. Part of him wished he didn't have to do it, but another part relished the thought. If it was impossible to bang a little sense *into* Boone's head, maybe it was possible to knock a little stupidity *out*. Nate waited until Boone turned away before bringing the butt of his pistol down on the back of his skull. He fell with a satisfying thud. Certain he'd been observed by at least three citizens, Nate started preparing his explanation for the sheriff.

∽

"You can't know how much I've missed you and everybody back home." Roberta had said that at least three times already, but it didn't seem enough. Sitting next to Carl, her hands in his, made her feel like she was getting back in touch with the life she thought she'd lost. Just looking into his warm eyes calmed some of the turmoil raging inside her.

"We've missed you, too," Carl said. "You have no idea how important you are to your friends."

"They're important to me, too." But honesty forced Roberta to admit she couldn't picture more than two or three. She hadn't realized how much coming to Texas had pushed Virginia into the back of her mind.

"Everybody will be shocked to hear about your

father, but they won't believe someone tried to burn you in your bed. What kind of savages do they have here in Texas?"

Roberta had been declaring herself a lost soul in the midst of strangers for so long it came as a complete surprise that her immediate feeling was one of resentment. "Not everyone is like that. There are good people here just as there are bad people in Virginia."

"Nobody who would murder your father in front of your eyes then try to burn you in your bed."

She remembered a man in the town next to where she'd grown up who'd been hanged for shooting his wife with a shotgun. Then there were the knife fights that occurred every Saturday night after people got liquored up. Maybe Texas wasn't as different from Virginia as she thought.

"That man is a foreigner," Prudence said.

Roberta had forgotten she was still in the room.

"If you haven't caught him, how do you know?" Carl asked.

"Nate says he's French and Spanish. That makes him a foreigner."

"How can you be sure it's this man?"

"Nate saw him peering in the bedroom window shortly before I came home. I saw him mounting the steps. He had his hand on his gun."

"What was Nate doing in your bedroom?"

The sharpness in Carl's voice was impossible to miss. The change in his expression was harder to define. Elements of surprise, disapproval, and ownership mingled with degrees of pique and confusion. It wasn't what she expected, and she didn't like it. Still, he was her friend, and she wanted him to understand. "He was there because I shot him."

"What?"

Carl's reaction was so incredulous she nearly laughed. "He came to help during the first attack. I thought he was one of the attackers."

"I still don't understand why he was in your bedroom."

Now she did laugh. Carl was jealous, which was ridiculous. They had been sweet on each other growing up, but that was years ago. "He wasn't in *my* bedroom. He was in my father's. The doctor said he was too seriously injured to move. Since I had shot him, it seemed only fair that I should take care of him. My feelings changed after I learned he had come to help."

"How did they change?"

Definitely jealous. She liked Carl, but she was over her girlish crush.

"I felt guilty for having shot a man, especially an innocent one. I still find it hard to believe I did it. I'd never done more than pick up a gun."

"I thought everybody in Texas practically slept with their guns."

"I can't speak for everybody, but I don't. Neither did Nate until diViere showed up."

"Mr. Dolan had one of his cowhands sleep at her place to make sure she was safe." That was probably the closest to approval Prudence could allow any man except Joe.

"He didn't do a very good job, did he?"

Roberta didn't understand why Carl was being so irksome, but she wasn't about to have Carlin's work belittled. "He was killed. His funeral is this afternoon."

Carl had the decency to look abashed. "I'm sorry. Was he a friend?"

"If I had to characterize our relationship, I'd say he was more like a younger brother. Old enough to do a man's work, but young enough to be tongue-tied around a pretty girl."

Carl chuckled. "He must have been mute around you."

That surprised her. Carl had never said she was pretty. As a gawky fourteen-year-old, she probably wasn't. "Carlin had no trouble talking to me." She smiled at the memory. "Sometimes, he could hardly stop. Most of the time it was about Nate. All three boys were in awe of him."

"They took turns staying at the farm at night," Prudence explained. "Joe was with her during the day."

"Is every man in Texas trying to take care of you?" Carl asked.

Before Roberta could tell Carl not to be ridiculous, she realized that a surprising number of men had been watching out for her. Though a month ago, she would have said no one in Slender Creek cared if she lived or died. Already that morning several women had come by to see her. Over the past few days a number of ranchers had ridden by the farm and stopped to speak, but she still didn't trust them. Regardless of who was responsible for the attacks on her and her father, they had provided the pretext by destroying the first dam.

"Now that Carl is here, I won't have to depend on Joe all the time," Roberta told Prudence. "I've felt guilty about having him spend all day with me then having to work in the saloon at night."

"Joe likes working on the farm," Prudence said. "If you were able to pay him, he'd stop working in the saloon."

"I couldn't pay him even before the fire. There's no chance I can now."

"How much money do you need?" Carl asked.

"You don't have any more money than I do."

Carl's smile was brilliant. "That's why I'm here. I just came into an inheritance, more than enough for us to be married. You can sell the farm and come back to Virginia with me."

Carl's announcement so surprised her, she blurted out, "I'm not going anywhere until I find out who killed my father."

"The sheriff will do that, so you might as well go home, where you belong."

It startled Roberta to realize she didn't think of Virginia as home. Sometime in the past five years, Texas had assumed that position. How had that happened? She'd never intended to stay in Texas any longer than necessary. She didn't even like Texas. It was hot, dry, and filled with men as wild as long-horns. She removed her hands from Carl's grasp and pulled back. "I'm not ready to get married. And even if I were, I couldn't take money from you."

Carl looked confused. "What are you going to do? You don't have a place to live, and the farm is in ruins."

"She can stay with me as long as she wants," Prudence volunteered.

"But why?" Carl asked.

"To find out who killed my father," Roberta repeated. "And while I'm waiting, I'll see what I can do with the farm. No one will want to buy it like it is now."

"They'd be crazy to buy it in any condition," Carl said. "You can't farm in this kind of country. Anybody knows that."

Roberta had always liked Carl, but he had a habit of thinking he knew all the answers. "All I need is a dam to provide water."

"A dam won't do any good if somebody keeps blowing it up—or if they burn you in your bed. You ought to forget all this and marry me as soon as we get back to Virginia."

Roberta had never felt quite so out of charity with Carl. "If I *were* going back to Virginia, I wouldn't travel with you without being married first. What kind of woman do you think I am?"

It was entertaining to see Carl scramble to make it clear he'd never once doubted her purity, but her amusement didn't last long. Ever since her father had brought her to Texas against her wishes, she'd proclaimed that she would go back to Virginia at the first opportunity. She *believed* she wanted to go back to the only place she ever felt was home, to the only people who she thought of as *real* friends. The possibility that she would fall in love with a Texan, even one who'd been transplanted from Arkansas, had never crossed her mind. The likelihood that she could think of Texas as home was equally remote.

Yet she was in danger of doing both. What's more, Prudence, Joe, Blossom, even Nate and Boone, could be counted on to do anything they could to help her. The doctor and Mrs. Pender had extended the hand of friendship. Men she didn't know had come to help after both attacks, their wives to give moral support. Maybe her anger over having been forced to move to Texas had blinded her to changes in her feelings. Her memories of Virginia were those of a child rather than of an adult. Would she feel differently, if she went back now?

∞

Everyone from Slender Creek and the surrounding ranches turned out for Carlin's funeral.

"You'd think he was somebody important rather than an ordinary cowhand," Boone complained.

"I think they're here because of the way he died," Nate said.

"Are any of these people family?" Carl asked.

All three men had accompanied Roberta to the funeral. Nate was there because Carlin had worked for him. Carl was there out of courtesy to Roberta. Boone was there because he wouldn't let Roberta go anywhere accompanied by another man, unless he was with her. Webb, Grady, and Russ were the only men from Nate's crew. Russ said the other men couldn't be spared from their work.

It was an awkward service. No one knew anything about Carlin before Nate hired him. No one knew if he had any family. They didn't even know his full name. The manner of his death hung over the service like a pall. No matter how hard people tried, they couldn't push aside the fear that a murderer was in their midst. No one from town wanted to make eye contact with the ranchers. The ranchers seemed equally uncomfortable with one another. Each spoke to Nate then went to a pew without talking to anyone else.

The service was short. There was little to say about Carlin, and no one wanted a sermon. Roberta had requested that Carlin be buried next to her father. It was the closest he would come to being buried near family.

"Don't you need to go back to the saloon?" Nate asked Boone as they left the cemetery.

"Why should I?"

"Business is always brisk after a funeral. People like a few drinks to take their mind off it."

"Blossom will take care of everything."

He wasn't going to get rid of Boone that easily, and he could see no way to separate Roberta from Carl without taking Roberta back to Prudence's house. If he couldn't have Roberta to himself, no one would. For the first time, he welcomed Prudence's presence. Yet it was Otis Parker who separated Roberta from Boone and Carl.

"I'm sorry about the death of your friend," the banker said, "but I'm horrified by the attack on you. Can you think of any reason for it?"

"None that makes any sense."

"I know this is not a good time, but if you have a few minutes you can spare, I would like to see you in my office."

"She's too upset to deal with business now," Carl said.

"What have you got to talk to her about?" Boone asked.

When Roberta turned to him, Nate hoped she was looking to him for help in escaping two men trying to control her life.

"I think that's a decision Roberta ought to make," Nate said.

"I agree," Otis concurred.

Boone and Carl started to argue, but Roberta stopped them both. "I'm perfectly capable of handling my own affairs. When I'm not, I'll let you know."

Carl and Boone watched her accompany Otis to the bank with varying degrees of dissatisfaction. Nate felt only pride. No matter how devastating the blow, Roberta didn't admit defeat. He fell a little bit more in love with her each day. She couldn't marry Boone or Carl. He was the only one who realized what a marvelous woman she was. He didn't want to own her. He didn't want to control her. He wanted to marry her because he loved the wonderful, vibrant woman she was. He wanted her to have the freedom and security to do anything she wanted. And he wanted to be at her side for the whole journey.

∞

"I don't understand why you changed your mind," Roberta said to Otis. "I'm in a worse financial position than I was when you turned me down earlier."

Otis squirmed in his chair, but his gaze didn't falter. "Two reasons," he said. "The people of

Slender Creek don't think anybody should be burned out of their home. We feel obliged to see that your home is rebuilt."

Roberta didn't know Otis well enough to have a definite opinion of his character, but she didn't believe that. The people of the town hadn't shown any interest in her or her father until the attacks. "What is your second reason?"

"The farm won't sell for a fraction of what it's worth without a house on it."

Roberta didn't find that credible, either. Her father owned the land, so the bank had no financial interest in it. After two fires and the dam being blown up twice, she was certain no one else would try to farm it. A rancher would pay next to nothing for it as grazing land and would have no use for a house. "How much of a loan are you offering?"

Otis mentioned a figure that was more than ample to cover the costs of rebuilding the house.

"Did Boone give you the money so I wouldn't know it was coming from him?"

"No."

His reply was so emphatic she had to believe him, but she was convinced there was something behind the offer she didn't see. "I want a copy of the contract to study. I intend to make sure there are no hidden tricks."

"Why do you think I'd try to trick you?"

"I don't think you're dishonest, but you're not telling me the whole truth."

"I will stake my personal reputation on this loan being sound and fair. If you have any questions about the agreement, I'll be happy to answer them."

Roberta decided she would learn nothing further for the time being. She was certain Boone had found a way to give her the money she had refused to take directly from him. She would figure it out. And when she did, Boone Riggins wouldn't like what she had to say.

❧

Roberta hadn't realized that seeing the ruins of her home would be so upsetting. Enough of the framework had survived that it looked like a skeleton with the flesh melted away. She had expected to be sad, angry, and depressed. She felt all of that, but the sight of the ruins brought home with stunning impact that she'd lost everything she owned. Even the clothes she wore now, and those she'd worn to Carlin's funeral, were borrowed. She had refused Boone's offer to provide her with a new wardrobe. He was still furious that she'd chosen instead to wear clothes given or lent to her by women in town.

"The house is a total loss," Carl said. "I wouldn't bother to rebuild."

Prudence hadn't wanted Roberta to visit the farm, but after one day of inactivity, Roberta was eager to get out and start making decisions about what to do next. If Joe hadn't already been at the farm, Prudence would have gone with Roberta rather than allow her to be alone with Carl.

"Of course I'm going to rebuild. I can't live with Prudence." She walked around the perimeter of the house. Seeing the charred remains of furniture, a pot, or a piece of glassware made the loss worse.

She'd never been strongly attached to the furnishings, but they had belonged to her mother. Seeing them destroyed was like losing a connection with her past.

Carl took her by the hand and turned her to face him. "It could be months until they find the person responsible for your father's death. Years. Maybe never. And what about the person who tried to burn you in your bed? You're not safe here."

Roberta withdrew her hand from Carl's grasp. "I still have to stay."

"We can be married here if you want."

Roberta could accept that Carl believed he was still in love and wanted to marry her, but she couldn't imagine why he thought all he had to do was show up without warning, crook his finger, and she'd run meekly off to Virginia with him. So much had changed in their lives, they didn't know each other anymore. "I'm not ready to get married, certainly not to a man I haven't seen in five years."

"But we were in love before you left."

"I was fourteen."

"My feelings haven't changed."

Roberta was losing patience with Carl's attempt to rush her into a lifelong commitment. "I've just lost my father, had most of my farm destroyed, and been burned out of my house. With Carlin's death on top of all that, I hardly know what I feel from minute to minute."

"You won't have to worry about any of that. I'll take care of everything."

"I don't *want* you to take care of everything. I have to do this myself."

"When they heard I was coming to Texas, your cousins, aunts, uncles, and friends told me they could hardly wait for you to come home."

Roberta had received several letters during the first two years she was in Texas encouraging her to come back at the first opportunity, but they stopped after that. "I miss everybody back home, too, but I can't just pick up and leave."

"Sure you can. You don't want to marry that Riggins fella, do you?"

"No."

"Then there's nobody to keep you here."

She was surprised he didn't mention Nate. Apparently he wasn't as perceptive as she thought. Did she want a future with Carl? She had no doubt that he'd make an admirable husband, but she wasn't looking for *admirable*. She was looking for extraordinary, unbelievable, a man so wonderful she couldn't imagine life without him. "I don't know if I can love you. I won't marry you unless I'm certain."

"Then let me convince you."

Without giving her time to object, Carl swept her into his embrace and kissed her hard. Despite her shock at his actions, his kiss didn't affect her nearly as powerfully as Nate's gentle kiss on her cheek. She was about to pull back when Carl went limp. A moment later he had slumped to the ground, and she found herself facing Joe, who had a large piece of lumber in his hands.

Chapter Fifteen

NATE PUT HIS HORSE INTO A FAST CANTER. HE WAS irritated that Prudence had let Roberta go off to her farm with Carl. It wasn't so much that he didn't trust Carl or believed Roberta was still in love with him. If Laveau had decided to go after Roberta, she wouldn't be safe even with Joe. She certainly wouldn't be protected with a man who was used to living in a settled, law-abiding Virginia community. It was a good thing he'd decided against riding out with Russ to see the work the cowhands were doing. He wouldn't have been back until nearly dark.

Why had Roberta decided to walk? This was Texas. Nobody walked when they could ride. It must have been Carl's decision. Virginians liked to walk everywhere they went, but they lived only a few miles apart. In Texas, neighbors were often separated by ten times that distance.

He turned into the lane to the farm. Even before he got close to the house, he saw a man sitting on the ground beside the burned-out shell. It was easy to recognize Carl, but what was he doing on the ground, and where was Roberta?

Carl looked up when Nate brought his horse to a stop. "Did you hit me over the head?"

"I just got here. What happened to you? Where is Roberta?"

Carl winced when he touched a spot on the back of his head. "I was kissing Roberta. The next thing I knew, I woke up with a splitting headache and Roberta was nowhere in sight."

"Where is Joe? Was he here when you got here?"

Carl got to his feet slowly. "I didn't see him, but Prudence said he'd be here as soon as the sun was up." He grimaced again. "Does that woman always tell people what to do?"

Nate wished Prudence hadn't chosen this morning to relax her guard. "You'd better get back to town and see the doctor."

"Roberta must be around here somewhere. I can't leave without her."

The man had to be nuts if he thought Roberta would leave him lying on the ground with a broken head. "What were you doing right before you kissed Roberta?" He prayed they were fighting, arguing, that she was trying to run away. He didn't think he could endure knowing she had fallen willingly into his arms.

"I was trying to convince her it was a waste of money to rebuild this house."

"Was this kiss part of your effort to convince her?"

"I would rebuild this house and a dozen more if it would make Roberta agree to marry me one hour sooner."

Nate guessed Carl had probably kissed Roberta

against her will. If Joe had heard them arguing, he could have interpreted the kiss as an attack. That would explain Carl's sore head. It would also account for Roberta's absence. But where had Joe taken her?

"I'm going to find Roberta."

"I'm coming with you."

"You don't have a horse, and I'm not going to wait until you find one. Go back to town."

Nate ignored Carl's protests. The ground was torn up near where Carl had fallen. A short distance away, he found only one set of footprints leading toward the barn. Apparently Roberta had struggled with Joe before he picked her up. Nate guessed he was taking her to the barn where he would hitch one of the mules to her buckboard. Sure enough, when he got to the barn, the buckboard and one mule were missing. Despite the cut up ground, Nate was able to pick out the tracks of the buckboard. Joe was headed toward the hills beyond the dam. Nate didn't believe Joe would do anything to hurt Roberta, but the man didn't have enough understanding to know how his good intentions could put Roberta in danger. Laveau could be hiding in the hills beyond the dam. So could the men who'd attacked the farm. Joe's brute strength would be a poor defense against bullets.

Nate wanted to urge his horse to greater speed, but it was increasingly difficult to follow the buckboard's tracks after the ground turned hard and rocky. He was sure Joe was headed toward the hills, but where? They stretched for miles to the north and west and were cut by rivers and canyons that provided hundreds of hiding places.

Once Nate reached the trees, it was easier to follow the trail. The buckboard wheels and the mule's hoofprints had left a clear trail through the dry leaves and grassy patches between trees. He'd gone only a short distance when he saw a small cabin ahead. The buckboard was drawn up at the front door. As Nate drew closer, he heard the sound of voices, Roberta's raised and angry, Joe's low and steady. He was relieved to know Roberta was safe, but how was he going to rescue her?

There was no possibility of getting Joe to release Roberta without going back to Slender Creek for Prudence. He also knew it was impossible to overpower Joe physically even if his shoulder had been fully healed. He wasn't willing to use a gun. Joe adored Roberta and was doing what Prudence had told him to do—protect her. It was Carl's fault for trying to force his attentions on Roberta. He'd have something to say about that once Roberta was safe.

His only solution was to tie Joe up. The problem was how to do it.

Nate dismounted. Putting his coiled rope over his shoulder and keeping out of the sight line from the only window, he worked his way through the trees to the cabin. It was hard to understand everything Roberta was saying, but it was evident she was trying to convince Joe to take her back. It was equally apparent Joe wasn't going to do it.

Taking a chance Joe wasn't looking through the window, Nate grabbed a quick glance inside the cabin. Crazy Joe's back was to the door, blocking Roberta from leaving. Nate considered trying to get Roberta's attention in hopes she could distract Joe long enough for him to get inside the cabin, but Joe might figure out from Roberta's reaction that somebody was outside.

His other choice was to wait until the argument seemed to be at its highest and rush in hoping he could reach Crazy Joe before the man realized Nate was there. Nate opted for the latter, but that left one pivotal, unanswered question. Had Crazy Joe barred the door? If he had, any approach from the outside was useless without Prudence.

Nate unholstered his gun, gripped it by the barrel, and waited. It wasn't long before Roberta raised her voice. Figuring this was as good a chance as he was going to get, he reached for the door, lifted the handle, and pushed.

Joe started to turn at the sound of the opening door. Nate's blow caught him on the side of his head hard enough to stun him but not enough to knock him out. With a curse, Nate swung around behind Joe and brought the butt of his pistol down on the man's head a second time. He was relieved when Joe sank to the floor.

"Is Carl okay?"

It would have been difficult for any utterance from Roberta to dismay Nate more than those three words. How could he hope she would come to love him when her first thought was for Carl.

"He has a sore head, but he's fine."

"Did you have to hit Joe so hard? He was just trying to protect me."

No thank you. No expression of relief. No concern that he might have been hurt or have strained his still healing wound. No pleasure in seeing him. He might as well have—

Roberta stepped up to him, gave him a quick kiss on the lips, then stepped back. She looked a bit bashful, maybe shy, neither attitude one he'd previously associated with her. That gave him hope. He didn't know a lot about women, but he did know that if a young woman could be completely comfortable in your presence, she wasn't romantically interested in you. He hadn't been in love long, but he already knew it was an uncomfortable condition, which subjected him to radical mood swings.

"I knew you'd find me. You've been looking out for me ever since you sent the boys to help Joe with the barn."

"I'm just a man trying to protect the woman I love. There's nothing special about that. Boone has been trying to do the same thing."

"Boone wants to own me, to lock me up in a fancy house and keep me there. You just want me to be safe and be myself."

Herself was who he fell in love with. Why would he want to change her? He would have liked to say more, but Crazy Joe was beginning to stir.

Roberta noticed, too. "Let me talk to him."

"Not until I tie him up. That man is stronger than an ox."

He had Joe bound hand and foot by the time the man became fully conscious. As soon as he caught sight of Nate, Joe struggled against the rope. Nate was glad he'd brought a rope they used for lassoing full-grown steers. Joe might have broken anything else.

"It's okay," Roberta said to Joe. "Nate is here to help me."

"Miss Prudence told Joe to protect Roberta."

"Nate isn't going to hurt me."

"Carl was hurting Roberta."

"He was just trying to convince me to marry him."

"He was hurting Roberta."

Nate agreed. Any man who tried to force Roberta to marry him was hurting her.

"We have to go back to town. Are you going to fight Nate if he unties you?"

"Miss Prudence doesn't trust Nate."

"I trust him."

"Miss Prudence doesn't trust Nate."

That seemed to leave only one option. Return to town and ask Prudence to come release Joe. Roberta appeared to have reached the same conclusion.

"I don't want to leave you here, but I will unless you promise not to fight Nate. Prudence told you not to let any man hurt me, but Nate doesn't want to hurt me."

Joe appeared to be thinking over the situation.

"You can drive the buckboard with Roberta just like you did coming here," Nate offered. "I'll follow on my horse."

After another pause, Joe came to a decision. "I will drive Roberta."

"What about Nate?" Roberta asked.

"I will not fight him unless he hurts Roberta. Carl hurt Roberta."

Nate untied Joe and stepped back, ready for anything the man might try. Instead, he got to his feet, looked first at Roberta then at Nate. "Joe protects Roberta."

"That's good," Nate said. "I hope you will always protect Roberta. I will protect her, too."

Joe seemed to understand because he smiled. "Joe will take Roberta to Miss Prudence. You will come, too."

The drive back to town was uneventful. Nate rode alongside the buckboard while Joe told Roberta about the farm he lived on as a child. They stopped at the farm, but Carl wasn't there.

Nate was relieved. He hadn't looked forward to explaining to Joe why he should let Carl ride to town in the buckboard. Prudence met them at the door. From her expression, Nate gathered Carl had already filled her ears with fears of Roberta's safety.

"What happened?" she asked before the buck-board came to a stop. Carl followed her out. When he saw Roberta sitting next to Joe, Nate thought Carl was going to have a fit. Nate insisted that they all go inside before they attempted an explanation.

"There's nothing else to be done," Prudence declared after she had received a full explanation. "I'll have to take him back to his family."

Roberta appeared as shocked as Nate felt. "I didn't know he had a family."

"I offered to look out for him when they threatened to lock him up."

"What will happen to him now?" Roberta asked.

"I'm not sure," Prudence said, "but he will not be locked up." She turned to Nate. "While I'm gone, Roberta will stay in my house. I depend on you to protect her."

"Why not me?" Carl asked. "I want to marry her."

"You're not the only one."

How Boone Riggins learned Roberta had returned to town was a mystery, but the man had a knack for turning up where he wasn't wanted.

"I asked her to marry me months ago," Boone told Carl.

"I asked her five years ago," Carl responded.

Prudence took Roberta by the hand and ushered her into the house. Once Roberta was inside, she turned back to the men gathered outside. "She's not marrying anybody today, so you can go away. Joe, tie the horse to the hitching post and come inside."

❧

"Why the hell did you give her money to rebuild her house?"

"All you had to do was nothing, and she would have married that Peterson guy and gone back to Virginia."

"Otis is just as responsible. He didn't have to agree to give her the money."

Several ranchers had descended on Nate, furious that he'd provided the money for Roberta's loan. He supposed he couldn't blame Otis for refusing to shoulder the blame. He had a business to think about. Nate let his gaze travel from one rancher to the other until he'd looked every man in the room in the eye. He was pleased to see that some had the decency to be embarrassed. Unfortunately, Frank Porter wasn't one of them.

"That's a knife in the back of every rancher in the

county," Frank said. "What are we supposed to do for water after she rebuilds that dam?"

"Let me make something very clear," Nate said to Frank. "I can and *will* do what I want with my own money. I won't ask for your approval, nor will I bend before your criticism." Frank sputtered, but Nate didn't give him a chance to speak. "I provided the money to rebuild her house, not the dam. If anyone else in Slender Creek had lost their home, the whole town could have come together to help rebuild it. What kind of men are you to single out an unmarried woman who recently lost her father, suffered extensive damage to her only source of income, then nearly died in a fire? If you had any decency, you'd be more concerned about finding out who's doing all of this than persecuting the victim of these senseless attacks."

Frank started to speak, but Ezra Kemp interrupted him. "We followed your advice to look for any strangers, but we haven't found any. None of my boys have seen anybody they don't know."

"Maybe Carl Peterson is behind it," Frank said. "He wants to marry her, and she won't leave."

"Don't be stupid!" Ches Hale burst out. "He wouldn't want to burn her house down with her in it, now would he?"

"That leaves this diViere character you were telling the sheriff about," Ezra said. "Have you seen him again?"

"I didn't see him. Roberta did. If he's behind these attacks, he won't be seen here, but he won't be far away. We know there were at least half a dozen men involved in the first attack. It's unlikely one man murdered Carlin and set the fire. I believe diViere is behind this because of me."

"That doesn't make any sense," Frank said.

"I'd agree with you except for two things. Someone dropped my hat during the first attack to incriminate me. They had no way of knowing I had changed my plans and come back early. DiViere was about to enter Roberta's house when he thought she was at the funeral. I believe he set fire to her house simply because she foiled his attempt to murder me in my bed. Since no one has seen any strangers around, someone in the county is helping him. I know all this is hard to believe, but it's the only explanation I can see."

"Nobody's that cruel," Ezra said.

"Laveau diViere is a thief, a murderer, and a traitor. Just last year he shot one of his partners then set the man's house ablaze with him in it." Nate had seen doubt in their eyes, but now some of that faded.

"If nobody can find him, how can we stop him?" Ezra asked.

"The best way is to find out who's helping him."

Each rancher reiterated that none of his men could be involved. "What about yours?" Frank Porter asked.

"Most of my crew are rounding up steers for a drive to market. I have only two young hands and a cook at the house. I know they weren't involved because one of them was killed."

They talked about finding diViere without coming up with anything definite. Frank Porter still grumbled about Nate providing money for Roberta, but Ezra told him to shut up. Nate was convinced it was out of guilt, but the ranchers volunteered enough men to rebuild Roberta's house without her having to pay for anything beyond materials. Nate knew their objections to his giving Roberta money were still there, but at least they were beginning to see that being good businessmen didn't preclude being decent human beings.

But they had raised a valid point about his own men. Russ had hired most of the crew while he'd been gone. It was time he took a more active interest in his ranch. Roberta was right about him avoiding being part of the community. He hadn't even had enough interest in his ranch to ride out with his men to see the condition of his range, his cows, even the size of his herd. He had full confidence in Russ as a foreman, but Nate was falling down on his responsibilities as a boss and a landowner.

First, though, he had to convince Roberta to move to his ranch.

❧

Blossom fixed Roberta with an inquisitive look, her head cocked at a slight angle. "Are you going to marry Nate? Everybody knows he's in love with you."

Roberta had been pleased when Blossom came to visit. She was bored being confined to the house, and tired of Carl apologizing for kissing her against her will. She had been sorely tempted to go back to the farm, but had promised Nate she wouldn't leave town unless he was with her.

"It wouldn't matter if he was madly in love with me," Roberta told her friend. "I'm going back to Virginia."

Prudence's home was as austere and dismaying as her personality. The walls were covered with a paper that set a crosslike figure against a dark background. There were no pictures, no decorative touches, and every chair in the room was straight-backed and uncomfortable. The floor was composed of bare boards, and the curtains at the windows blocked nearly all sunlight. Roberta thought it was like living in a cave and found it thoroughly depressing.

Blossom sat forward, her look turned serious. "If you're determined to go back to Virginia, I think you ought to marry Carl. He loves you, and that's where you both want to live."

"I know he's been spending half his day in the saloon trying to convince you to talk me into marrying him, but it's not going to work."

"Why not? He wants to take you back to Virginia where you'll never have to see a rancher again. He will build any kind of house you want and fill it with enough servants for a princess. Besides, Virginia's not hot as hell and dry as a desert. You always said you hated the Texas heat, and you can't tell me you like working in the dirt from morning till night."

Roberta *didn't* like working in the dirt regardless of the time of day, but she had discovered that she derived satisfaction from knowing that she could do strenuous work. It gave her a sense of accomplishment she'd never had before, a sense of self-worth that she was starting to enjoy. Her father's death, as much of a tragedy as that was, had changed the way people saw her. She was no longer the rarely seen, and even less often thought of, daughter of Robert

Tryon. She was being regarded as a person in her own right for the first time in her life. She doubted she could explain to Blossom why that was so important to her.

"Things have been changing so quickly, I don't know what I think. I need time to figure out what to do."

"There's nothing to figure out," Blossom insisted. "Your farm is ruined, and your house is gone. You've got a perfectly wonderful man who wants to marry you and take you away from the attacks, the fires, and the dirt. No woman in her right mind would hesitate."

But was she in her right mind? So much had happened—the circumstances surrounding her had changed so drastically—she could be sure of only two things. She was strongly attracted to Nate, and she had to know who killed her father. She was sure the same person had tried to kill her. She couldn't go into a marriage, knowing that kind of danger might follow her.

"Why are you so anxious for me to marry Carl?" she asked Blossom. "Do you think Boone will marry you if I leave?"

"Boone wouldn't marry me if I were the only woman in Slender Creek." Blossom looked away. "Boone loves money, but he's ashamed of being a saloon owner. He wants a wife who'll give him class. You're the only one who can do that."

Roberta couldn't help but laugh. "I'm a farmer's daughter. That's almost worse."

"Not in his eyes."

"Why?"

They were interrupted by a knock on the door. Blossom got up and looked out the window. "You can ask Boone himself. That's him at the door."

"Tell him to go away."

"Tell him yourself. I'm not in love with him anymore, but I need my job."

Roberta decided she might as well see Boone. It was only fair that she try to make him understand she wasn't going to marry him.

"You don't need me hanging around for this conversation." Blossom grinned. "You can tell me all the juicy parts later."

"Just for that, you can let Boone in on your way out."

Boone appeared surprised to see Blossom when she opened the door. "I'm just going," she told him.

"Come in," Roberta said, when Blossom had left. "I've been meaning to talk to you."

Boone gave her a huge smile. "It's about time you decided to marry me. Now, I can get rid of the Peterson fella. I'm tired of him hanging about in the saloon. I can't understand what you see in him."

"Carl and I were very close before I moved from Virginia. He's a good friend."

"I shouldn't complain. He's very free with his money."

"Carl was always generous, even before he came into his inheritance."

Boone's gaze narrowed. "You didn't invite me in here to tell me you're going to marry him, did you? I know you're always talking about going back to Virginia, but—"

"I'm not going to marry Carl. Sit down. I feel awkward standing like this."

Boone chose a chair and frowned when he sat down.

"Don't bother to change. The rest are all the same."

"Just like Prudence. Hard and inflexible. But I don't want to talk about Prudence. I want to talk about us getting married."

"That's what I wanted to talk about."

"We can have the wedding as soon as you want. Buy any dress you want. We can go to San Antonio if you can't find anything here."

"You can't think I'd let you pay for my wedding dress?" That wasn't what she wanted to say.

"I know Otis gave you a loan, but you can give the money back. I'll build you a bigger and better house than any in Slender Creek."

"Stop!" If she didn't slow him down, he'd have the preacher at the door before she could tell him she wasn't going to marry him. "Boone, listen to me. I'm not going to marry you."

Boone looked at her like she had lost her mind.

"I like you," Roberta persisted, "but I don't love you. I'm sorry if you truly believed I would marry you, but I've been telling you for months that I wouldn't."

"It's that Peterson guy," Boone boomed. "He's turned your head with his talk about this fortune he's inherited. I bet it's not nearly as much as he'd like you to think."

"It has nothing to do with Carl or his inheritance. I think it's important that two people love each other before they decide to marry."

"I do love you."

"I'm sorry, Boone, but I don't love you. I never have."

"Of course you love me."

"I have *never* told you or anybody else that I loved you. You've got to stop telling yourself what you want to hear and listen to me. *I'm not going to marry you*. It's not something I just decided. I've been saying the same thing for months."

"Who is it?" Boone demanded.

"What do you mean?"

"Who are you going to marry?" he demanded.

"I haven't decided to marry anyone."

"No woman turns down a man like me without thinking she's got a better bird in hand. That could be only two people. Nate Dolan or Carl Peterson. Which one is it?"

"I'm not turning you down because I'm going to marry someone else. I'm turning you down because I don't love you."

"It's got to be Nate Dolan. You didn't say anything about not marrying me until he started paying attention to you. Are you going to rebuild your house?"

"Why do you want to know?"

"You should know Nate Dolan gave Otis the money he lent to you."

Chapter Sixteen

IF ROBERTA HADN'T BEEN SO UPSET OVER THE attempt on her life and sidetracked with Carl's unexpected arrival, she would have kept after Otis until she found out who was behind the loan. Instead, she'd let herself be swayed by Otis's talk about community responsibility and not allowing anyone to be without a home. "It doesn't matter where Otis got the money," Roberta insisted. "The loan is from the bank, not Nate." Inwardly, though, she cringed at being caught in a trap not of her making.

"You're in love with him, aren't you?"

"Who I may or may not be in love with doesn't concern you. I *can* tell you that I have no plans at present to marry anyone."

"You should marry Peterson and go back to Virginia. Nate won't stop chasing diViere. If the man is as dangerous as Nate is telling everyone, Nate will be dead and you a widow." Boone heaved a sigh and stood. "I'd better get back to the saloon. With Crazy Joe gone, I've got no one to make sure there's no trouble."

Roberta no sooner closed the door behind Boone

than she had to face the problem of Nate having provided the money for her loan. She'd accepted the lumber for her barn directly from Boone with a promise to repay him, so how could she accuse Nate of doing anything wrong?

She needed to talk to him right away.

≈✥≈

"There's no need for you to go with us, boss," Russ said to Nate. "All we're doing is counting steers. We haven't started to round them up and trail brand them."

"I'm not going because I think you need the help," Nate told his foreman. "I just want to look over the herd. Do you realize I haven't gone beyond the corrals in more than a year?"

"I've tried to see you didn't even need to leave the house. You said you wanted to devote all your time to your search for diViere."

"You've done an outstanding job, but now it's time I started to act like a rancher."

"Don't you trust me to do the job? Have I done anything to make you think I've made any mistakes?"

"Nothing at all." Nate hoped Russ wasn't going to make this an issue of his ability to do his job. Since he'd been back, Nate had noticed that Russ had a tendency to act like it was his ranch, that he could make decisions without consulting his boss. Nate had no one to blame but himself. From the beginning he'd left Russ free to run the ranch pretty much as he saw fit. He'd even let Russ hire most of the crew. "You don't have to ride with me. I don't want to get in the way of your work."

"It'll be easier if I show you around. I know the most important things for you to see."

"Have it your way," Nate said to Russ. "Just know I intend to be in the saddle most of the day."

"Do you think you're strong enough for that?"

"I used to ride all night."

"That was more than ten years ago."

Nate wasn't sure why Russ was trying so hard to keep him at the ranch house. Except for an occasional tenderness when he overextended himself, he felt fully recovered. "If I get too tired, I can come home. Now let's saddle up. I've wasted too much of the day already." He had meant to ride out earlier, but several small delays had taken up most of the morning. He wouldn't cover as much ground as he had hoped, but there would be plenty of time in the days ahead. Laveau was in the area. Nate only had to wait for him to show his hand.

During their walk to the corrals, roping the horses, and saddling up, Russ kept up a running monologue of what he would show Nate and the changes or improvements he hoped to make. Despite appearing otherwise, Nate couldn't shake the feeling Russ was worried about something else. He supposed he would learn what it was during their ride. They had just mounted up when the sound of a galloping horse caught Nate's attention. A buggy was being driven at a breakneck pace toward the ranch house.

Roberta held the reins.

Putting his horse into a quick gallop, Nate rode to meet her, but she didn't stop until she'd brought her buggy to a stop at the house. She turned to him, her face a mask of shock.

"Someone tried to kill me."

Nate didn't let Roberta say anything more until he'd gotten her inside, settled her in a comfortable chair, and Benny had provided her with a cup of hot coffee. "Now, tell me why you ignored everything Prudence and I have said and drove out here by yourself?" That's not what he really wanted to say. He wanted to crush her in his embrace, tell her she was never to go anywhere without him, and promise to be at her side for the rest of her life. But there would be time for that later.

"I came because Boone told me you gave Otis the money he lent me to rebuild my house. If I'm going to consider marrying you, I need to make sure I'm not beholden to you in any way."

For a moment, Nate forgot about everything else. Roberta was thinking about marrying him. She'd never said that before. "We'll talk about that later. Tell me why you think someone tried to kill you."

"Someone shot at me."

"Did you see anyone? Did they follow you? Was it a rifle or a gun?" A rifle could mean someone was hunting and made a poor shot. A gun was more ominous.

"I didn't see anyone, and I can't tell a rifle from a gun."

"Did they fire more than once?"

"No."

"It was probably someone hunting or target practicing," Russ said. He had followed them inside but hadn't spoken until now. Instead of his usual antagonism toward Roberta, he looked unusually solemn.

"I was on Nate's range when it happened," Roberta told him.

"My men are all busy counting steers," Russ said. "It couldn't have been one of them. Besides, I don't allow hunting for anything except deer and wild hogs, and they aren't out during the day."

"I'm not accusing anybody, just telling you what happened."

Nate could tell Roberta was getting overly agitated. "You're not leaving this house until we figure this out. I'll send one of the boys into town for everything you need."

"She can't stay here," Russ objected.

"She can, and she will," Nate declared.

"What about the men? Her reputation?"

"The men will be on guard duty twenty-four hours a day. They won't have time to do anything that might jeopardize her reputation."

"What about you?"

"If you think I'd do anything to besmirch the honor of the woman I love and intend to marry, you'd better start looking for a new job."

Russ stumbled over himself apologizing. "I was just thinking about what other people might say."

"Protecting Roberta is more important than worrying about idle gossip."

"Russ is right," Roberta said. "I shouldn't stay."

"There's no place else to stay unless you intend to take up Boone's offer to use his house."

Roberta colored. "I told him I wasn't going to

marry him. That's why he got angry enough to tell me about the loan."

"Forget about the loan. You're not going back to the farm. You're going to marry me."

Roberta glanced at Russ then back at Nate. "I said I was *thinking* about marrying you. I haven't decided yet."

"You'll have plenty of time to do all the thinking you need. Russ will stay with you while I see about getting your room ready. Meanwhile, make a list of what the boys need to bring from Prudence's house. Be specific. They're not used to being around women."

Nate didn't wait for Roberta or Russ to raise any objections. His main objective was to keep Roberta safe, but he didn't intend to waste an opportunity to have her to himself without Boone and Carl Peterson showing up whenever they wanted. In the coming days, he intended to do everything in his power to make her forget Virginia.

But he wouldn't forget Laveau.

❧

Roberta hadn't been at the ranch three hours before Carl arrived, demanding that she return to town immediately. When she tried to explain why she'd decided to stay at Nate's ranch, he made an ugly remark, which ended with Nate knocking him down and throwing him out of the house. He left, vowing not to return until she regained her senses. Since he wouldn't believe she was being sensible unless she agreed to marry him, she hoped he wouldn't come back.

Now, it was two days later, and she was facing a meeting with Prudence. Grady had galloped up the lane two minutes ago to say he'd seen her on her way from town. "I'll get the boss." With that, Grady disappeared with the alacrity of a guilty little boy. He said he was going to stay in the bunkhouse until she left.

Roberta suffered from mixed feelings. She was appreciative of everyone's efforts to make her feel safe and comfortable. Benny spent entire afternoons in the kitchen fixing meals she was certain the cowhands had never seen before. Nate, Grady, Webb, and Russ circled around her like orbiting moons. Nate had ordered the entire contents of a dress shop brought out to the ranch for her selection. She had refused to let him pay for anything. Instead, she dipped into the money Otis lent her.

She enjoyed being spoiled. It had never happened before, but it wasn't long before she started to feel restless. She became so desperate she cleaned the house despite Nate's objections that Russ had a standing arrangement for someone from Slender Creek to clean once a month. She threatened to take on the washing if she couldn't find something else to do. Now, she had to face Prudence. She really would have preferred doing the washing.

Nate came to her side on the porch. "You don't have to see her if you don't want to."

"Of course I do. Prudence can be a trial some-times, but she's been a stalwart friend."

"She won't be very nice about your being here."

The two days spent with Nate had been some

of the best of her life. She'd made up her mind to marry him.

Prudence's lips remained pursed all the way from the buggy to the parlor. Not even a bountiful display of Benny's sweets could keep her from getting straight to the purpose of her journey.

"I was shocked when I returned to find you'd moved in with Nate Dolan."

"I didn't *move in* with Nate. I was coming to tell him I couldn't accept his loan when someone shot at me. Nate thought I wouldn't be safe alone in your house. He has two men watching outside during the day. At night, I lock my bedroom door, and either he or one of the boys stands guard."

Prudence appeared distressed on hearing of a second attack, but it didn't alter her belief that Roberta was endangering her immortal soul. "Now that I have returned, you can come back to my house."

"Roberta will stay here until we can find out who's trying to kill her," Nate said. "If you think your presence will preserve her reputation, you're welcome to stay here as well."

Roberta hoped her surprise didn't show. Nate must love her more than she thought to offer to let Prudence stay in his house.

Prudence appeared to struggle with herself before reaching a decision. "I'm strongly tempted to accept your offer, but since Roberta has already been here several days, I think my energy might be better spent encouraging the sheriff to make a greater effort to apprehend this monstrous criminal who seems determined to harm Roberta for no reason beyond wanton cruelty. I don't doubt that you will keep her safe." She turned to Roberta. "Someone must harvest your crops, or you will become completely dependent on Mr. Dolan."

"Roberta asked me to hire a man to manage the farm until she can take over again."

The gaze Prudence directed at Nate was not entirely friendly. "You seem to have thought of everything."

"I have good reason to try."

Roberta felt warmth flood her cheeks. She still marveled that she had always remained unmoved by Boone's most extravagant declarations of love while even the mildest allusion to Nate's love caused her to blush and stare at her hands in her lap. She didn't need anyone to tell her love was the difference. It's just that she hadn't expected such a reaction at all.

Prudence's gaze remained locked on Nate. "If that's how you feel, you should be talking to the preacher."

"I will as soon as I can get Roberta to agree."

Prudence swung her gaze to Roberta. "Are you in love with this man?"

Prudence wasn't one to mince words or waste time. Roberta was tempted to equivocate, but she decided it was past time for that. "Yes, but I'm not ready to get married."

"You've got three men wanting to marry you. It's time you stopped dithering and made up your mind."

That stung. "I've convinced Boone I won't marry him, and I'm waiting for Carl to realize the girl he fell in love with five years ago doesn't exist anymore."

"Tell him."

"I have, but he's not ready to believe it."

"Then I shall tell him. I have several things I must do in town, so I need to be going." She stood. "If this man is willing to marry you, you are more fortunate than you know."

Having decided it was time to go, Prudence didn't linger. She was out the door, in her buggy, and driving away in a matter of minutes.

Nate turned to Roberta. "That went better than expected."

"You cut the ground out from under her when you offered to let her move in."

"I was hoping she wouldn't take me up on my offer."

"So was I. I'd have had to move back to her house."

Both laughed as they went inside, but they turned serious soon enough. "When are you going to agree to marry me?" Nate asked. "I don't want to sound like Prudence, but the longer you stay here unmarried, the more likely people will whisper."

"They've been talking out loud about me ever since my father and I moved here."

Nate stopped and turned her to face him. "What are you going to do if we don't find Laveau?"

Roberta shrugged in frustration. "I don't know. I feel too up in the air to make important decisions. Not knowing makes me feel like tomorrow might arrive and change everything. What am I going to do about the attacks on me? Even if I married you, I couldn't stay cooped up in this house. Most likely they would stop if I moved back to Virginia. It's got to have something to do with the farm."

"I don't have to stay in Texas and ranch. I grew up the son of a merchant. I could do that again."

"And live in the same town with Carl?"

"We don't have to go back to your hometown. We don't even have to go to Virginia."

Roberta felt her agitation growing. "But you like Texas, and you like being a rancher."

"I could just as easily have gone to half a dozen other places and done as many different things. I followed my commanding officer to Texas and became a rancher because that's what I learned working for him. I'm in love with you. I will go wherever you need to go, do whatever I need to do so you can be safe and happy."

A wave of love for this man swept over Roberta like a torrent of flood waters rushing down from the hills to the north. She had done nothing to deserve such a love. There must be dozens of women who were more worthy. She wasn't beautiful, rich, or sweet and charming. She wasn't brilliant, sophisticated, or the leader of local society. She was a farmer's daughter who liked being in charge of her own life even if it meant working in the fields. Why should a man like Nate love her so much he was willing to go anywhere, do anything that would make her happy?

For the first time in her life, someone would make important decisions based on what she wanted. That, in itself, was scary enough, but Nate's happiness was equally important. Whatever choices she made had to be made with both of them in mind. And none of that could be decided until they solved the mysteries of who killed her father… and why someone wanted her dead.

She turned to Nate. The love glowing in his eyes nearly overwhelmed her. "I do love you, more than I thought possible, but I can't marry you yet. It may not make sense to you, but I can't do that until I know who killed my father. It's as though my life went into limbo that night. I can't move forward, and I can't move backward. I don't *want* to be like this, but I can't help myself."

"That's how I felt when Caleb died."

"How did you get over it?"

"I vowed to hunt Laveau down and bring him to justice."

"But you haven't done that."

"Taking on that task freed me to get on with the rest of my life. It doesn't overshadow everything else."

"Can't you see it already has? You bought a ranch you don't run. You live in a town you know nothing about. You're never in one place long enough to put down roots."

"I was here long enough to fall in love with you."

"Only because I shot you. Have you thought of how different things would be if you hadn't come back early?" She didn't wait for Nate to respond. "I have. You would have ignored me just as you did before. What if you fell in love with me because it was the first time you stopped long enough to get to know a woman? What about the second time you stop? Or the third?"

She hadn't thought about that last point until now. But having thought of it, wasn't it a valid question?

Falling in love with Nate had also caused her to question her decision to go back to Virginia. Why was the distance between falling in love and it being a good idea to get married so great? Why did her head and her heart have to be in constant conflict?

"You can be sure of one thing. I will love you at least as much in the future as I do now. I'm not without some experience with women. You're the only one who has made me want to stop long enough to fall in love. I hadn't ignored you before. I just thought I had things I needed to do first. I realize now I was wrong."

Roberta wasn't sure she could interpret his actions the same way, but she didn't resist when he drew her close to him.

"My first concern is to keep you safe, but I'm going to do my best to make you believe I love you enough to last a lifetime."

"Why me?"

"Because I can't imagine anything worse than spending the rest of my life without you."

That stopped Roberta for a moment. "You really mean that, don't you?" She felt impelled to ask the question even though it was impossible to doubt the sincerity in his eyes.

Rather than respond with words, Nate answered with a kiss. Roberta had been kissed often enough to know it was going to be different this time. It wasn't a rushed kiss or a tentative buss unsure of its welcome. It wasn't forceful or timid. Nate moved with the measured assurance of a man certain of his mission and his ability to accomplish it. It was that assurance that drew Roberta forward to meet him, to welcome him, to accept his offering with joy as well as relief.

His lips were soft yet firm, warm yet cool, asking but expecting. The kiss was his gift to her, yet one she wanted to share rather than merely receive.

She moved into his embrace, her body coming to rest against his. He was taller by quite a few inches, yet they fit comfortably. It was no strain to tilt her head to meet his kiss. It happened as easily as if she'd done it a thousand times. But she'd never experienced this kiss. No one had or ever would. It was for her alone. A sigh escaped her, and she leaned into Nate's body.

"Is that a sign of approval?"

What a needless question. Would she be virtually wallowing in his embrace if it weren't? "If you think you can do better, you can try again."

Nate chuckled softly into her hair. "I plan to try several times."

Roberta could find nothing objectionable about that or the kiss that followed. She wasn't sure it was better than the first, but it was good enough. Besides, she was too busy enjoying it to bother judging it.

For a man who claimed to have limited experience with women, Nate had managed to learn to kiss quite convincingly. His lips were gentle, encouraging her to be an equal partner in the kiss, but behind that gentleness she could sense sizzling passion held on a tight rein. A passion so fiery, so hard held, it both frightened and aroused her. How was it possible that she had been able to ignite such a fire in this man? What would happen if he ever lost control?

Somehow she knew he never would. Not with her. He nibbled the corner of her mouth and tugged at her lower lip with his teeth. He covered her mouth with his own, only to draw back when her breath started to come in gasps. She had always thought of a kiss as a peck on the cheek or a quick buss on the lips. She had never imagined it could be an experience that could last as long as she wanted, involving not one kiss but an unlimited number delivered in an amazing number of unique ways. The mere thought made her breathless.

Maybe it was the kisses that made her breathless. Or the nearness of Nate's body. Or the rapidly expanding world of possibilities. Or the fact that she loved this man more deeply than she had ever thought possible. Maybe it was everything coming together when she least expected it. Maybe it didn't matter what it was as long as all the reasons had their origin in Nate.

Suddenly she was tired of restraint. She wanted to taste the passion she could feel bubbling beneath the surface. She slid her arms around Nate's neck and pulled him into a kiss that was neither timid nor unsure.

Nate's response was not what she'd expected.

Chapter Seventeen

NATE'S ARMS CLOSED AROUND HER WAIST. LIFTING her off the floor, he pressed their bodies together with such force she could hardly breathe. His mouth came down on hers hungrily, forcing her head backward. There was nothing polite or gentlemanly about his kiss. It was rough, marauding, entirely selfish. It demanded all she could give, took all there was to take. Her mouth felt ravished, her lips bruised, her body held immobile by arms that closed around her like iron bands.

It took only a moment for an answering hunger to gush from her with a strength she would have found incredible if she'd stopped long enough to consider it. Instead, she wrapped herself around Nate and kissed him back with all the strength she could muster. She felt wild, unfettered, abandoned, free. Not once did she stop to think her actions might not be ladylike. Not once did she care if they were. She wanted Nate to know he wasn't the only one who could love deeply, passionately, without reservation.

Her response was visceral. It required no thought, no plan of action, no rationalization. It came from a place that felt primitive, uninhibited, without limits. Nothing was unacceptable as long as it grew out of their love for each other. The more unacceptable it would have been from another man, the more meaningful it was for the two of them. It made everything between them special, unique, unshared, unsampled, in many ways unexpected and unimagined.

Somewhere along the fringes of conscious thought, Roberta was belatedly aware that a door had opened, and she heard the voices of two men in a vigorous argument. Grady and Webb were already in the room before Roberta and Nate could pull more than a fraction of their awareness from each other. The two boys could hardly have looked more stunned if they'd walked in on Roberta and Nate in a carnal embrace. Both tried to make excuses, but all they managed to do was produce a series of unintelligible sounds consisting mostly of gabbling noises and gusty breaths.

Nate released her from his embrace but kept his arm around her waist. "Stop sounding like two pigs fighting over a mud hole and act like men. We were just kissing. If you manage to survive your shock, you'll see me do it again." He turned to Roberta with a sly grin. "As often as she'll let me."

It was an effort for Roberta to appear as unselfconscious as Nate. Her own behavior was mildly shocking to her. To have it observed by the boys was embarrassing. As far as she knew, *nice* women didn't act as she had. She didn't want to change the way she responded to Nate, but she wanted it to remain between the two of them.

Nate released Roberta before turning back to the boys. "What did you want?"

Webb's mouth opened. When nothing came out, he nudged Grady, who jumped like he'd been stuck with a cattle prod. He turned from Webb to Nate, a look of panic in his eyes, before he found his voice. "Uh, nothing. We can talk about it later."

"It's clearly something, or you two wouldn't have burst in here arguing." The boys looked abashed. "You might as well tell me what it is."

Webb seemed unsure, but Nate's smile appeared to reassure him he wasn't about to be physically ejected from the room. "We were trying to figure out why Russ never lets us ride with the rest of the men. We're honored to be asked to make sure nothing happens to you," he hastened to assure Roberta, "but staying at the house all the time makes us feel like Russ doesn't think we can do the work."

"I've wondered the same thing, but I've had so much for you to do here it seemed pointless to bring it up. As soon as I'm sure Roberta isn't in danger, I'll see that you ride with the rest of the crew. Is there anything else you wanted to ask?"

"No!" both boys answered at once. "We'll get back to work."

They practically stumbled over each other getting out of the room. The moment the door closed behind them, Roberta turned to Nate and burst out laughing. Seeing her laugh seemed to set him off. "I thought they were going to faint," she said, when she was finally able to talk. "I've never seen two boys so shocked."

"I expect they'll eat their supper without taking their eyes off their plates," Nate said. "It'll be days before they can look either one of us in the face."

That set Roberta off again.

"They probably thought I was about to disgrace you right here in the middle of the floor."

"The way I was wrapped around you, I'm not surprised." Just remembering caused Roberta to grow warm. Realizing she wanted to do it again made her blush. Nate stepped close and took her hands in his.

"You aren't sorry, are you?"

"No. Just a little embarrassed. I had no idea I could act like that."

Nate smiled. "I take that as a compliment."

"Do you want a rapacious female practically attacking you?"

"You didn't see me trying to run away, did you?"

Roberta grinned. "It's just something I have to get used to."

"You'll grow accustomed more quickly if we practice often. Say at least once an hour."

Roberta pulled her hands from his grasp. "You'll have those boys thinking I'm a woman without principle or decorum."

"They wouldn't dare. They adore you."

"They're afraid of me, you mean."

"Let's just say they have a healthy respect for what I'll do to them if they let anything happen to you."

Remembering what it had cost Carlin to protect her drove all thoughts of romance from her mind. It also reminded her of the danger that seemed to lurk around every corner. She moved away from Nate and turned her gaze toward the window that looked out over the lane leading up to the ranch house. "I'm not sure it's right to ask them to risk their lives for me." She turned back to Nate. "They're just boys. They've got their whole lives before them."

"They won't if they let anything happen to you. I asked them if they wanted me to bring in someone else to guard you. Both assured me they would still watch over you even if I brought in a dozen men. They want to know who killed Carlin as much as we do."

"We're not making any progress, are we?"

"I know who's behind it. We just have to find a way to catch him."

"How?"

"The sheriff is working on it, and every rancher in the county is anxious to prove he's not responsible. We'll find him and everybody who's working with him. It'll just take time."

Roberta wasn't as confident. DiViere had escaped punishment for seven years. Why did Nate think they were going to catch him now, especially after Nate had devoted two years to trying to bring him to justice without success? Nate must have known what she was thinking.

"He's been practically invulnerable since the war. In the beginning, he was shielded by the Union Army. Now he's got the carpetbagger administration throwing a curtain of protection around him. But he's grown more violent, more brazen, less inhibited by fear of consequences. He'll make a mistake, and then we'll catch him."

Roberta was afraid to think of the kind of mistake that would require. DiViere had come close to killing both of them. She felt helpless to aid in catching a man who seemed more a figment of her imagination than flesh and blood. It was only the lack of another suspect that caused the sheriff and the ranchers to accept Nate's belief that diViere was the real villain.

"I want to sell the farm." The words were out of her mouth before she knew she'd made the decision.

Nate was taken by surprise. "Are you sure?"

"Yes." Her thoughts weren't in order yet, but she was certain she'd made the right decision. "It cost my father his life, and it has endangered mine."

"What will you do?"

"I don't know. I just know I can't go back to that farm." She stopped even as the next sentence was forming in her brain. If she didn't go back, wouldn't that mean she was giving up, letting the attackers win? She had sworn she wouldn't leave until they found her father's killer. If the attacks were somehow tied to the farm, selling it might mean never knowing who or why. She suddenly felt weighted down by an unmovable burden. "I have to go back. I have to rebuild the house, plant the fields."

At first she expected Nate to argue with her, but she realized he'd known all along she would go back. He'd also known why.

"I'll help you."

"I have to do this alone."

"You can decide what kind of house you want, what to plant in which fields, even whether to rebuild the dam, but you can't believe for one minute that

I'll allow you to go to that farm alone. I don't know what kind of twisted reasoning has caused Laveau to focus his hatred on you, but he won't give up."

"I'm a grown woman. I can take care of myself."

"I'm a grown man, and I love you. That makes it my job to make sure nothing happens to you."

Roberta decided she could accept that line of reasoning.

❧

"Boone is trying to pretend he hasn't spent the last year telling everybody you were going to marry him. Prudence told him to stop making a fool of himself, that her memory hadn't failed even if his had."

Roberta welcomed Blossom's visit, but she was surprised Carl had accompanied her. Even more surprising, Carl's attention was focused more on Blossom than Roberta.

"He still can't believe you turned him down," Blossom added. "He thinks he's the most eligible man in Slender Creek, and any other woman would jump at the chance to marry him."

"I wasn't in love with him."

"Boone doesn't understand the concept of love. To him, marriage is the joining of assets—pretty much the same as a successful business alliance."

"He told me he was too busy to get married right now," Carl informed Roberta. "He's considering opening a bank to compete with Otis Parker."

"Between the saloon and his restaurant, he collects more cash in a week than anybody in town," Blossom added.

"Doesn't he pay most of it out in wages and purchasing supplies?" Nate asked.

Blossom winked at Roberta before turning back to Nate. "He's just making noise to detract people from talking about how Roberta prefers you to him. Boone can't stand to come in second."

Roberta tried not to blush. She was sure a lot of people believed she was doing a lot more than *preferring* Nate to Boone, but she was uncomfortable having it mentioned so openly.

"When are you going to announce your engagement?" Blossom asked.

"I haven't asked Roberta to marry me so there's no engagement to announce."

Blossom didn't hide her surprise. "Don't try to tell me you aren't in love with each other."

"We won't," Nate said.

"And she's practically living in your house."

"She's here so I can protect her," Nate said. "And she's going to stay here until this is over."

"I understand that, but not everybody in Slender Creek does."

"If Prudence has been telling people Roberta is doing anything she shouldn't—"

Blossom didn't let him finish. "Prudence has defended Roberta. She cornered Sally Erskine in the general store yesterday and accused her of spreading malicious gossip. She told Sally she'd make her life a living hell if she said one more word against Roberta. She finished by saying Roberta wouldn't be having a seven-month baby who weighed nearly nine pounds."

Roberta didn't feel the slightest inclination to join in Nate's amusement at Sally's discomfiture. She was horrified her personal life was the subject of widespread gossip.

"Roberta knows I want to marry her," Nate told Blossom, "but she doesn't feel she can make that decision as long as she doesn't know who wants her dead."

Blossom looked hard at Nate. "Then you've got to find who it is. I don't like what people are saying any more than Prudence."

"Me either," Carl added.

"I know Laveau is behind it all," Nate said. "What I don't know is why he targeted Roberta and her father. Even more important, I don't know what locals are helping him."

Blossom insisted no one within a hundred miles would do such terrible things, but Nate told her if she'd been in the war, she wouldn't say that. When Carl agreed with Nate, Blossom turned to Roberta. "I guess every man in the county has been in the saloon at one time or another. There's not one I met who would try to burn you in your bed."

"Laveau did that." Nate didn't equivocate. "I'm sure he killed Carlin, too. I suspect he killed Roberta's father, but we won't have any way to prove it until we find out who's helping him."

"There might be a dozen men who'd set fire to a barn or trample crops for money, including some of the men who work with Russ." When Nate looked thoughtful, Blossom asked, "Do you suspect anyone?"

"No, but I think all the ranchers, including myself, have made a mistake in thinking we know where our men are all the time. Roberta has told me my obsession with Laveau has kept me from becoming part of the community. It has also kept me from paying attention to my own ranch. I've let Russ do virtually all the hiring. I don't even know the men who work for me."

"It's up to you and the other men in Slender Creek to catch whoever is behind it," Blossom stated. "I don't like knowing there's a murderer around. I could have been talking to him in the saloon."

"You won't find Laveau in a saloon unless he's planning something," Nate said. "He considers himself an aristocrat."

Blossom sniffed. "Then I certainly haven't seen him. The men I meet think more of their horses than of themselves."

They talked for a while longer without coming to any conclusions. "Are you coming to church this week?" Blossom asked Roberta when she rose to go.

"I don't know."

"People are concerned about you. Not everybody is as mean-spirited as Sally Erskine."

"She can go if she wants," Nate offered. "If necessary, I'll take every man on the place to make sure she's safe."

❧

As it turned out, that wasn't necessary. Every rancher in the county sent a few cowhands. Roberta ended up being escorted by more than twenty riders. The townspeople apparently took the phalanx of riders as proof that the ranchers believed her safety was the only reason she was at Nate's spread. Not even the most inveterate gossiper was ready to pit herself against such a show of force.

Roberta was nearly overcome by the warm reception. She welcomed Mrs. Pender's genuine concern and blushed when the doctor whispered that being locked away with Nate twenty-four hours a day was a perfect opportunity to get him to the altar before some enterprising woman stole him away. She was pleased to discover the ranchers were as concerned about her safety as they were about having their names cleared of suspicion. The preacher even praised her for bringing to church twenty men who'd never previously darkened its doors. Not used to such attention, she was relieved when the service ended. But rather than make her escape to the ranch, Nate said he was taking her to eat at Boone's restaurant. After that, they were going to see the sheriff. Nate said it was time they came up with a way to end the stalemate.

Roberta had rarely eaten at Boone's restaurant. Nate never had. Their appearance together was something of a minor social event. Within twenty minutes the restaurant was filled with people Roberta was sure hadn't eaten there more often than she had. What surprised her most was that nearly everyone spoke to her, offered to help any way they could, and said they hoped the guilty people would soon be found so she wouldn't have to live in fear. Roberta had never felt that she was part of the community, but it was apparent the people of Slender Creek did. Still, she was relieved when the meal was over. She was uncomfortable knowing everyone in the room was watching her, wondering what she was thinking, coming up with their own version of the relationship between her and Nate.

The sheriff wasn't happy to see them.

"It's Sunday," he complained when he answered the door.

"Murder never takes a day off," Nate told him.

"Come in," the sheriff grudgingly invited. "My wife has gone to visit her sister."

"This isn't a social visit," Nate reminded him.

Roberta had never felt particularly nostalgic about the house she left in Virginia or the farmhouse her father had built, but frilly curtains at the windows of the sheriff's home, knotted rag rugs scattered over the board floor, comfortable chairs in soft colors, and decorative touches that softened the edges of western austerity made her long for a real home of her own. It was feminine without losing any of the strength and individualism associated with Texas. For the first time, she didn't feel like Texas was an alien land.

"What have you got in mind?" the sheriff asked as soon as they were seated.

"We need to think of something that will bring the attackers out in the open. As long as they stay in hiding, there's no chance of catching them. You know I believe Laveau has someone locally helping him."

"I don't agree with you, but let's forget that for the moment."

"Every rancher needs to know where his cowhands are every hour of every day. If that means checking on them in the middle of the night, that's what they have to do. If it means bringing them in from the range so they can sleep in the bunkhouse, they have to do that as well. I'm including myself," Nate added before the sheriff could object. "I've been more negligent than anyone. I can't expect the other ranchers to do something I'm not willing to do myself."

"They're not going to like it, but they'll do it," the sheriff said. "When you insisted somebody local had to be involved, they started suspecting each other."

"Laveau is not going to step out in the open, so our only choice is to find out who's helping him."

"So how do you plan to draw them out of hiding?"

"I'm going to rebuild my house," Roberta said. "Do you have a better suggestion?"

"If this Laveau character is really after one or both of you, you could be the bait in a trap."

"That's an option I'm willing to consider, but not with Roberta," Nate said. "Laveau is really after me. I feel guilty that I've somehow caused her family to suffer through no fault of their own."

"She could sell her ranch and leave. That would solve everybody's problem."

Roberta disagreed. "Someone killed my father and Carlin, and tried to kill me. That won't change regardless of where Nate might go."

The sheriff didn't look pleased "Neither one of you lives in Slender Creek, but you've brought your troubles down on us."

Nate's reaction was instantaneous. "If you don't like your job, or are afraid to do it, you ought to resign. You were hired to defend everyone in the county, not just the people who live in town."

For a moment Roberta was afraid the two men would get into an argument, but the sheriff backed down. Maybe he recognized that as a veteran of the war, Nate wouldn't respect anyone who appeared reluctant to face danger. Maybe he realized others might think like Nate.

"Let me know when you start rebuilding," the sheriff said. "I'll see about getting someone to watch at night."

"The ranchers have volunteered to help any way they can," Roberta told him.

"Do they know you intend to rebuild?"

"Yes."

"But you don't trust any of them, do you?"

"Until I know who's helping diViere, I won't know who I can trust."

"That's if this Laveau character is involved like you think he is."

"You'd better hope so," Nate told him. "If not, you've got a cold-blooded murderer living in Slender Creek."

Roberta could tell there was something different about this evening. It wasn't just that Nate looked at her differently. She *felt* different. And not just because she was wearing a new dress. Not just because Nate seemed more handsome than ever. There came a point in every relationship when it either made that essential leap forward, or it began a slow retreat.

She had been at Nate's ranch for more than a week, long enough for the initial uneasiness to wear off. Long enough for the initial excitement to fade. Long enough for her confinement to cause boredom to set in. Long enough for her to become impatient to leave.

None of that had happened. Every moment with him increased her desire for more time to spend with him. The more she knew about him, the more she wanted to know. He rarely mentioned his brother—he *never* mentioned his parents—but she knew they had cast a shadow over him that he hadn't been able to shake. She was determined to discover the hold they had on him and break it. But that was for another time. Tonight was to be enjoyed for whatever promise it would bring.

Nate looked at her across the table. "Would you like anything else to eat?"

"I think I'd better stop. It was a delicious dinner, and I don't want to spoil it."

Benny had spent every afternoon for the last week preparing a series of dinners so extravagant each one surpassed the previous one. According to Grady, the hands hardly knew what they were eating. Roberta wasn't familiar with everything, either—Benny's Italian heritage had found its way into his food—but it was all delicious.

"More wine?"

That was the newest addition. Nate was used to wine because it was part of Cade's wife's Spanish and French heritage. From what she knew of the effects of beer and liquor, Roberta had approached it with trepidation. She was surprised to find she liked it. "I haven't finished my glass."

"Why don't we take it on the porch? It's a lovely evening."

Since going to church for the first time, they had been to town twice. They had also started spending time outside the house, even though Nate didn't like to venture farther than the porch or a walk around the house for a little exercise. Roberta leaned against the porch rail and looked out over the flat prairie that spread before her in all directions. Not long ago it had looked like an alien landscape. She had missed her Virginia mountains often shrouded in a blue haze. She felt the absence of the tree-covered hills that protected her small town from the winter winds that whistled down the valley. She missed the colors of fall and the snow that often covered the ground at Christmas.

Somehow, without her knowing it, that had changed. The mountains had become roadblocks that closed her off from the rest of the world, the changing leaves a harbinger of a long, difficult winter.

The Texas prairie, once a barren and inhospitable landscape, had taken on a new character. Its openness was an invitation to become part of its heartbeat. The brown of winter was offset by the burst of color that heralded the arrival of spring, the gnarled, sturdy oaks a testimonial to their survival. Even the lowly cactus, a plant she once considered one of nature's least desirable creations, had become a fellow traveler that offered flowers and fruit. And the grass, the countless miles of it that waved in the spring breeze and braved the summer heat, the foundation of an economy that depended on cows to survive.

Now that she had come to understand this place called Texas, she could see its roughness was an essential part of its strength, could respect the perseverance required of those who chose to make it their home, could accept its bounty without bemoaning that which it withheld.

"What are you looking at?" Nate asked.

"At so much I never saw before."

"Is that a good thing?"

She turned and smiled. "It's a very good thing. I don't know why I could never see any of this before."

Nate came to stand beside her. "What do you see?"

"That Texas is a place I could learn to call home."

"What has changed?"

The answer was simple. "You."

"I don't understand."

She smiled again, cupped his cheek with her hand. He didn't understand his own worth, something else she intended to change. "I wanted to go back to Virginia because I was trying to recapture the past. It took seeing Carl to realize the past existed more in my imagination than in reality. I blamed Texas for the trouble over the dam, my father's death, my not becoming part of the community. I failed to see that it's the people who matter, not where you live. Most important of all, I failed to see you for who you are."

Nate looked so surprised she leaned forward to give him a quick kiss. Instead, Nate reached for her, folded her into a crushing embrace, and kissed her with such force she was certain her lips would be bruised. But all thought of that was swept away by the passion behind the kiss, by the heat that roared through her with the speed of a wildfire. Her words had unleashed some hard-held emotion that exploded from its captivity inside Nate with such force that his whole body shook. A moment later, he realized he was holding Roberta with uncomfortable pressure. He released her, shocked at what he'd done.

"I didn't mean to hurt you. Do you want to go inside?"

"It only hurt a little. Anyway, I don't want to go inside. I might miss the chance you'd kiss me like that again."

He looked confused. "I hurt you. Don't deny it."

"You couldn't kiss me like that unless your feelings for me were so strong you couldn't control them. Do you know how wonderful it is to know I can instill such feelings in a man like you? It makes me feel important, powerful, no longer *a woman people ignore.*"

Surprise held him silent a moment. "How can I make you feel powerful? I'm not important. I've never done anything worth remembering."

"You did several things important to me. You gave my father good advice, defended him against the other ranchers, and encouraged him to stand his ground. And you forgave me for shooting you."

"That was nothing."

"You sent Carlin, Grady, and Webb to help me rebuild my barn and stand watch over me. When that wasn't enough, you brought me to your ranch and reordered everything for my safety and comfort."

"I'm in love with you. I'd have to kill anybody who hurt you."

"Don't you understand what it means to have a man feel that strongly about you, to do that much for you even when he should have been concentrating on recovering from a gunshot wound?"

"Any man would do the same."

"Any man didn't. *You* did." She couldn't tell whether he didn't believe her or was *afraid* to believe her. "You've spent your life doing things for other people. Taking care of your brother, fighting in the war, helping your friend defend his ranch from squatters, and trying to bring Laveau to justice for things he's done to others, some of them strangers you've never seen. You helped my father, and now you're helping me. You're even trying to help the ranchers prove they weren't responsible for my father's death."

"Is that how you see what I've done?" The idea seemed incredible to him.

"How else can I see it?"

"That I failed to protect my brother or bring Laveau to justice."

"No one succeeds at everything. What's most important is that you tried."

"Do you *really* believe that?"

"Yes. Besides, you convinced me you're the most wonderful man in Texas, and I'd be a fool to let anyone else marry you."

His smile was slow in coming, but when it finally bloomed, his blue eyes sparkled with happiness. "So you've finally decided to marry me. Since Prudence dislikes men, I was beginning to think I might have to settle for Blossom."

The idea of Prudence and Nate together threatened to pitch Roberta into a fit of giggles. "You thought no such thing. You knew I was in love with you. I told you."

"You said you can't marry me yet. That gives you plenty of time to wiggle out of your commitment."

Being reminded of her refusal to marry him drew a cloud over her mood. "I'm sorry, but I just can't do it."

"I won't rush you, but I do have a request."

"What is that?"

"Will you make love to me?"

Chapter Eighteen

IN THAT MOMENT, ROBERTA KNEW WHAT WAS different about this evening. She hadn't had the courage to put it into words, but she wanted to make love to Nate. It didn't matter that Prudence would be horrified, that the women of Slender Creek would disapprove, that some would say it was what she'd been doing all along. She loved Nate and wanted to be with him in this most meaningful way. It annoyed her that he could put this change in their relationship into words when she couldn't.

How should she answer? A simple yes couldn't express how much she looked forward to being in his arms. A mere look or a nod of her head was cowardly, indicative of a reluctance she didn't feel. Yet a lot of words were unnecessary. "I was hoping you would ask me."

He seemed unprepared for her quick acceptance.

"If you didn't believe I wanted to make love to you as much as you wanted to make love to me, why would you ask?"

"Women don't always express their love the way men do."

Roberta repressed a laugh. "I'm not going to ask you to explain that."

Nate breathed a sigh of relief. "Good. I was trying to decide whether to claim a sudden illness or state that I'd heard a noise I needed to investigate."

Roberta did laugh. "I'd rather you tell me why you chose this night."

"I've been thinking about it for days but telling myself I couldn't say anything because it might scare you away. Tonight the words came out on their own."

"Are you saying you're so deeply in love with me you can't control your own words?"

"I wasn't going to put it that way, but that just about describes it. If I could *say* the things I want to say, *do* the things I want to do, you'd probably saddle a horse and ride straight to town."

The sun had disappeared beyond the horizon leaving the earth swathed in a bluish haze that deepened the shadows and turned the trees into inky splotches set against the orange-streaked sky. The heat of the day had begun to subside, hastened on its way by a gentle breeze.

"I promise to hear you out before I decide whether to stay or run away."

Nate took her hands. "I know you won't run away. I'm just afraid of asking too much."

"I've said I want to make love to you. What more could be too much?"

"You're not here by choice. You're living in fear of being harmed without reason. The situation has given rise to a lot of cruel speculation. Under the circumstances, anything I say or do could be too much."

Roberta squeezed Nate's hands and tugged them to her breast. "The events of last few weeks have forced me to learn a lot in a short time. I know what I want to do with the farm right now, and what I want to do with it in the future. I know why I thought I wanted to go back to Virginia, and I know why I thought I disliked Texas. Most important, I know I'm in love with you, that I want to be your wife, and that I want to make love to you as soon as you'll let me. What other people think of my choices isn't important. Only what you think."

Nate tugged his hands from Roberta's grasp, put them around her waist, and pulled her to him. "I never thought the day would come when a woman would say that to me. That you should be that woman… well, it takes my breath away. I don't know what I've done to deserve you, but if you'll tell me what it was, I promise to do it as often as possible."

"You're supposed to make me tremble with passion, not shake with laughter."

"I mean it with every fiber of my being."

"I know. I just find it hard to believe anybody can care that much about what I think."

"Even the man who loves you?"

"Nobody has ever loved me the way you do. It'll take some time to get used to."

"I'm not sure I'll ever get used to it."

"Let's make a pact. Whenever one of us says or does something wonderful or unexpected, no matter how far it is from anything we ever believed could happen, we will do our best to… no… we *will* believe it."

Nate's hold on her tightened. "We will not doubt that we deserve to be loved as few people have been loved. We will listen to no one but each other. We won't hesitate to say we could live a day without each other but fervently hope we'll never have to. Now let's seal all we've promised with a kiss."

Roberta didn't need any prompting. She had been yearning to wrap her arms around Nate's neck and pull him down into a kiss of such power she'd feel weak in the knees. Nor did the kiss disappoint her. It was neither subtle nor tentative. It reached out and claimed her for its own. There was no room for hesitation, no possibility of resistance. She yielded willingly.

She hadn't thought it possible, but this kiss was different from all the rest. Its meaning didn't come from the power or the passion behind it, but rather from their embracing a love that needed no explanation, justification, or ratification. It was complete in itself, binding them together with a permanence beyond that of ceremonies or documents. When they broke the kiss, she felt as if final approval had been granted to their union. Without a word, they turned and went inside.

Roberta had never seen Nate's bedroom. Like the rest of the house, it contained no pictures or personal items that reflected the man who lived there. The dull yellow walls were bare, flat surfaces empty, bedspread and chair coverings plain, colors predominantly shades of brown. The room might be in character with the man Nate used to be, but it had nothing in common with the man he'd become.

The single lighted lamp by the bedside cast the room in a pale yellow glow that hinted at a welcome, a bit of warmth, and a softening of the near emptiness of the room.

Nate's kisses were gentle and persuasive, inviting her to join him as he explored what it meant to belong completely to another person. He placed kisses at random spots—her lips, the corner of her mouth, her cheek, nose, ears, and back to her mouth—before pausing to give her an opportunity to do the same.

She had to stand on her tiptoes and pull his head down. She liked that he was tall. She liked even better that he was within reach. She'd never thought to explore the possibilities of a kiss like this, but was eager to begin. His lips were soft, his cheeks rough, his forehead smooth, his nose teasing. She especially liked the feel of him, the power in his arms, the breadth of his shoulders, the firmness of his back. She liked leaning against that strength, being wrapped in it, being protected by it. She loved the freedom to explore him even as he explored her. It not only signified that she was an equal in this relationship, it opened to her the excitement of claiming as her own the body of the man nature had created for her.

By this simple gesture, Nate had opened himself to her and had said: *I am yours. Take me.*

Roberta felt humbled by the enormity of such a gift. At the same time, she was aware of the enormous responsibility such a gift brought with it. She had always assumed she would place all that she was in the hands of the man she married, to be loved and valued any way he chose. She hadn't imagined he would do the same.

Breaking off the last kiss, she wrapped her arms around him, moved into his welcoming embrace, and rested her head on his shoulder. There was something about being close to him, about pressing her body against his, that confirmed what she was feeling. There was warmth, security, strength, a place to belong, a place where she fit. And the questions and worries were held at bay. She felt at peace. Safe.

Nate started to work the buttons on the back of her dress, but she didn't have much thought to give to that when he was nuzzling her neck, scattering kisses along her jaw, and tugging provocatively on her earlobe. The experience was novel and exhilarating. She'd never thought kisses on her neck could kindle such sensations in her any more than she'd attributed the same capability to her earlobes. Or her back. Or any other place Nate chose to kiss or touch. Her body was host to several small fires that threatened to unite and turn into a conflagration.

Her mother had never told her that being in love and being held by a man could be like this. Her father had never talked about love at all. Blossom hadn't talked about anything other than the practical advantages of marriage. Except for Joe, Prudence had treated all men like a plague. How could Roberta have anticipated such a wondrous experience? It was impossible to think rationally. It was hard to think at all. She didn't even want to. She wanted to abandon herself to the moment, to luxuriate in everything sensual, for fear it would never be like this again.

She didn't realize Nate had finished unfastening the buttons at the back of her dress until he slipped it off one shoulder and covered the newly exposed flesh with kisses. Tremors raced through her body causing her to lean against Nate for support. Weakness invaded her limbs, yet she was buoyed by an energy that burned through her like a smoldering fire. She offered no resistance when he slipped the dress from her other shoulder and let it fall to her waist.

Gathering what little of her wits she could summon, she began to unbutton Nate's shirt. The kisses he planted on her neck and scattered down her arms caused her fingers to fumble, but the sight of Nate's bare chest kept her at her task. The scar from his gunshot wound momentarily startled her, but placing her hands flat against his warm skin enabled her to overcome her shyness.

She had never touched a man in this way. She wasn't sure she'd even thought of doing it. It was a kind of intimacy she hadn't thought possible… or even desirable. She'd been wrong. It was quite possible and very desirable. She let her hands play over Nate's chest, luxuriating in the warmth of him, soaking up the feel of him, marveling at the play of muscles under his skin, drinking in the sight of him as she pushed the shirt off his shoulders. It was an exotic experience, something completely alien to her, but something she wanted to do for the rest of her life.

She lost her way when Nate turned his attentions to her breasts. When he undid her shift, she was prepared to feel his hands on her sensitive skin, not his mouth. She gasped for breath, her body went rigid, her hands froze in place.

"Did I hurt you?"

It was a struggle to utter the single syllable, "No." Thoroughly aroused, her body responded on its own to a stimulation that was at once unanticipated and nearly unbearable in its intensity. She moved against Nate until he took her nipple in his mouth. Lost to sensation, she found herself removing clothing until she stood naked.

Nate seemed almost as surprised as she was, but not so astonished he couldn't remove his own clothes nearly as quickly.

Nate was beautiful. And he was frightening. Over the years she'd come up with various hazy images of how she thought the perfect man would look. That image had become concrete when she fell in love with Nate. It became luminous in its beauty as he stood before her. It was his arousal that made her edgy. It looked more like a weapon than an instrument of love.

"I won't hurt you."

She struggled to believe him.

"If anything makes you uncomfortable, let me know and I'll stop."

She couldn't imagine stopping now. Not even her trepidation could make her draw back.

Nate drew her over to the bed. He lay down and invited her to lie beside him. Roberta steeled herself for what would happen next. Her anxieties were calmed when Nate took her in his arms and kissed her deeply. He continued to kiss her as his hands moved over her breasts, along her side, across her back, and down to her thighs. His touch was a gentle caress, but it left a trail of flame in its wake that enveloped her body, until she was unable to remain still. She didn't know what to do, how to tell him. On one hand she wanted the torment to stop. On the other, she hoped it would never end. She alternately pressed against him then pulled away.

When his hand moved between her thighs, she was certain she wanted to roll away. Instead, she pressed forward to meet him. When his finger invaded her, she intended to flee but found herself wanting more. When that came, she wasn't sure she would survive. She jumped so sharply Nate withdrew.

"I hurt you."

"No." She tried to explain, but she wouldn't have been able to get the words out even if she'd been able to put them together.

Nate pulled away. "Maybe we'd better not—"

"No!" She pulled him to her. "Don't stop. It didn't hurt. I just didn't expect it to be so... powerful." That wasn't the right word, but she couldn't think of a term that combined explosive force with mind-numbing pleasure. She didn't want to try. She just wanted to feel that way again. When he placed his hand on her hip, she moved it lower. When he was reluctant to enter her, she pushed against him.

She braced herself for an explosive force. Instead she felt a gentle, sweet pleasure that grew steadily until it flooded her whole being with a yearning that was a combination of pleasure and an aching need for release. She felt suspended between the two, waiting for the tension to break.

When it did, rather than feel let down, she was sent spinning into the air only to float gently back to earth. As she did, Nate entered her.

Before she could be fearful that she couldn't contain him, he began a gentle movement within her that started her soaring once more. She rose to meet him, fell away, and rose again. Gradually she fell deeper and deeper into the embrace of an experience that seemed to take her out of herself, to separate her from the world that surrounded her. Then she gradually lost contact with her body. All that remained was a cauldron of acutely heightened sensual pleasures that threatened to shatter her being and scatter it to the winds.

When it finally did shatter, she felt disembodied, like a light that burst into a fierce glow in a dark world. She was vaguely aware of Nate reaching his climax and joining her in the knowledge that she had been transformed. In this moment, she had been created anew.

❧

A knock on the door awakened Roberta. In the same moment she remembered making love to Nate the previous evening, she realized she was in her own bedroom. She was also naked. She was surprised she hadn't come awake when Nate moved her. She certainly would have if he'd attempted to redress her.

Benny's muffled voice came from the other side of the door. "The boss said not to wake you, but you've been asleep so long I got worried."

"I'm fine. I just overslept."

"The coffee's hot. I'll fix your breakfast when you're ready."

"Give me about twenty minutes."

"No problem."

She didn't need that much time to get dressed, but she needed every minute to adjust to what had happened the previous evening. It would take time to absorb it mentally and emotionally. She already felt different physically. She was a little sore, but she felt more alive than ever. She had twice her usual energy. She would try to talk Nate into letting her go into town or at least go for a ride. She couldn't imagine staying indoors all day.

Nate had placed her clothes on a chair. She slipped into her shift but decided to wear a different dress. She wondered if seeing Nate would be awkward. She didn't want to act like nothing had happened, that nothing had changed, yet she didn't know what to say. Having to keep it a secret was awkward, but in a way that made it even more special. It was something the rest of the world couldn't share. It was just for the two of them.

Several things had changed. She would have to reconsider her refusal to marry Nate until after her father's killer had been caught. Then there was the question of whether to stay in Texas. She didn't dislike Texas as much as she had thought, but what was she going to do about diViere? As long as Nate stayed in Texas, he wouldn't be able to ignore the threat that man posed. Even if he promised not to go after diViere, diViere might still come after him. She could live in Texas, but she couldn't marry Nate knowing he would either kill diViere or be killed by him. Nate had said he would consider moving to Virginia, but would he think that was running away? Nate wasn't a coward, and she could never do anything that would make him feel like one.

It took a few minutes to dress and brush her hair, but when she left the room, her mind was still unsettled. Her love for Nate was greater than ever, but the problems separating them hadn't changed.

Nate had told Webb and Grady to be ready to ride out that morning, but he couldn't leave before he'd seen Roberta. He hadn't pushed her into making love, but he needed to make sure she had no regrets. Last night had convinced him he had to do everything he could to talk her into marrying him as soon as possible. They might never find her father's killer, and he couldn't imagine spending the rest of his life without her. He was certain she felt the same about him, but he knew catching her father's murderer was vitally important to her. He didn't want that or anything else to come between them.

"It's been more than twenty minutes," he said to Benny.

"Women aren't too good with clocks," the cook answered. "My mother wouldn't even look at one."

Benny was Italian. Roberta was American. That wasn't the same. Was she late because she was reluctant to face him? Would she feel ashamed if others knew they'd spent the night together? He had worried about that last night when he carried her from his bed back to her room. Should he have waited until they were married to make love to her? He wasn't sure he could have. It had been a strain to wait as long as he had. Worrying wasn't going to solve anything, though he would have the answer the instant she entered the room.

"My coffee's cold," Nate noted.

"I'm making some more," Benny said. "It has gotten stronger than Miss Roberta likes it."

Grady and Webb liked Roberta, but Benny practically idolized her. If she had asked for some exotic food, Benny would have ransacked Texas to find it. Nate tensed when he heard Roberta's footsteps approaching the room. Benny spoke first.

"I've got fresh coffee," he announced the moment Roberta stepped through the door. "It'll be ready as soon as you sit down."

"I hope you've made a big breakfast. I'm famished."

The minute Roberta flashed her usual smile at Benny, Nate knew everything was all right. When she smiled at him, he knew things were going to be even better than that.

"Eggs, sliced ham, roasted potatoes, and hot bread. I can fix more if you want."

Roberta rewarded Benny with a huge smile. "That's more than enough. I hope Nate realizes how fortunate he is to have you. I think you ought to ask him for a raise."

Benny blushed so furiously Nate laughed. "I'd double his salary if his cooking could convince you to marry me tomorrow."

Benny looked horrified. "No woman can get

married that quickly. My sister took six months. She would have taken twice that long if her husband hadn't threatened to find another bride."

"I have no family, only three dresses, and no house," Roberta told him. "I could get married now."

"It would take me a week just to fix the food. Then you have to decide whether to get married here or in the church." Benny was growing more Italian by the moment. His hands were as much in motion as his mouth. "And who is going to handle all the decorations? And you have to have a dress. No bride can get married in an old dress."

Nate hadn't thought about wedding preparations, but it was clear Benny would never forgive either of them if he wasn't an integral part of the preparations. And it looked like Nate's notion of a simple ceremony was just that, a foolish notion. He really didn't care. He'd wait as long as he must to marry Roberta.

"You don't have to worry about any of that just yet," Roberta told Benny. "I'm not marrying anybody tomorrow or next week. I promise to give you at least a week's notice when I do."

"I don't think a week will be enough." Benny busied himself getting Roberta's breakfast, but that didn't stop him from listing at least two dozen things he considered essential to any wedding. Nate would have been alarmed if Roberta hadn't given him a shy smile and winked. All was well.

"After breakfast I'm going to take the boys and ride out to where Russ and the rest of the crew are working," Nate said when Benny set Roberta's breakfast before her. "We'll probably be gone most of the day, which will give you plenty of time to discuss wedding plans. My only request is that you choose the earliest date possible."

⁂

"We aren't headed to where Russ said they were working," Grady told Nate when they rode away from the ranch house.

"I thought we'd ride over as much of the ranch as we can before joining Russ and the rest of the crew," Nate told him. "I want to see a lot more than just what Russ is doing. You two don't know any more about the place than I do."

"That's because Russ doesn't think we can do the work," Grady complained.

"I told him he wouldn't know until he let us try," Webb added. "But he said he didn't have time to waste on three overgrown kids."

Webb's inadvertent reference to Carlin caused the boys to fall silent. They felt as guilty about not being the one on guard that night as Nate did about sending the boy into Laveau's path. "I have confidence in your abilities, or I wouldn't have hired you," Nate told them.

Nate didn't know that he'd ever felt happier with his life or more optimistic about his future. He was in love with a woman who loved him as much in return. He had made enough connections in the community that he no longer felt like an outsider. On top of that, he had the best ranch in the area and the most loyal crew. Considering that he'd neglected all of that because of his obsession with Laveau, he didn't deserve to be so lucky. He'd have to do better in the future. He couldn't depend on luck all the time.

The spring rains had been heavier than usual and the temperatures had been cooler. The carpets of bluebonnets that covered the hills earlier had faded, but the colorful heads of Indian paintbrush, gaillardia, coreopsis, and an occasional white poppy were scattered through the grasses and the prickly pear cactus that appeared in rocky outcroppings. A flock of wild turkeys had the boys talking of roast turkey and dressing, while a poky armadillo elicited only scorn. Groves of post oaks provided shade from the heat of the sun, while rivulets of cool water trickled down from hills covered with maple and hickory trees. On a day such as this, how could anything go wrong?

The first crack in perfection appeared when Nate came upon a yearling with an unfamiliar brand. It wasn't unusual for cattle from several ranches to mix during the winter, or for a rancher to have cattle bearing more than one brand. Nate hadn't paid attention to his ranch like he should, but he had learned the brands of all the neighboring ranchers. This wasn't one of them.

"Have you seen this brand before?" he asked the boys.

"No," Grady replied.

"Have any ranchers bought new herds since I was here last year?"

"Not that I heard," Webb replied. "Maybe it's a stray from another county."

That was the most probable explanation, but it didn't satisfy Nate. The yearling looked too young to have wandered that far from its mother. He was trying to put that out of his mind and pay attention to the condition of the range and the grazing cattle when he came upon another yearling with the same brand. When they sighted a third, there was only one possible explanation.

Someone was attempting to steal cattle by branding newly weaned calves. Once the calf had left its mother, it was impossible to tell who owned it.

"Boss, I don't think those yearlings wandered in from another county," Brady said.

"I think somebody's trying to steal your cows," Webb chimed in.

Nate had already reached that conclusion. It was the implications that flowed from that conclusion that now occupied his mind.

First, if anyone was branding his cattle, Russ should have known about it and put a stop to it. Also, he should have told Nate about it and warned the other ranchers. There were two possible reasons Russ hadn't done that. One, Russ didn't know about the branding. Nate considered that unlikely. He'd found these three yearlings in the space of half an hour. He was sure there were more. Russ and the rest of the crew were out on the range every day. It was highly unlikely that none of them had sighted these year-lings. The other possibility was that Russ *did* know about the branding and hadn't said anything. For that to make sense, Russ would have to benefit in some way. And the most logical way for him to profit was to be doing the branding himself.

"What are you thinking, boss?" Brady asked.

"That I've been a fool."

He could make excuses for his failure to oversee his own ranch—he was off looking for Laveau; he was recovering from a gunshot wound; he was falling in love and trying to convince Roberta to marry him—but he knew none of those reasons exonerated him. Other ranchers had done more and still knew what was happening on their ranches and in their bunkhouses.

A series of possibilities lay before him, some of which made the hair on the back of his neck stand up. The most alarming was that Russ had to know he couldn't hide the branding for long, that once Nate was back in the saddle he was certain to find these calves. Either Russ had made no attempt to keep the calves in an out-of-the-way part of the ranch, or he'd been careless and let these three escape. Russ was *never* careless, so why did he believe he didn't need to hide the calves? Because Nate would never see them. Why would Nate never see them?

Because Nate would be dead!

"What's wrong, boss?" Webb asked. "You look like you've seen a ghost."

"Is it your wound?" Grady wanted to know. "Maybe we ought to go back."

"I'm thinking."

"About what?"

"I'll let you know in a minute."

How could Russ get rid of Nate in a way that wouldn't throw suspicion on himself? One was to have Nate implicated in the murder of Robert Tryon. Another would be to have Laveau murder him while he was recovering in Roberta's house. A third would have been to make it appear he hadn't recovered from his wound. It was the connection with Laveau that he found hardest to accept. If Nate was right, while he was off looking for Laveau, the bastard was right here making plans to destroy him. And using his own foreman and crew to do it! Worst of all, an innocent man died. If Russ was involved in the fire that nearly killed Roberta, that made it two innocent men.

It was hard to accept all this, but there were too many questions to ignore. Why hadn't Russ introduced the new crew members to Nate? Why had he insisted that they eat in the bunkhouse? Why hadn't he allowed the men Nate hired to work with the men Russ had hired? Why had he insisted that Roberta was trying to poison Nate?

Too many conjectures based on speculation. Nate would have dismissed most of them if it hadn't been for the connection with Laveau. Once that man was involved, anything was possible, no matter how unbelievable. If the worst was true, what was he going to do about it?

The first thing was to make sure Roberta was protected. If what he thought was true, she wasn't safe at the ranch. Once her safety was assured, he would have to find a way to catch Russ in the act of branding his calves with a brand Russ had undoubtedly registered in his own name. Hopefully, a threat of hanging would induce him to reveal Laveau's part in the attacks. If it had been Laveau who killed both men, not even the corrupt governor could save him.

Having made his decision, Nate told the boys, "We're heading back to the house."

During the ride back, Nate told them what he'd been thinking. Neither of the boys liked Russ, but they couldn't believe he would be involved in anything so terrible. They asked questions and raised objections, but by the time they had unsaddled their horses and turned them into the corral, they agreed that Nate was probably right.

"What do you want us to do?"

The boys were still young, but Nate was proud of how they'd matured, how they were eager to be involved in what came next. "I need proof of the crew's involvement in the attacks as well as the rustling. I can't ask you boys to search the bunk-house, so I'll do that. I need to know if they're doing the branding in one place or wherever they happen to find a likely weanling. Do you think one of you could follow them without being caught?"

"I'll do it," Webb volunteered.

"Grady, I want you to mix with the crew when they come in. Don't do anything that will attract attention. Just listen for something that might tell us what's going on. Roberta has announced that she's going to rebuild her house. I want to know if anyone leaves this ranch during the night. I don't care who it is or why. I want to know. I don't think any Slender Creek rancher will come within ten miles of that farm at night, so if anything happens, it'll be those who attacked it before. I want to know if any of my crew is involved." After clearing up a few details, the boys left Nate to begin his search of the bunkhouse.

He didn't like going behind his men's backs, but if they were guilty, he wasn't going to get any straight answers. He needed evidence before he could make an accusation or ask the sheriff to make an arrest. If his own men were involved, it was because he'd paid so little attention to his ranch and depended so heavily on Russ that he didn't know what was going on.

The bunkhouse had been built to accommodate a dozen men to a degree of comfort unique in the county. Ten bunks were lined up against the wall with each man having his own space. Trunks, bedrolls, and saddlebags containing personal property were stowed under beds or on racks built into the wall. Boots were placed alongside bunks while chaps and coats were hung on pegs. Other items could be stored in the small chests of drawers that Nate had supplied for each man. Russ had used the space for the last two bunks to set up a table so the men could eat their meals in the bunkhouse. That should have been a sign to Nate that something wasn't right. Cowhands never wanted to eat in the bunkhouse, and cooks didn't want to go to the trouble of carrying food and dishes to a second location.

Not knowing who occupied which bunk, Nate started with the first one on his right. He found the hood in saddlebags under the bed. He found the second hood inside a bedroll. By the time he finished, he had found seven hoods. Every member of his crew, except the three boys he'd hired, was involved in the attack on Roberta's farm. Cold fury consumed him. What kind of men were they to have been involved in killing two innocent men and the attempt to kill Roberta? And how could he have let himself become so consumed by his search for Laveau that he hadn't known something was wrong?

He guessed that he, too, was supposed to die, which would free Russ to claim the freshly branded calves. Nate's will left everything to be divided among the surviving members of the Night Riders. By the time one of them could have arrived to take over the ranch, Russ would have had plenty of time to leave with the calves.

Webb had left, but Grady was waiting for him outside the bunkhouse. "I found the masks," Nate told him. "From now on be very careful what you do or say. Tell Webb to do the same. I'm not sure these men would stop at killing. Don't say anything to Benny. The less he knows, the better. I'm going to take Roberta into town. I'll be back with the sheriff as soon as I can."

Chapter Nineteen

"I CAN'T BELIEVE IT," BLOSSOM SAID, WHEN NATE explained why he'd brought Roberta to stay with her. "Russ has busted his butt to take care of that ranch. He didn't think anybody around here was good enough to work for you, so he hired men from outside the county. Everybody knows he was beside himself with worry when you were shot."

Nate didn't tell her about the masks. Roberta had been so angry when he told her that she was ready to go after Russ herself. It had taken all of his persuasive abilities to convince her to stay with Blossom while he and the sheriff went after Russ and the other men.

"It appears he's a better actor than anyone would have suspected," Nate told Blossom, "but there's no doubt about the branded calves."

"What are you going to do about it?"

"First, make sure Roberta is safe. There's more to this than stealing a few calves, even a few hundred. I can replace calves, but no one can replace Roberta."

Blossom put her arm over Roberta's shoulder. "I'll make sure she's safe. I'm just surprised you didn't take her to Prudence."

"He was afraid she wouldn't let me out again." Roberta didn't look at Nate. "She's sure our relationship is improper."

"So get married, and she'll have nothing to complain about," Blossom advised.

"All in good time," Nate told her.

"Do you know where to find this man you say Russ is working for?" Blossom asked.

"No. Once we get an official arrest warrant, I'll offer a reward big enough to have every man in Texas on his trail."

It was less trouble enlisting the sheriff's help than it had been to convince Roberta to stay safely tucked away in Blossom's room.

"Are you telling me your own men have been doing this, and you knew nothing about it?" the sheriff asked, stunned and angry.

"I'm not proud of that, but I'm not about to deny it."

"You say you just found out today?"

"This morning."

"And you've got proof?"

"I've found seven masks in the bunkhouse. I also found several just weaned calves bearing a fresh brand that doesn't belong to anyone in the county."

"I'm glad you've got something more than *intuition* to go on this time," the sheriff said once Nate explained the situation. "Give me half an hour to round up some deputies, and I'll be ready to go."

The half hour went slowly for Nate. He had little to do besides think of how decisions he'd made led up to this moment. It wasn't merely because

Laveau was responsible for Caleb's death. It wasn't just because his parents had favored Caleb over him. It was *really* because he'd let other people's actions devalue himself in his own eyes. As a consequence, he'd let his life turn into a pursuit that had little to do with him. He had to stop letting the past control his life. He didn't have to forgive or forget, but had to break its hold. He had thought it didn't really matter whether he lived or died as long as Laveau paid for what he'd done.

But Laveau's death wouldn't bring Caleb back, and he now had the best reason in the world to want to live: Roberta. He could hardly wait until she became his wife. Laveau could cheat half of the country if he wanted, but as long as he stayed out of Texas, Nate planned to stay home. He had a ranch to run and an inheritance to build for the children he hoped to have. But most of all, he wanted to spend every moment possible with Roberta. He wanted to wake up with her in the morning, sit across the table from her at meals, share the events of the day, plan the rest of their lives together. He'd wasted too much time struggling against what he couldn't change, trying to justify what didn't need justification. He wouldn't do that anymore.

The ride to the ranch was uncomfortable. The sheriff didn't stop needling Nate about the culprits being his own men. Nor did he think much of Nate's plan to confront Russ with the evidence of his crime in hopes he would implicate Laveau in the murders.

"Russ is not fool enough to stick his head in a noose just because you want it there."

"He won't hang for branding calves he hasn't stolen, but he will hang for killing two men and attempting to kill a woman."

"Hell, we could hang him just for trying to kill Roberta."

"Be sure you tell him that."

Grady was waiting when they returned. "They're not back yet."

"This is a waste of time," the sheriff complained. "They'll see us and make a run for it."

"Not if you hide in the barn."

"I'll let you know when the crew gets here."

The deputies weren't happy about having to hide, but Nate told them Russ would probably come straight to the house. "The only time I've had this many men here was a meeting of the ranchers. If he sees all of you, he'll know something is wrong."

The men grumbled, but the sheriff told them to stop acting like children and do what they were told. Much to Nate's surprise, they did.

The sheriff spent the next twenty minutes taking a tour of the house, complimenting Nate on leaving the place as he'd found it, and telling him the previous owner was a much better rancher than Nate would ever be. He topped it off by telling Nate he'd done his best to help someone else buy the ranch. Nate was almost relieved when Russ entered the house. His foreman pulled up short when he saw the sheriff.

"Is something wrong?" Russ asked.

"Are all the men back?" Nate responded.

"Yeah. They just finished putting their horses in the corral, so I came to tell Benny to take their supper out to them." When Nate was home, Russ ate in the house so they could talk about the ranch.

"The sheriff wants to talk with the men, to ask them if they've seen anything unusual recently."

"Like what?"

"I'll let the sheriff explain what he's looking for."

"I can save you the trouble," he told the sheriff. "We haven't seen anybody or anything we haven't seen just about every day for the last year."

"I'd rather talk to the men myself," the sheriff said. "You never know when something I say might trigger a memory of some detail that hadn't seemed important at the time."

Russ tried to convince the sheriff that talking to the men was useless, but he didn't appear to suspect anything was wrong.

The crew looked surprised when Nate entered the bunkhouse. The flare-up of tension was tangible when the sheriff followed. It didn't ease when Russ entered last. Nate had never been one to make snap judgments about people before he knew anything about them, but he knew right away that these weren't the kind of men he wanted working for him. He could see it in the way their bodies stiffened, in the way their eyes cut to where they'd left their guns, but there was also a look about them that said they were rough men, old enough to have charted their own courses in life. He was astounded by the number of weapons. Each man appeared to have one or two guns in addition to that many rifles. Why would a law-abiding cowhand need so many weapons?

He wouldn't.

"The sheriff is trying to find out who's responsible for the attacks on Roberta Tryon's farm," Nate told the men. "He wants to ask some questions about what you may have seen or heard in the past weeks. Give him any help you can."

Nate left to bring the deputies to the bunkhouse, but Webb rode up just then. From the boy's grim expression, Nate knew he'd found something incriminating.

As soon as Webb could dismount where he wasn't visible from the bunkhouse windows, he told Nate, "I found where they've been doing the branding." He reached for his bedroll, which looked uncharacteristically rigid, and pulled out a branding iron. "I found this lying behind a rock. They didn't even bother to hide it well."

Having gotten a look at the men in Russ's crew, Nate knew he couldn't expect them to sit still while the deputies filed in one at a time. The chances were good that he wouldn't get more than two deputies inside before one of the men went for his gun. In such a confined space, someone was bound to be killed. He made a quick change of plans. The sheriff had brought six men. Nate figured he and two men could get inside before any shooting started. Counting the sheriff, that would be four inside the bunkhouse. He would place the other men, plus Webb and Grady, at six windows. At a signal from Nate, they would knock out a pane and take aim at one specific cowhand with orders to shoot if the man went for a gun. With four men inside the bunkhouse and six outside, Nate hoped to avoid a shoot-out.

It took longer than he wanted to explain his plan and position the deputies. He hoped the sheriff had been able to allay any suspicion that something was about to happen.

With one last look to make sure everyone was in place, Nate opened the bunkhouse door. Two deputies followed so quickly one stumbled over Nate's heel. They were only just in time. "Now!" Nate shouted as one of the cowhands went for a rifle leaning against the wall.

To the accompaniment of glass from six broken windows crashing to the bunkhouse floor, Nate put a bullet in the wall next to the rifle. The concussion in the confines of the bunkhouse was deafening.

"We're being attacked!" Russ shouted. "Go for your guns!"

A bullet into the floor at Russ's feet stopped him in his tracks. He looked at Nate in shocked amazement. "What the hell is going on?"

"The sheriff is here to arrest you and these men," Nate stated. "All of you move to the center of the room." Despite the rifles at the windows, Nate wanted the men away from their weapons. They were slow to move from their bunks, but when the sheriff grabbed one by the collar and threw him into the middle of the bunkhouse, the others followed reluctantly. Keeping the men tightly bunched, Nate called the deputies inside. Moments later they had a rifle trained on each cowhand.

"Arrest us for what?" Russ asked. "We haven't done anything."

Nate had hung the branding iron from his belt in

the back. He reached around and brought it forward. "I've seen the cows you've been branding with this iron. I can take the sheriff to the location of your fire."

"I've never seen that branding iron," Russ said, "and neither have my men."

Nate wondered if Russ realized he'd said *my* men rather than *your* men. "The fire is on my land, the iron was found on my land, and the cows are on my land. I'm certain when I write the cattlemen's association I'll find this brand isn't registered in my name."

"You can't arrest us for rustling," one of the men said. "We ain't taken any cows. If you make a count, you'll find they're all here."

"You can't prove we branded those calves," Russ objected.

Nate waited until Russ realized what he'd said. "How did you know it was calves that were branded? I purposely said cows."

Russ scrambled to cover his mistake. "Cows are already branded. Covering an old brand or working it into a new one is nearly impossible. It would be much easier to brand calves."

"But nearly impossible to brand them as soon as they were weaned unless you were around them every day."

Several men glanced toward Russ, but he wasn't giving anything away.

"I was angry about the branding," Nate continued, "but it's being responsible for the deaths of Robert Tryon and Carlin that will hang all of you."

For a moment, Nate wasn't sure that having all the weapons on his side was going to keep the men under control. They shouted denials as well as threats, but in the end, it was staring down the barrels of ten rifles that brought them under control.

"We didn't have nothing to do with that," one of the men stated. "You can't prove nothing."

Nate directed two of the deputies to put down their weapons and begin a systematic search of the room. It was clear, even before the deputies found the first mask, that the crew knew what they were looking for. When the fifth masked turned up, one of the cowhands turned to Russ. "He hired us to trample crops and set the barn on fire, and that's all we did. We didn't have nothing to do with shooting that old man and that kid."

The others were eager to agree, but Nate didn't speak until the seventh mask was found—Russ's mask. He turned to the sheriff. "Do you think we have enough evidence to hang them?"

"Rustling, destroying crops, burning a barn and a house, two murders and one attempted murder. Hell, I don't need no judge. That's enough to hang them right here, and nobody will say nothing except good riddance."

Russ spoke up. "We did everything except the murders."

"Who did?" the sheriff asked. "What's his name? What does he look like?"

"I never got a good look at him. He only came here at night. He gave me a name, but I'm sure it's made up."

"What was it?" Nate asked.

"Gilbert Travis. He didn't sound like nobody named Gilbert. He sounded foreign."

"Laveau diViere had a Spanish mother and a French father," Nate told the sheriff. "Gilbert Travis is the name he gave Roberta when she found him outside her house."

"Where can I find this diViere?" the sheriff asked Russ.

"I don't know. Whenever he was here, he'd tell me when we were to meet the next time. If he came some other time, I'd find a note inside the barn door."

"How did he pay you?"

When Russ was slow to answer, Nate had a sudden inspiration. "He didn't pay you at all, did he? The lure he held out was having free access to my cattle once I was dead."

Russ's silence was an admission that Nate had guessed correctly. "He gave me the branding iron and registered it in my name."

Poor fool, Nate thought to himself. He was certain Laveau had registered the brand in his own name. After Nate's death, Laveau would have had Russ arrested for rustling and ended up with the calves himself.

"I'm arresting all of you," the sheriff said. "A judge will decide your punishment. Don't do nothing stupid like trying to get away. I'm ordering the deputies to shoot first and worry about whether you're guilty later."

It took some time to get all the men on their horses with their hands tied to their saddle horns. Russ was the last to mount up.

"Why did you do it?" Nate asked. "I paid you more than any foreman in the county. I let you run this place like it was yours." As soon as the words were out of his mouth, Nate knew he had the answer.

"I guess I spent too much time thinking what it would be like if it really was mine," Russ said. "When you were away, it felt like it was."

Nate refused to feel guilty. Russ had hired men he knew wouldn't shy away from criminal activity. He'd branded calves that didn't belong to him, and he'd destroyed property. Most significantly, he'd done this knowing that he could only benefit if Nate died. This was more than daydreaming about *what if*. He'd actively participated in a plan that involved murder.

Nate finally had a witness who could testify against Laveau. Now all he had to do was find him.

❧

Roberta told herself she shouldn't be nervous, it was too early to worry, but it wasn't too early to get bored. That had happened within an hour of Blossom leaving for work. There was nothing to do in the confines of the single room her friend rented on the upper floor of Mrs. Blanton's rooming house. Since Blossom spent nearly all her waking hours in the saloon, there was little in her room that wasn't related to undressing, bathing, sleeping, and dressing again. Roberta had studied all the pictures, virtually inventoried the contents of the room while searching in vain for something to read. If she hadn't been able to look out a window that overlooked the main street, she probably would have disregarded Nate's request that she not leave the room until he came for her.

It was through that window that she saw Nate and the sheriff bringing Russ and six other men into town, their hands tied to the pommels of their saddles. Even though Nate had explained what he found and what he was certain had been done, it was hard to believe Russ was guilty. Killers were black-hearted, evil men. Russ was just unlikeable.

It was interesting to see the townspeople tumble out of houses, stores, offices, and saloons to gape at the caval-cade as it went by. She didn't know how many would recognize the six cowhands, but everybody knew Russ. As the foreman of the largest ranch in the county, he'd been an important member of the community. It had to be a shock to find out he was a criminal. Everyone in town would have the whole story before suppertime. It would be the only topic of conversation.

The town didn't have a jail big enough to hold that many men. Except for the occasional drunk, there had been no need for a jail. The sheriff's job had been so close to ceremonial that several complained about having to pay him a salary. She guessed that would change now.

Her window also overlooked three alleys. It was a movement in one that caught her eye as she was about to turn away. She didn't recognize the man at first, but there was something about him that made her look again. When he turned in her direction, she knew he was the man she'd seen about to enter her house the day of her father's funeral, the man who said his name was Gilbert Travis.

The man Nate said was Laveau diViere.

She didn't know why he would risk being in

Slender Creek, but she had to warn Nate. She was down the stairs, out the door, and running down the street in a matter of seconds. People spoke as she ran past. Some wanted to know why she was running—an action considered unladylike—but she didn't care what they asked or what they thought. It only mattered that she reach Nate before diViere.

When she burst into the sheriff's office, her breath came in gasps and a lock of hair had fallen in her face.

Nate hurried to meet her. "What are you doing here? I told you not to leave the room until I came for you."

"I saw him," she said between gulping breaths.

"Who?"

"The man you said was Laveau diViere."

That name was like a pistol shot fired over the heads of a noisy crowd. Every head in the room turned to her, their various conversations forgotten.

Nate's grip on her wrists tightened. "When?"

"Barely a minute ago. I was looking out the window when you and the sheriff came into town. I was about to turn away when I saw him in the alley between Bill Lambert's law office and Priscilla Bradberry's dress shop."

"What was he doing?"

"Watching you."

"What did he do after we passed?" the sheriff asked.

"He went back down the alley. I wanted to follow him, but I knew I had to tell Nate first."

"Go back to where you're staying and leave finding him to us," the sheriff told Roberta.

"I'm going with you," Nate said to the sheriff, "but I have to take Roberta back first."

"Don't take long. If this diViere character is as slick as you say, he won't stay around long."

"I can help," Roberta protested. "I know what he looks like. You don't."

"You just tell me what he's wearing," the sheriff said. "Nate has already told me what he looks like."

"He's dressed like a cowhand," she told him. "That's why I wasn't sure who he was until he turned in my direction."

Nate tensed. "Did he see you?"

"I don't see how he could. I didn't open the window. Besides, he was watching you."

"See her back to the house, but be quick about it," the sheriff told Nate.

Roberta didn't like being shuffled off to sit in a room, waiting for someone to tell her what was happening—or what had *already* happened while she sat uselessly behind pulled curtains.

Nate stopped when they reached the front door. "I don't have to warn you to stay inside this time. And stay away from the window. There have been times when I would have sworn Laveau could see through walls."

"I hope you find him quickly," she told him. "I've already organized Blossom's drawers and rearranged her closet. If you take too long, I'll start on Mrs. Blanton's rooms."

Much to her surprise, Nate kissed her right there in the street. Roberta kissed him back with equal enthusiasm and hoped Prudence wasn't looking out the window.

"I'll be back as soon as I can."

Resigned to her enforced incarceration, Roberta turned and went inside. A strange sensation came over her when she closed the door, a feeling that her mother used to characterize as someone stepping on her grave. She shoved it aside. It had to be nerves brought on by seeing diViere and being afraid he meant to shoot Nate. She called out to Mrs. Blanton, but her voice echoed through the silent house. It looked like she would have no one with whom to pass the time, until Nate came back. She didn't want to return to Blossom's room, but she felt uncomfortable staying in Mrs. Blanton's part of the house when that lady wasn't there.

Reluctantly, she climbed the stairs.

The moment she stepped through the doorway into Blossom's room, she knew something was wrong. She started to step back, but it was too late. Laveau diViere grabbed her and twisted her arm behind her with such violent force she thought she might faint from the pain. With his other hand, he gripped her by the back of the neck.

"There's a vein in your neck that takes blood to the brain. If I put enough pressure on it, you'll pass out. If I continue the pressure, you'll die."

"What do you want?" Her voice sounded amazingly calm, a calm that she didn't feel.

"I wanted Nate dead, but I'm fairly certain you warned him that I'm here. I saw you looking at me from your window. A moment later you came out and headed toward the sheriff's office. It wasn't hard to guess what you meant to do."

"Why didn't you leave? Everyone is looking for you."

They hadn't moved from the doorway. Roberta hoped Mrs. Blanton would return yet was afraid of what diViere would do if she did. She hoped he wouldn't force her to sit. She had a better chance of escape if she remained standing.

"I didn't leave because I haven't done what I came to do."

She knew, but she had to ask. "What is that?"

"Kill Nate Dolan."

She knew it was hopeless the instant she felt her body go into action, but she was so enraged she couldn't stop herself. She kicked back with her foot and tried to twist out of diViere's hold at the same time. She couldn't break his grip, but she felt the impact of her foot against his flesh and heard him grunt. It was the last thing she heard.

❦

She was tied to a chair when she woke up.

"That was a foolish thing to do."

Her gaze shifted until she saw diViere standing at the window.

"Why didn't you kill me? You killed my father. Carlin too."

DiViere didn't answer, just looked out the window.

"Why did you kill my father? He didn't know you. He'd never seen you in his life."

"He did know me." DiViere spoke without turning around. "I needed his help. I offered to pay him handsomely, but he refused."

"What did you want him to do?"

"Help me destroy Nate Dolan."

"My father would never do anything like that. He was an honorable man."

"He's now a dead man. What good did his honor do him?"

Roberta had never doubted diViere was an evil man, but his callous indifference took her breath away. Taking a human life was of no more importance to him than killing an animal for food or a wolf because he preyed on livestock. He was now planning to execute Nate with the same nonchalance. She had to do something to stop him, but she couldn't while she was tied up.

"It was very foolish of you to fall in love with him. Boone Riggins would have been a much wiser choice."

"I didn't intend to fall in love with Nate. It just happened."

"I could never understand that kind of undisciplined emotion. Nate was an admirable adversary until he fell in love with you. In a way, I'll miss him."

"Why do you want to kill him?"

"He's ruined several of my enterprises. I don't allow anyone to do that."

"Won't being a murderer make it impossible for you to continue these *enterprises*?"

He turned to her, his face a study in scorn. "Thanks to the war, there's not a man in the country over twenty-five who hasn't killed someone."

The knot binding her hands was loose. Apparently tying up captives wasn't one of Laveau's skills. She couldn't untie it, but it was possible that by applying pressure, she could stretch it enough to slip one hand out. Either diViere was too busy watching for Nate to notice her struggles, or he didn't think she had any chance of success. The rough rope cut into the tender flesh of her wrists, but she did her best to ignore the pain. There would be plenty of time for that later. Right now warning Nate was the only thing of importance.

"You really are an annoying woman." DiViere didn't turn away from the window when he spoke.

"If you hadn't attacked our farm and murdered my father, I would never have known of your existence." That must have angered him because he turned to her.

"I thought you would go back to Virginia after the attack. I was sure of it when Peterson came to get you."

"What do you know about Peterson?"

He had turned back to the window. "He appears to have transferred his interest to Blossom. It would seem age has faded your charms."

"Nate doesn't think so." It was odd that even in a moment like this, vanity could rear its head. She tried to channel it into her effort to escape. She had succeeded in loosening the knot a little, but not enough to get her hand out. The pain in her wrist had grown until it was hardly bearable, but she concentrated on how to escape from the room once her hands were free.

"Nate is a fool. He didn't have enough sense to know he was worth two of his brother."

Roberta didn't know how long the sheriff would

search for diViere, but at some point they would stop, and Nate would come to her. She had to be free before then, but she wasn't making enough progress. She pulled hard against the rope, but as it loosened on one wrist, it tightened on the other. Pain in one wrist increased the pain in the other. Suddenly, diViere tensed and stared out the window like a cat whose prey had just come into view. That could only mean one thing.

Nate was coming.

Pain was no longer important. Roberta had only seconds to warn Nate. She pulled against the rope with all her strength. Her efforts were fueled by the look of satisfaction she saw forming on diViere's face. The horrible man actually looked forward to what he was about to do. The pleasure he derived from that anticipation gave her the forbearance to ignore the pain and the strength to jerk one hand free. DiViere was so captivated by the anticipation of reaching his goal that he appeared unaware of the small sounds that should have warned him something had gone amiss. She wrenched her other hand free, rose to her feet, and was halfway across the room before diViere realized anything was wrong. He sprang after her, but nearly lost his balance when he slipped on a small rug in the center of the room. That gave Roberta time to wrench open the door and run for the stairs, but diViere was as agile as a cat. He recovered his balance and was after her in an instant.

He caught her partway down the stairs just as Nate entered the front door.

For a moment, the three of them froze in place.

Then, with a particularly vicious curse, diViere flung her down the stairs.

Chapter Twenty

"YOU SHOULDN'T HAVE TRIED TO BREAK MY FALL,"
Roberta said to Nate.

"I didn't fall in love with you to have you break
your neck before I could talk you into marrying me,"
Nate responded.

"I already agreed to marry you," she reminded him.

"You have too many conditions to make it count."

"If you want this arm set properly, you'll be
still and stop trying to look at her," Dr. Danforth
scolded Nate.

"It's worth a broken arm to look at her."

"What have you done to him?" the doctor asked
Roberta. "He never used to talk like an idiot."

"I didn't do anything."

"First you shot him, and then you broke his arm.
I wouldn't call that nothing."

When diViere pushed Roberta down the rest
of the stairs, Nate had rushed forward to break her
fall. Roberta had twisted away to keep from falling
directly on him. Nate had responded by turning so
abruptly he was off balance when he caught her. His
left arm was under him when they fell to the floor.

It had given DiViere just the distraction he needed to get away.

Dr. Danforth winked at Roberta. "He should stay away from you. I don't think you're good for his health."

Roberta returned the doctor's wink. "Maybe I should sell my farm and go back to Virginia."

"I've got another arm and two legs," Nate declared. "I'll sacrifice all three before I let you get away from me."

"Looks like he's beyond saving," the doctor said. "Take him home and see if you can keep him from breaking anything else."

"She's not going back until she's married."

Prudence had remained silent while the doctor set Nate's arm, but her frown hadn't eased. Roberta was pleased to see it reflected more worry and concern than disapproval.

"I agree with you," Nate told Prudence, "but I can't get Roberta to agree."

"Nonsense," Prudence stated. "She's been in love with you from the first. She's just being stubborn."

"I am not," Roberta insisted. "I said I couldn't marry him until I knew who killed my father."

"You know that now."

"I have one other condition." She turned to Nate. "You can't go after him. I know what you're going to say, but having you alive is more important than catching Laveau diViere. That won't bring my father back. If it would, I'd go after him myself."

Laveau had escaped while they lay in a tangle at the bottom of the stairs. No one had seen him leave the house or leave town. They found Mrs. Blanton in the kitchen. She'd been gagged and tied to the leg of her cast iron stove.

"I can't leave him free to come after you anytime he feels like it," Nate objected.

"If he had been determined to kill either of us, he could have done it while we were lying at the foot of the stairs. For some reason, he changed his mind."

"You don't know Laveau."

"I'm not sure you do. He respects you."

Nate looked at her in disbelief. "Why do you say that?"

"He said you were a worthy adversary, worth two of your brother. I think shooting you while you were unable to defend yourself wouldn't have satisfied whatever is driving him."

"He hates me."

"I don't think so, but that doesn't matter. You've got to promise you won't go after him."

Nate was silent. Roberta could sympathize with the struggle going on inside him. Dropping his pursuit of Laveau went against his sense of responsibility to her and their future together. It also went against his sense of what it meant to be a man. In the eyes of some, maybe even in his own, it was a sign of cowardice. Then there was the frustration of giving up on a chase that had occupied him for more than two years. She knew what she was asking was virtually impossible, but she couldn't do anything else. She had already lost her father. It would kill her to lose him, too.

Nate must have reached a decision because he

sighed and turned toward her with a faint but under-standing smile. "I can offer you a compromise. As long as Laveau stays away from us, I won't go after him. But if he ever threatens you again, I won't stop until he's dead."

That wasn't what Roberta wanted to hear, but she was certain Nate had given as much ground as he could without losing respect for himself.

"That's good enough," Prudence announced. "She'll marry you today if you want."

Roberta was tempted to tell Prudence to mind her own business for once, but Nate was waiting for her answer. After what she'd put him through, she couldn't make him wait longer. "I will marry you anytime, anyplace you want. Just let me tell Blossom and give Benny time to bake at least one cake. Neither one will forgive me if they miss our wedding."

><>

"He knew I would have come after him with a shotgun if he hadn't brought you to see me," Pilar was saying to Roberta. "I've been trying to get him married for years."

Roberta and Nate had waited a week before they were married, but the celebration Prudence organized was restrained compared to Pilar's party. She had used Rafe and Maria's annual visit from California as an excuse to get all the Night Riders together.

Roberta had enjoyed meeting the men she'd heard so much about, but it was more interesting to see the women they'd chosen to be their wives. She was enchanted by Cade and Pilar's two sons, but

Pilar's grandmother scared her. She could virtually see the generations of aristocratic Spanish ancestors lined up behind Donna Isabella Cordoba diViere. The woman's backbone was unbending, her gaze unwavering. It was impossible to know what was behind those unblinking black eyes until she looked at Cade's older son, Carlos. It was obvious she adored her handsome great-grandson.

"Did you really shoot Nate?" asked a handsome man accompanied by a plain wife with an adorable daughter.

"Not intentionally."

"Did you mean to break his arm?" That from a scrawny old man who claimed to be the reason his grandson was so handsome.

"Of course not."

"And he still married you?"

"I had already asked her," Nate said. "It was too late to back out."

"Sounds like you married a natural disaster." That from a man with a ruined face.

"I figured if I could survive the war, I could survive being married to her."

"It does not sound like you have been doing very well." That from a blond giant with a charming European accent. Nate's arm was out of splints, but it was still in a sling.

There was a lot of kidding back and forth, but it was obvious the men held one another in considerable affection. They shared stories about the war and about driving the squatters from the diViere ranch. The two old people exchanged a couple of swipes at each other, but it appeared that they had developed a grudging respect for each other.

Because of the large number of people invited, the festivities were taking place in the courtyard. A generous space enclosed by three walls of the hacienda, it featured a pool in the center, which was surrounded by several trees that weren't yet large enough to offer more than token shade. Despite the presence of more than twenty adults, the conversation centered on babies and small children. Roberta was too newly married to be ready for children, but she enjoyed watching the parents, especially the fathers. While some seemed comfortable in their roles, others seemed at a loss as to what to make of these miniature people.

"What are you going to do with your farm?" Pilar asked Roberta.

"I'm going to turn it into a pasture for the blooded-bull Nate has bought. I don't even want to hear the word *dam*."

"From what Cade tells me, more people will be building dams. I wonder what's keeping Carlos?" she asked of no one in particular. "It shouldn't take him this long to find his new coat."

Donna Isabella had turned a lifetime's experience in embroidery to making fancy clothes for her two great-grandsons. Five-year-old Carlos was particularly proud of the coat she had given him for his birthday.

"He's probably bringing *all* of his coats for us to see."

"He told me he likes the new one better than all the others. I'm sure—"

A smothered shriek drew all eyes toward Felicity

Holt. She held her infant son pressed tight to her chest. With a look of terror in her eyes, she was pointing to the terrace on the second floor of the hacienda.

Laveau diViere stood on the terrace. In front of him he held Carlos Wheeler, who was wearing his new coat. Laveau pressed a small pistol against the boy's temple.

"I'd appreciate it if no one moved, especially you, Cade," he said. "I'd hate to shoot this boy because you couldn't stand still long enough to listen to a few words."

"Hurt that boy, and I'll kill you myself." Cade looked as though only Pilar's restraining hand kept him from racing toward the stairs that led to the balcony.

"He won't hurt him," Rafe Jerry assured Cade. "He knows he'd never get out of here alive if he did."

"Do you think I care about that?" Laveau shouted. "I hate all of you. You have made my life a misery."

"You have come home at last. I thought I would never live to see this happy day."

Everyone's attention had been so focused on Laveau they hadn't noticed Donna Isabella was already climbing the stairs to the balcony.

"Do you still love me, Grandmama?" Laveau asked.

"I have always loved you," she responded. "I have longed for the day you would return."

Cade attempted to break away from his wife, but she held on to him as though their lives depended on it. They exchanged fierce whispers. Roberta couldn't hear what she said, but Cade stopped fighting his wife.

"That's right," Laveau shouted at his sister. "Think of your precious husband rather than your son. I would never have believed my sister would turn herself into a whore, but money is more important than family. I could have made even more money if you hadn't helped them drive me away. I've had to scramble for a living while you lived in luxury on *my* inheritance."

"I sent you your share every year," Pilar shouted at him. "You have never had to work. If you had left everybody alone, we'd have forgotten about you."

That apparently was the wrong thing to say. For a moment Roberta thought Laveau would shoot the boy and die in a hail of bullets.

"Don't let them upset you, my son," Donna Isabella said. "It is jealousy that drives their words."

Donna Isabella had appeared on the balcony next to Laveau. "Let me have your pistol. I have brought you a larger gun. I will hold the boy while you take your vengeance on the men who've made your life a misery."

Roberta couldn't believe that a great-grandmother would do such a thing. Surely she knew Laveau was evil. He would kill the boy before he let them take him.

Donna Isabella held a rifle out to Laveau. The light of insanity gleamed in his eyes. He hesitated only an instant before reaching for it. Once it was in his hand, he gave his grandmother the pistol. With a laugh he turned toward those gathered below, but it was a laugh that ended in a scream. The sound of a pistol being fired broke the spell, and the men charged up the stairs followed by their wives. When they reached the balcony, they found Laveau lying on the floor, bleeding from a wound in his stomach. Donna

Isabella clutched Carlos to her bosom, the pistol still pointed at Laveau.

"When my home was taken from me along with everything our family had cherished for generations, you did not come home to save me or your sister. It was Cade Wheeler and his friends who risked their lives to do what you should have done."

"I came home, but they drove me away."

"You came home to kill the man who gave me back my dignity, married my granddaughter, and gave me the most beautiful great-grandsons in the world. You have wandered the country leaving evil in your wake. How could you think I would let you hurt anyone in this place?"

"But they're Wheelers. You hate them."

"I was wrong, and I have asked the Virgin to forgive me. Tonight I will ask Her to forgive me for what I have done today." Then she deliberately shot Laveau in the stomach a second time. "You have brought much pain to people you betrayed. It is only fair that you spend your last hours in pain."

Then she shot him again.

❧

Roberta was relieved to find a quiet corner where she could retreat with Nate after all the upset over Laveau's death finally subsided. The official report would state that Donna Isabelle had shot Laveau to keep him from killing her great-grandson. As far as the law was concerned, justice was satisfied. For the Night Riders and their families, it wasn't so simple. A danger-filled, seven-year odyssey crowded with nearly every emotion from rage to heartbreak had come to a shocking conclusion. Despite struggling under the burden of having had a son's life threatened and losing a brother at the hands of her grandmother, Pilar begged her guests to stay. She'd said now her life could go on without the shadow that had hung over it for seven years.

Roberta felt much the same. Her father's killer had been punished and the threat to her happiness removed.

"Do you want to go home?" Nate asked.

"Yes, but I don't think we should leave just yet. Having guests is helping Pilar get through the crisis."

"How do you feel about Laveau's death?"

"He's no longer a part of our lives so I'm free to forget him. I'd much rather spend my time thinking about you."

"Are you sure you'll be happy in Texas? I wouldn't mind moving to Virginia."

"Carl's coming after me made me realize I'm not the same person who left Virginia."

Nate smiled. "And who are you now?"

"I want to be a person in my own right, not a mere extension of my husband. I want you to teach me to ride so I can be next to you when you survey the ranch. I want to be part of the business decisions you make. If anything were to happen to you, I want to be capable of insuring our children's inheritance."

"So you do want children?"

Roberta felt something go soft inside. "I want little boys as handsome as Carlos and little girls as pretty as Owen and Hetta's daughter."

"As long as the girls look like you, I wouldn't care if we have a full house."

When a shadow crossed his face, Roberta knew he was thinking of Caleb. "We will love all our children so much they'll never have reason to wonder if we love them less than one of the others. I never had brothers or sisters, and I've lost both parents. I have lots of love stored up. As wonderful as you are, not even you can use it all."

Nate shook his head. "You're the one who's wonderful."

She kissed him on the lips. "I had to be to deserve you. Now tell me what you think we ought to name our first son."

About the Author

Leigh Greenwood is the author of the popular Seven Brides series and the Cowboys series. The proud father of three grown children, Leigh resides in Charlotte, North Carolina. Please visit Leigh's website at: www.leigh-greenwood.com. You can email Leigh at: Leighgwood@aol.com, or write him at: P.O. Box 470761, Charlotte, NC 28226. A SASE would be appreciated.